PRECIOUS
FRIENDS

PRECIOUS FRIENDS

MURDER IN SAG HARBOR

ANGELO PERROTTA MYSTERIES

FRANK SPINELLI

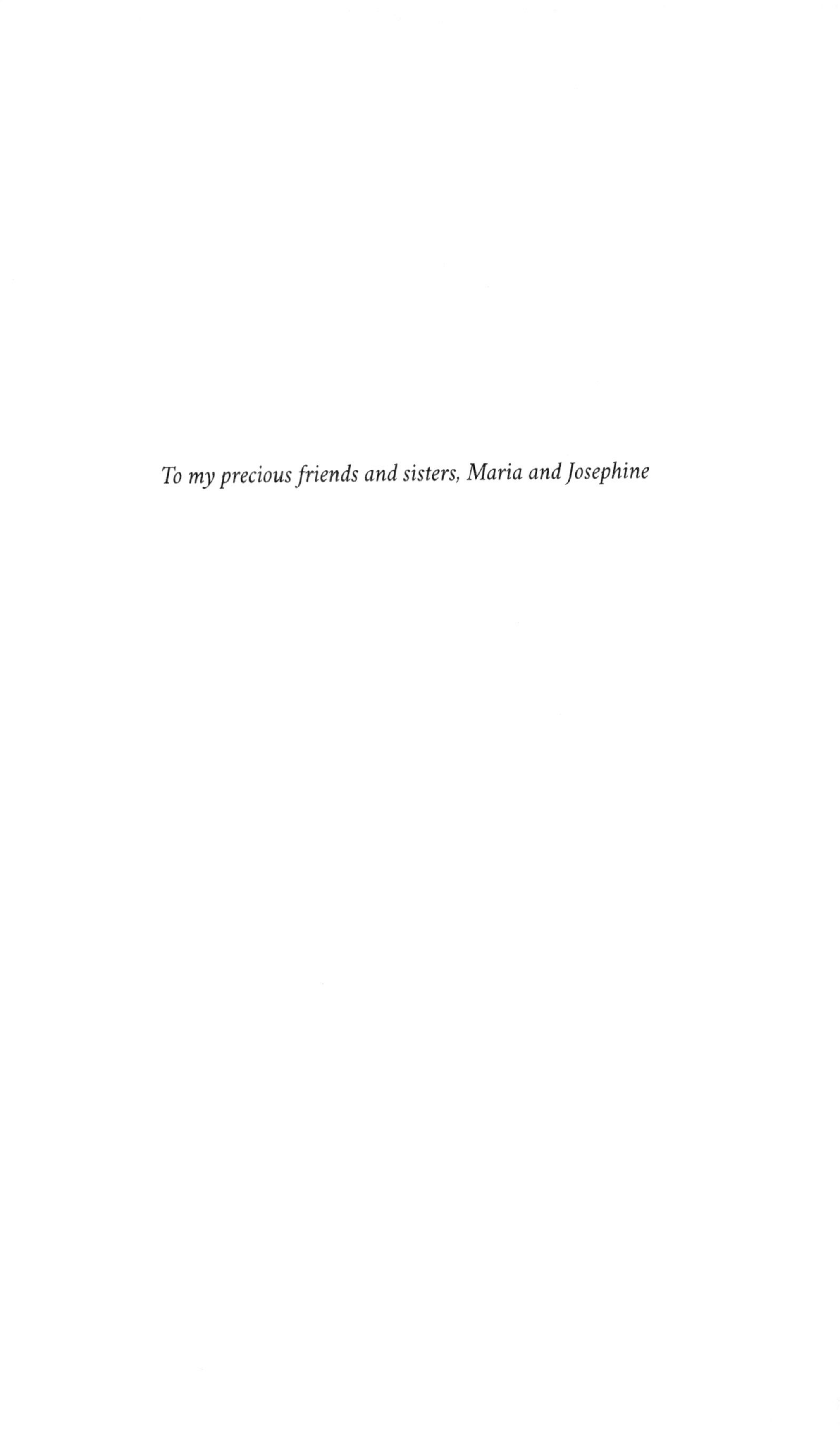

To my precious friends and sisters, Maria and Josephine

Contents

Praise for Precious Friends

"An absolute delight! *Precious Friends: Murder in Sag Harbor* is more than a suspenseful murder mystery. Full of twists and turns that will keep you on the edge of your seat, this entertaining read is set in the high society of the Hamptons where public opinion turns deadly. Great storyline, excellent characterization, and real-life issues. Such a fun read! Each time I was forced to put down the book to attend to my own real-life responsibilities, I couldn't wait to get back to it. Spinelli's smooth writing style and finesse at doling out snippets of information at a time kept me wanting more. Drama, romance, and mystery all rolled into an enjoyable read with a satisfying conclusion."—**Ivanka Fear**, author of Blue Water Mysteries and Jake and Mallory Thrillers

"What a mystery! So much going on that will keep you guessing until the end. The setting was perfect for the intrigue going on as the characters circle around each other, some in friendship, others in intrigue and murder thrown into the mix."—**Erik S. Meyers**, author of the Sally Witherspoon mystery series

"*Precious Friends: Murder in Sag Harbor* is an unsettling murder mystery that emerges from a seething cauldron of domestic unhappiness. Frank Spinelli's considerable skills weave an increasingly tense and intentionally confusing web that places J.B. Pulaski, a college professor, and Mike Fogarty, his husband, at its center. Two uncomfortable themes that run through the narrative are mid-life crisis and marital infidelity. Murder and chicanery are, believe it or not, secondary leitmotifs. This is not a tale of personal heroism, but of a very human struggle with imperfection."—**Ulysses Grant**

fight to gain a foothold in a tale of infidelity, blackmail, old grudges, and murder. *Precious Friends* is the modern and gay version of *The Great Gatsby* where power, prestige, and presence are at the forefront of society and gossip is the fuel that motors the action. Move this to the top of your pile of books, buckle up, and enjoy the ride."—**Matt Cost**, award-winning author of *Glow Trap*

"Precious Friends, teases, tempts, and then ropes the reader like a barbed-wire lasso. Sparkling with biting dialogue, posh locales, and razor-sharp narrative, Frank Spinelli's gin-swilling characters are heroic or cruel or sexy or conniving…or all of the above. *Precious Friends* is seductive, precious fun."—**Nick Nolan**, author of *Tales from Ballena Beach*

Chapter One

J B Pulaski had never thought about confessing to murder before. But watching his husband Mike grinding against their young Latino guest—the performative spectacle of it, the deliberate boundary-crossing—JB decided tonight might be the perfect time to try.

The Latino's name was Dan Vega, and he was housesitting for JB's best friend, Rakesh, while he vacationed in Puerto Vallarta for three weeks. *One more week*, JB reminded himself. *Seven more days until Dan heads back to Miami.*

If Dan wasn't planning on returning home, JB didn't doubt that he would become Mike's number one stray. All night, JB heard the whispering of *"Who's that?"* and *"What's his name?"* Dan's light-brown eyes, mocha complexion, and glistening dark curls had snared everyone's attention. What JB despised most was the way Mike danced after one too many cocktails. The way his body transformed from composed to predatory the moment he spotted a new conquest.

Dancing, like sipping cocktails and engaging in small talk, was an unavoidable ritual of socializing out east—cultural lubricants intertwined as naturally as Montauk oysters and mignonette. Social gatherings in the Hamptons often represented a collision between the banal and the vapid.

How could anyone survive a conversation about the audacity of new money erecting tasteless McMansions in Bridgehampton, the Sisyphean parking nightmare at Main Beach, the comparative outrage of farm stand heirloom tomato prices, the culinary pretensions of Nick & Toni's new chef—or life in general—without a stiff drink in hand?

JB's eyes focused on the conga line snaking past him with Mike leading the way. Mike looked over his shoulder at Dan, his smile about to crack his face in half. They were so close they were practically conjoined. Just then, Dan must have said something stunningly obscene because Mike threw his head back, whinnying that braying laugh he reserved for random handsome men who said anything remotely funny.

The luau was in full swing around him—thirty guests in floral print shirts and vibrant sarongs. A juxtaposition of older, rich gays plus a smattering of their favorite jewel-encrusted fag hags and assorted corporate fruit flies, swimming amongst the young, poor, and hopeful. A tableau of desperation masked as festivity. Social events such as this occurred only in those precious few months that spanned from Memorial Day until Labor Day.

The conga line dissolved, and there was Dan, shifting nervously in the hallway of JB's Sag Harbor home. "How are you, JB?"

It wasn't so much a bizarre question as a bizarre time to ask it. This ritualistic probing around was typically accomplished in the first few moments of a conversation; wooden planks laid down in a bridge that would lead to friendship or, in this case, away from it.

"I want to tell you two things," Dan continued with sudden enthusiasm. "Rakesh called today and asked if I could stay on another week. Apparently, Andy's mother is sick, and they're going straight to Tampa to visit her." He burst into laughter, doubling over. "I was thinking Rakesh and Andy could never go *straight* anywhere."

Mike had a knack for finding strays like Dan—clingy, silly, and juvenile. Adult men who acted younger than their age. Men who held maturity at arm's length, deferring it with fluttering lashes, shrugging accountability with pouty lips. What was it about this gay generation that let them play perpetual adolescent when JB had younger students who were mature beyond their years?

"And the second thing?" JB pressed.

"Oh yeah, the second thing is, I want to say how cool you are for letting me hang with Mike. Some husbands get salty, but you're not, right? Anyway, I just wanted to say, I think you're cool as F, and kind of sexy in your own way."

It hit JB then, even though he already knew. *They're fucking.* Of course they were. He'd been down this road before. This was the part where Mike's strays checked in with the husband to make sure their feelings were intact. Dan didn't dare burn bridges, especially ones that led to the Hamptons.

"I see no reason to be uncool," JB said. "Life is too short. If I was upset with someone, I'd simply kill them."

The left side of Dan's mouth slid into a twitchy smile. "Kill?"

"Do you recall the Sag Harbor murders?"

"Jamie and Tom? Of course, I remember. I house-sat for them a month before they were found dead last summer."

"Oh, that's right," JB said as though it had slipped his mind.

"You killed Jamie and Tom?"

"Uh-huh."

Dan's smile grew smaller. "You're fucking with me." He forced a laugh, which may well have been a hiccup.

"I'm not kidding." JB's eyes sharpened. "Mike was part of a throuple. That is what you kids call a threesome nowadays, correct?"

"Throuple?"

"The murdered couple plus Mike. They were a throuple. Except they had grown too attached to Mike. He may have told you this story, so I apologize if you're hearing it again. It wasn't that I cared all that much, me being cool as F and all, but it was their personalities that drove me insane."

A server came by and proffered a pewter tray of mini ahi tuna tostadas with little sugared orchids.

"Thank you." JB chewed, exposing all his teeth to Dan.

"You're trying to scare me." Dan chuckled, but JB saw the wheels churning. The question must be swirling in the poor boy's head: *why is he confessing to murder?*

"I don't think I am." Finally, JB was having fun at his own party. "Not that it matters."

"I don't believe you."

"Is it so unbelievable?" JB waited, but Dan never responded. "I think you do believe me. Again, not that it matters."

Silence followed. JB attempted to hide the smirk tugging at the corners of his mouth.

"I don't think it's funny to joke about murdered friends," Dan said.

"They weren't friends of mine. I wouldn't murder my friends. What could be more uncool?"

"Of Mike's, then."

"That makes all the difference in the world."

"Still, it's not funny." Dan turned to leave.

"I'll try to do better next time, but do me a favor, Dan...mum's the word about the murders. Mike doesn't know."

Dan appeared dazed as he walked away. JB watched him hurry across the living room and exit the front door without saying goodbye to Mike.

JB headed for the bar to order a celebratory Scotch. Dan would wake up tomorrow still thinking he had been the victim of JB's prank, though he would be wondering a little, too. Enough to ask a few people some questions about JB's attitude toward his husband's extramarital activities.

At forty-eight, Joseph Byron Pulaski—JB to the select few he allowed close—cut an imposing figure: six-foot-four of lean, sinewy strength meticulously maintained through disciplined keto, punishing leg routines, intermittent fasting, and hot yoga sessions that left him drenched but centered. These weren't simply vanity projects but necessary fortifications against what he called "life's relentless assault."

Tonight's assault came in the form of a Hawaiian luau—a godforsaken party JB had agreed to cohost only after Mike's poisonous dart of gossip two weeks prior: "Word on the street is that we're always the guests—never the hosts. People are starting to whisper, wondering if you're one of those controlling husbands who hates having people in his home."

Through the refracted bottom of his tumbler, JB observed the assembled guests as a trio of multiracial Ken dolls greeted them with leis and passed canapés adorned with pineapple slices and syrupy cherries. The servers wore uniforms handpicked by Mike: Hawaiian shirts and matching shorts— green, yellow, and red—bought a size too small.

JB's attention drifted to the wall behind the bartender—a gallery of moments curated over seventeen years. There was the party at Rakesh's, where JB and Mike had first declared their exclusivity: Mike, luminous and golden, his hair like a halo of sunlight. A wedding photo of JB and Mike in pristine white tuxedos, champagne flutes raised in a salute, and there, clutching JB's leg, was Emilio—their adopted son—completing a portrait of hard-won happiness.

When had he last felt such joy?

The weight of fatherhood had crushed Mike initially. JB understood—Mike didn't see parenthood as a milestone, but as yet another grim signpost on the slippery winding road toward death. But Emilio had changed everything for JB. Their son brought such happiness to his life, a bright spot in what had become an increasingly dark landscape.

That shadow had descended precisely fourteen months ago, in Angelo Perrotta's medical office. Elevated PSA levels. The words "prostate cancer" spoken with the clinical detachment of a weather report. JB had known the awful truth before the biopsy confirmed it.

Almost immediately, Mike splintered from the man JB had met in a bar on Christmas night. Mike, six years JB's junior, had always viewed aging as an affliction he couldn't bear to confront. JB's cancer pushed him over the edge. In the days that followed, Mike's mood turned rancid. He skulked around the house with a drink in his hand, neglecting Emilio and unwilling to manage the household.

Then came the knock that changed everything.

Mike had met Jamie Friend and Tom Fitzsimmons at the gym—Miami residents who'd come to Sag Harbor to escape the heat, only to land in hot water with JB when they began an affair with his husband. Lean with thick hair curling beneath his trucker cap, Jamie stood in their doorway like the beginning of bad vintage porn. Tom, shorter and symmetrical, possessed all the telltale signs of an aging queen waging a failing war against Father Time: Botox, skin burnished by tanning beds, blindingly white veneers, and the unmistakable artifice of hair plugs.

In that moment, JB understood with crushing clarity: Mike had found someone—or rather, two someones—to occupy his time while JB underwent cancer treatment.

Mike's affair with the couple had lasted two months. Two months of JB undergoing the worst experience of his life, moving into the bedroom above the garage, ostensibly because he didn't want Mike to see the urine bag strapped to his. The truth was more complex—JB had moved out in a magnanimous gesture to prove he was evolved enough to handle Mike's infidelity. How pathetic and sexless he'd felt, such a far cry from the man he was before the chemo and radiation, when sex was as vital as oxygen.

JB recalled with peculiar relish the last time he'd seen Jamie and Tom. Mike had invited them for dinner last August. Jamie had focused his attention on JB, bragging about the potential deal their houseguest had brokered with a Mexican billionaire—in return, they'd agreed to make him a partner.

"That is the dumbest business decision I have ever heard," JB had said, standing to refresh his drink. "You should be more judicious about the kinds of people you get in bed with. How well do you know this houseguest? Throw him a few bucks. Call it a finder's fee, but if you ask me, don't make him a partner."

Three weeks later, that couple was found dead in their garage.

Apparent double suicide. Carbon monoxide poisoning. Their bodies sprawled in the front seat of their idling Mercedes G-Wagon.

JB had experienced a certain decadent delight when he heard the news.

Someone tugged on JB's arm, interrupting his dark contemplation. It was his doctor and good friend, Angelo Perrotta. "Great party." He had offered JB that exact compliment ten minutes earlier.

"Are you not having a good time?"

Angelo shuddered as though he'd accidentally belched at a formal dinner party. "What? Of course. Why do you ask?"

"You seem overly attentive, like I'm your pregnant wife. Don't worry. I'll let you know when my water breaks."

Angelo offered a confused expression, then chuckled. "You're such a kidder."

"That I am."

"Jason and I are heading out." Angelo paused before adding, "For what it's worth, I think you're incredibly patient."

JB thought that if Angelo continued, he'd ruin everything by laughing in his face. Instead, he spoke directly in Angelo's ear. "I'm not as good as you think. I have evil inside me. I squash it down so no one can see it."

"I don't believe that."

"Go home."

An awkward void opened once Angelo walked away. JB stepped outside to clear his head. He realized Angelo hadn't asked him about Dan. Hadn't commented on how cute he was, or asked anything about him at all. Not like all the other wide-eyed, teeth-baring guests stealing voracious glances at JB, silently hoping for a catfight.

"What are you doing out here?" Mike asked.

"Taking a break from all the fun."

"Have you seen Dan?"

JB smiled more than he had the entire evening. "No, I have not."

"Did you say anything to him?"

JB stared directly into Mike's eyes. "I don't recall."

"I saw you talking to him," Mike insisted. "What were you two talking about?"

"My garden, or was that with Angelo?"

Mike tottered slightly as he stepped closer, and JB took his elbow to steady him. "I know you must have said something because Dan left without saying goodbye."

"Are you sure you didn't say anything to offend him?" JB countered. "Looks like someone may have been overserved tonight."

Mike hesitated, thinking. "No, I don't think so."

"Would you like me to fix you a cup of coffee?" JB suggested as he rubbed Mike's shoulders. "I'm happy to do it."

"I hope I didn't say or do anything to offend Dan."

"I'm sure you didn't," JB insisted. "Now, go back to your party. I'll fix you a cup of coffee."

JB stood on the porch a few moments longer, observing this human reef of symbiotic relationships. Dan would be arriving at Rakesh's house by now. JB wondered if he'd frightened him. Dan would be thinking, *what if JB had killed Jamie and Tom? Maybe that's why he's so odd. He's a murderer.*

That gave JB great comfort.

In the distance, he could hear Mike's laughter echoing from inside the house, already searching for his next conquest. JB had learned something valuable tonight: the truth, when wielded properly, could be the most effective lie of all.

He had to be careful not to reveal too much of it.

Chapter Two

One week after the luau, Rakesh invited JB to The American Hotel restaurant for lunch. The Sag Harbor staple epitomized old-world elegance, with the hushed exclusivity of a private club, yet its prominent perch on Main Street did not elude the lofty locals and trendy tourists who were drawn to its refined interior.

Rakesh sat up after taking a long sip of his martini. He had a prominent jaw, the kind an artist would sculpt, a jaw that revealed the man he had become. The thin frame, the sharp tongue, and calculating dark eyes that JB could read easily were all that remained of his college roommate.

"I heard Mike was drunk out of his mind at your luau," Rakesh began without preamble.

"When hasn't Mike been drunk at a party?"

"Word on the street was that he couldn't keep his hands off Dan Vega."

JB took an extended pause. "Mike is going through a little midlife crisis."

"Oh, please. Next, you'll tell me a girl in trouble is a temporary thing. Mike parades his strays around town like he's competing in the Westminster Dog Show."

"It's temporary, and the less attention I pay to it, the better."

"Mike's midlife crisis began precisely after your diagnosis."

JB bristled. They both knew the timeline—the cancer, the treatment, Mike's immediate retreat into the arms of Jamie and Tom.

"How's Andy? And how did I not know he had family in Tampa?"

"There's not much to tell. Andy's hillbilly family from rural Tampa is not something I care to discuss. Besides, Andy wasn't close to them, and he never introduced them to me. He insisted I return home from Puerto Vallarta. Poor thing managed everything on his own. With his mother gone, Andy doesn't have any family except for some loser half-brother named JR, who's serving time for drug dealing"—Rakesh bowed his head—"and please keep that between us."

"You didn't attend the funeral?"

"Could you imagine this"—Rakesh indicated himself—"in a Baptist church in some Podunk town?" Rakesh lifted his martini glass to his lips and took a long pull. "How did two elitist snobs like us find ourselves married to poor white trash? Why couldn't you have loved me? We had such fun back in college." Rakesh sniggered as he reached over and squeezed JB's hand. "We could have been the power couple of our generation."

"Mike is not white trash." JB pulled his hand away. "Neither is Andy."

Rakesh broke off the end of the baguette and buttered it with deliberate precision. "Andy's mother's affairs were a mess, and my darling husband has become a world-class drunk."

"I'm sorry to hear that."

"It began last summer." Rakesh took a hearty bite of the heel. "He pulled himself together. Now it seems like it's escalating again."

"Why didn't you tell me?"

"Oh, I don't know. Maybe it was around the time you were diagnosed with cancer."

JB traced the condensation on his frosted glass. "What have we done to our husbands?"

"Done?" Rakesh fixed JB with a glare. "I'll tell you what we've done. We've given two men a life they only dreamed of."

"Is that what you think? That they should be grateful?"

JB could recall on demand every detail of every moment about meeting Mike that Christmas night—luminous, golden, talking for hours about his family without pause or pretense. The way Mike had pulled him into a world of warmth and light JB had only glimpsed in others' lives.

"Ground control to Major Tom." Rakesh waved his hand in front of JB's eyes. "You still walk miles in the forest of your thoughts."

"I won't give up on Mike." JB leaned forward. "My urologist said there's a chance my erections will come back. And since I cut back on my drinking, I haven't worn an adult diaper in weeks."

"I love that for you." Rakesh raised his glass in a mock toast, his smile as practiced as his accent. "Dan Vega called me yesterday." Rakesh's eyes glittered with something between amusement and concern. "Apparently, you regaled him with tales of your homicidal prowess at the party."

"It was a joke."

"Was it?" Rakesh beckoned the server. "Clear the table and bring us two martinis. Make them doubles."

"Not for me."

"You're having one too." Rakesh waited until the server left before continuing. "Dan was quite shaken. He wanted to know if I thought you were serious."

"What did you tell him?"

"I told him you were a pretentious academic with a dark sense of humor." Rakesh paused. "But honestly, JB, the way you've been behaving lately…"

"How have I been behaving?"

"Like a man with nothing left to lose."

The server set down two frosted martini glasses and poured. Rakesh took a long sip and smacked his lips together.

"Besides," Rakesh continued, "if you had killed Jamie and Tom, you would have done it much more elegantly. Poison, perhaps. Something literary. Carbon monoxide is so…pedestrian."

JB found himself smiling despite everything. "You think I'm too sophisticated for murder?"

"I think you're too smart to get caught." Rakesh's voice carried a note of genuine affection. "That means you shouldn't go around confessing to crimes you didn't commit."

"How do you know I didn't commit them?"

Rakesh stared at him for several seconds before leaning back in his chair. "Because I know you, Joseph Byron. You're many things—arrogant, controlling, occasionally cruel—but you're not a killer."

"Everyone's a killer under the right circumstances."

"And what would those circumstances be?" Rakesh swirled his martini so the olive performed a lazy pirouette.

JB thought about Mike grinding against Dan at the luau, about moving above the garage while Jamie and Tom occupied his bed.

JB lowered his voice. "When someone threatens everything you've built."

Rakesh set down his glass with deliberate care. "JB, listen to me carefully. Whatever you're planning—stop. Mike isn't worth it."

"Mike is my husband."

"Mike is a beautiful man with the emotional depth of a puddle. He panicked when you got sick, and instead of dealing with it like an adult, he ran into the arms of the first two men who paid attention to him."

What gnawed at JB wasn't the casual brutality of Rakesh's assessment. It was this unspoken agreement among so many gay men he knew—infidelity carefully draped in silence like expensive fabric over secondhand furniture. An accepted secret. "You've never liked Mike."

"That's irrelevant. What's relevant is that you're spiraling into something dangerous." Rakesh reached across the table and gripped JB's wrist. "I get it," Rakesh continued. "You feel guilty for not being able to satisfy your husband, so you granted him a hall pass with Jamie and Tom, but they're dead now. You're still alive."

"Like I said, I won't give up on Mike."

"Do me one favor—don't tell anyone else you killed that couple. Promise?"

JB looked down at Rakesh's manicured fingers, remembering all the times this man had steadied him—through school, through coming out to his parents, through cancer.

"I promise," JB said, "I won't tell *anyone* else."

Chapter Three

JB was reading in the study when Mike appeared in the doorway, phone in hand, his face a mixture of confusion and rage. "Have you lost your mind?" Mike asked in a harsh whisper. "What would make you do such a thing?"

JB set down his book. "Do what?"

"Dan thinks you were trying to scare him off." Mike stepped into the room, closing the door behind him. "He said it's obvious you don't want him hanging around me."

"What a coward." JB walked to the bar cart and poured himself a Scotch. "Would you like me to fix you a drink?"

"Dan is not a coward."

JB measured vodka into a second glass.

"I was only having a little fun." JB handed Mike the vodka. "Does Dan really think I killed Jamie and Tom?"

"Of course, he doesn't think you killed them," Mike roared, then caught himself, lowering his voice with a glance toward the door. "Dan thinks you're pathetic. In fact, he feels sorry for you because—"

JB leaned in. "Go ahead. Say it. Because I had cancer! Well, tell that dimwit I don't need his sympathy."

Mike met his gaze directly. "I don't think you understand how serious a claim this is!"

"It was a joke."

"There's nothing funny about confessing to murder." Mike drained his drink in one gulp. "Dan wants nothing to do with me."

"Well, that was my plan."

"You're crazy. You need help."

"*I* need help!" JB let out a bitter laugh. "Mike, I've been your partner for the past seventeen years. If anyone can speak to you with complete honesty, it's me. Over the past year, you haven't simply tested the boundaries of our relationship as part of some garden-variety midlife crisis. You've gone out of your way to humiliate yourself, me, and most of all our son. And for what? To nab the attention of a lapdog like Dan Vega? He is the most vapid, self-absorbed person we've ever met. Have you no self-respect after being associated with a dead couple?"

Mike's mouth opened, then closed. Something shifted in his expression—a flicker of shock, quickly replaced by disgust. "I always knew you were a snob. My sister warned me before we got married. 'Go ahead and marry him,' she said, 'but know that JB sees himself on some great pedestal looking down at you.' God, she was right."

"That's a shame," JB sighed. "Out of your entire family, Leslie's the one I like the most."

Mike stared at JB, his expression crumbling from anger into something wounded. Slowly, he slid down the wall until he was sitting on the floor, hands covering his face.

JB crouched beside him. "I can't believe you're crying over Dan Vega. Is he worth your tears?"

Mike's head snapped up, his eyes blazing. "I'm not crying over him, you self-centered ass. I'm crying over us. Over what we've become."

"We haven't become anything." JB reached for Mike's shoulders. "I love you."

Mike recoiled from JB's touch, his body tensing. "Love? You think this is love? Scaring away someone who pays attention to me?"

"What will it take to win you back?" JB's grip tightened on Mike's shoulders. "To be like we were before? You were happy with Jamie and Tom. Maybe—" he hesitated, then pushed forward—"maybe we could find someone to join us. A third."

Mike went still. "A third...with us?"

"Someone we both like. Someone who could help us reconnect." JB's voice took on a desperate edge. "I know I can't give you everything you need right now, medically speaking, but maybe—"

"Stop." Mike pulled away from JB's grasp and struggled to his feet. "Just stop."

He walked toward the door, movements mechanical, like someone sleepwalking. At the threshold, he paused without turning around.

"JB, I need you to understand something. This isn't about sex. This isn't about Jamie and Tom or Dan. This is about the fact that the man I married—the man who used to laugh at my jokes and hold me during a thunderstorm—that man disappeared the day you got diagnosed. And the person who's left…" Mike choked up. "I don't even recognize him anymore."

Mike left without another word. Moments later, JB heard the front door slam.

* * *

Three days later, Mike still hadn't emerged from his funk. JB did his best to shield Emilio from Mike's behavior. He took their son sunning at the beach, kayaking in the bay, and practicing yoga. But every time they returned home, they found Mike lying on the couch with a glass of vodka in his hand.

To break the cycle, JB decided to surprise Mike. He figured Mike would come out of his funk with a trip to the city. Mike was too outgoing and social to sulk indefinitely. JB knew how much Mike enjoyed musicals, so he planned to buy tickets, no matter the price, to *Hamilton*.

That afternoon, Rakesh called to invite JB for a drink. He arrived at The American Hotel lounge after six and found Rakesh seated at the bar. "Well, there he is," Rakesh said. "Congratulations."

JB sat next to him. "For what?"

"For redefining slut-shaming for a whole new generation of Hester Prynnes."

JB motioned to the bartender. "I'll have what he's having."

"Bring me another while you're at it," Rakesh added. "We're celebrating.

I'm only sorry I ever doubted you."

JB ran a hand through his hair, cringing at the thinness of his pate. "I seriously have no idea what you're talking about."

"Mike deserves it with the way he's been carrying on. No one will sleep with him now."

As Rakesh reached for his glass, JB gripped his wrist. "What are you talking about?"

"Your diabolical plan. The one where you told Dan you killed Jamie and Tom. It hasn't backfired, as I'm sure Mike had hoped. Instead, folks from Southampton to Montauk are touting your actions as heroic. Not to mention how cavalier you were, defending your marriage with words, not a sword. I don't think we'll see the likes of Dan Vega around here for a long, long time."

A slow dawning of comprehension rose on JB's face. "Oh, I see. Now that I have the townsfolk's support, you've suddenly fallen in line."

Rakesh rubbed his hands together with mischievous delight. "I'm only happy everyone now sees Mike for who he truly is."

"You never liked Mike. You made up your mind about him the minute I introduced you two that night we had dinner at Elmo's."

"I didn't stay for dinner."

A memory surfaced: a very gay restaurant in the heart of Chelsea, muscle boys in tight Raymond Dragon T-shirts, frothy pink cosmopolitans, and Mike, overcompensating, nervous, treating the meeting with Rakesh like a job interview he was woefully unqualified for.

"Oh, they hired a new pianist," Rakesh said, pivoting away from the subject. "Gianni Cuomo. Sounds Italian."

JB stared at the flyer of a man in a black tuxedo. Marquee-idol good looks and a reedy frame. Exactly Mike's type.

"I'm taking Mike into the city Friday night. We're seeing *Hamilton*."

Rakesh held his mouth open. "Well, aren't you the romantic one, Professor Pulaski?"

His ears burned. "I think the trip will help us. I do."

Rakesh raised his glass, smiling. "Well, cheers to that."

* * *

The following weekend in Manhattan was a success.

JB surprised Mike with a shopping spree at Bloomingdale's. They exited the department store, carrying shopping bags rife with new clothes. JB stole a glance at their reflection in the window on Fifth Avenue. Tall, attractive, happy—that was what JB saw staring back at him. They left Bloomingdale's, having magically become the couple they once were. The spell lasted the entire weekend.

After the theater, JB and Mike dined late and extravagantly at Joe Allen's, and they did spend too much money. They sipped martinis and shared a porterhouse in a quiet booth set against the exposed brick wall. Mike, as always, recited his glowing review. He couldn't contain his giddy recollection of scene after scene as though he'd memorized the book. The golden glow of the candlelight illuminated Mike's features as if he were on stage himself.

JB ordered another round and excused himself to use the restroom. Once he returned, Mike tucked his cell phone in his pocket. JB noticed but said nothing.

They returned to the Tribeca apartment after dinner. JB played music he knew Mike would like. '70s classics. Stevie singing about being afraid of changing. Mike stepped out of the bathroom, towel-drying his hair. Beads of water glistened on his smooth, bare shoulders. "Oh, my God. I haven't heard this one in forever."

JB sat on the bed, still completely dressed except for his shoes. He was reading the *Sunday Times*, which he'd bought at a deli on their way home. Mike sprawled out next to him, wearing only boxer shorts, his face beaming as he gazed at the ceiling.

JB was tempted to ask Mike if he could sleep with him, embrace him, feel the scratch of Mike's stubble on his chest.

But then Mike stood up and turned off the music. "Come to think of it, I never liked that Fleetwood Mac song."

"I thought you loved that song." JB kissed Mike on the forehead. He decided he wouldn't jeopardize the good night they'd spent together with his silly request. "I'm going to wash up before bed."

"Night," Mike replied. "Did you call Emilio at any point this evening?"

"I called him at intermission." JB smiled as he closed the bedroom door behind him.

This moment was as whole and perfect and smooth as an egg.

Chapter Four

The weekend in Manhattan marked a turning point. From then on, JB devoted himself to Mike's happiness, though he still fretted his husband would grow bored or lonely. And so, JB arranged two more theater outings that month. In response, Mike began preparing dinner nightly and, noting JB's preferences, carefully placed his prized *The New Yorker* issues on his study desk rather than scattering them across the coffee table as before. More than anything, JB made a point of telling their friends about Mike's renewed thoughtfulness, as though collecting witnesses to their reconciliation.

One afternoon, JB was reading when Mike appeared in the front doorway, breathless and excited. "You were right!"

JB set down his book. "Right about what?"

"We've been invited to the Beltrams' Fourth of July party."

And there it was: physical proof that JB and Mike had not become Hamptons *persona non grata*.

It amused JB to watch Mike's giddy reaction to a party invitation—his enthusiasm as pure and unbridled as a child transfixed by a magician's sleight of hand, marveling at a quarter conjured from thin air. Mike and Rakesh shared this quality, though Rakesh approached such invitations with a different intensity. Where Mike saw an opportunity to dress up, to mingle and charm, Rakesh viewed each invitation as a carefully calibrated measure of social standing, a map illustrating the intricate topography of Hamptons hierarchy.

Neither appealed to JB.

Gus and Winnie Beltram owned a sprawling farmhouse in East Hampton. Winnie had become the most sought-after Hamptons caterer soon after opening her specialty food store fifteen years ago. A television producer had taken a chance on the witty woman with the affable demeanor, offering her a show. Twelve years and ten bestselling cookbooks later, Winnie Beltram had become a household name with her wildly popular show, *Chef's Kiss*.

"Low to the ground," was how Winnie described herself. "Built for stamina, not speed, with solid hips that spawned no babies." She once told JB, "Gus and I are fond of children—just not across the board as a species." Winnie had transformed herself into an appealing avatar for millions of viewers worldwide who saw her as the embodiment of that rare kind of television personality—a comfortingly ordinary-looking woman of a certain age who entertained out of sheer enjoyment rather than a female obligation.

The Beltrams' parties had achieved legendary status, with people like Mike and Rakesh savagely vying for invitations with the desperation of bargain hunters on Black Friday. Snagging a coveted invitation meant breaching their inner circle, which granted you access to former Bravolebrities desperately clinging to relevance, aging starlets perpetually "between projects," disgraced politicians and morning TV show hosts, nepo babies launching another failed line of activewear, and an assortment of absurdly wealthy businessmen escorting their striking yet frighteningly identical trophy wives. Most coveted of all, attending a Beltram affair meant having your photograph featured in the "Who's Who" section of *Hamptons Magazine*. A prize Rakesh and Mike would kill for in a steel cage match.

But this year felt different. JB couldn't help wondering if Gus and Winnie might deliberately exclude them—a calculated move to distance themselves from the controversy JB had manufactured.

Apparently not.

JB picked up his book to resume reading when a realization swept over him: The pages between his fingers were pages now, not an escape.

Finally, at last, he had reclaimed his life—not just in name, but in spirit.

* * *

Two days before the party, JB overheard Mike on the phone in his bedroom. JB hadn't meant to eavesdrop, but Mike's hushed voice had piqued JB's interest.

"Yes, we were invited," Mike said, his tone sharp with annoyance. "Why wouldn't we be?"

There was a pause, followed by Mike's nervous laugh.

"Don't be ridiculous," Mike replied. "I'm holding the invitation in my hand, and it's addressed to Joseph Byron Pulaski and Michael Fogarty."

Another pause followed.

"Well, they can stare all they like. JB's been on his best behavior lately. Obviously, Gus and Winnie found his prank harmless even if you didn't."

JB backed away before Mike could discover him. Had they been invited out of genuine goodwill, or were they simply this year's oddity? It didn't matter, JB told himself. He would prove to the Hamptons elite that Joseph Byron Pulaski could not be reduced to some traveling sideshow attraction.

* * *

The Beltrams' home, a massive cedar structure Winnie had remodeled herself, stood on an eminence thirty feet from the street. Recently, they'd added a library to the existing structure that led to a large glass solarium with a vaulted roof.

Guests mingled, sipping cocktails. Only clear beverages were served since everything—the couches, the floors, the walls—were white, as were everyone invited. Cerulean pillows adorned the sofa. Lapis pottery from a local designer sat on bleached bookshelves. The Beltrams' estate—"the farmhouse," they called it—was a humble-brag JB hated more than the ten-million-dollar home itself.

The solarium, on the other hand, was a gem: a vaulted ceiling with bleached cedar support beams. Oversized couches ran along the room's perimeter with substantial coffee tables you could actually rest your feet on, even set a drink without a coaster. Candles shimmered. Flowers glowed everywhere. This was JB's type of room.

All their friends were there. JB scanned the room for Dan Vega but found no sight of him. Mike headed straight to the bar. JB made his way to the hosts stationed at the solarium's entrance. His gaze settled on Gus—a stocky figure whose appearance seemed a testament to culinary indulgence. Short and deeply tanned, with limp hair hanging like a neglected houseplant, Gus filled out a billowy nautical-striped shirt that strained against his pronounced belly. The unmistakable silhouette of a man married to a chef.

Privately, Rakesh had nicknamed him "Nipples McGillicuddy," "Gussy Nips," and JB's favorite, "Mr. Utters"—a tribute to Gus's penchant for translucent shirts that offered an unwanted anatomical exhibition.

"Nice to see you." JB kissed Winnie on the cheek. She offered a quizzical expression accompanied by uncomfortable laughter, her eyes flickering over his shoulder as if something more fascinating were happening elsewhere—sea lions balancing balls on their noses.

Gus, typically giddy and chatty, appeared instantly awkward. "Well, this is a surprise," he said with exaggerated affectation. "We weren't expecting you."

JB, at a loss, stuttered, "Oh, but I thought we were—"

A photographer crouched in front of them, poised to snap a photo, when Gus waved him away. "Dear, isn't that Tony and Gabe?" Winnie nudged his back. "Let's go and congratulate them. I hear they're expecting twins."

They retreated quickly, weaving and bobbing and smiling and laughing among the guests that formed and broke and reformed around them before JB fully comprehended that Winnie and Gus meant to escape him. Panic rising, JB's mind raced to piece together this perplexing situation.

I need a drink.

The bar had been set up at the end of the room before the sheer expanse of glass that framed a wall-sized panorama of lawn. Guests multiplied like an infestation in anticipation of the fireworks. JB ordered a Scotch. *Were we invited by accident?* Some oversight by a party planner using an outdated guest list? Suddenly, it seemed as if guests were turning away when their gaze met his. Pockets of whispering and pointing. JB downed his drink.

He told himself he didn't care about the whispering and pointing, but that was a lie.

JB signaled the bartender for a double when Rakesh joined him. "Mike looks good. Is he working out more?"

JB drained his second Scotch and ordered another. At first, Rakesh's question confused him because at this party—filled with hyperbolic chatter, glittering jewels, and wandering hands—he was still too focused on the Beltrams' snub. But then, emerging through the fog of JB's growing inebriation, Mike appeared—more handsome, more confident, as if this Mike had gone into his winter storage and dusted off his younger self. JB squeezed his eyes and looked again. That was when JB noticed Mike chatting up a younger man dressed in a black suit. In that moment, he saw it all: the head tilted back, the harsh laughter, the flirtatious touch. Mike had found a new stray.

"Who is that talking to Mike?" JB asked, Scotch sloshing in his glass.

"What's wrong?"

Panic burst inside JB's chest like a firecracker as he strained to recall where he'd seen this young man before. The slick black hair, the olive complexion, and the thin mustache—they belonged to the new pianist from The American Hotel lounge.

"Hello!" Rakesh snapped his fingers, pulling JB from his spiral. "What's the matter?"

The Scotch had taken possession of JB's tongue. "When I arrived, Gus Beltram said he was surprised to see me."

Rakesh blinked in perplexity. "Nipples McGillicuddy said that?"

"We must have received the invite by mistake."

JB watched Rakesh absorb this information. "Oh my God, you've been gay-cotted?"

Shots echoed overhead, showering the dark sky with glowing lights—red, blue, and white—like a series of exploding chrysanthemums. The fireworks had begun, their brilliant colors reflecting in the glass walls, casting the room in shifting shades of color that matched JB's disorientation.

The evening transformed into something darker than a celebration of independence. JB scanned the crowded room for Mike, but there was no sign of him, which meant one of two things: either he was drunk, or he'd taken his new stray somewhere clandestine. It was not impossible that both were true.

"I need another drink." JB turned to the bartender. "Double Scotch."

Rakesh swiped a hand down his face. "I can't believe I'm going to say this, but you need to slow down."

JB seized the glass from the bar, his gaze locking onto Gus with the crackling intensity of a cherry bomb. JB could taste the hate in his heart like metal on his tongue. The rumors, although never corroborated, depicted Gus as a man who harbored certain inclinations but never acted on them—a secret shellacked under a bronze patina of elitism. Gus's eyes narrowed, regarding JB not merely as an unwelcome guest, but as something far more contemptible: an intruder violating the sanctity of their carefully curated gathering.

An interloper!

"I know you're upset." Rakesh gripped JB's arm, adopting the placating tone of a father speaking to a volatile toddler. "But don't do anything foolish. At least for my sake."

JB supposed Rakesh was being part snide, part facetious to defuse the situation, but JB felt only fury. A dam broke inside him—he sensed a terrible reversal unfolding, some social disaster whereby he had been lured here for some public stoning right out of a Shirley Jackson story.

"You know what?" JB said, commandeering the room, ungainly, a shred of confidence still alive in him. He stepped forward, wrenching his arm free from Rakesh's grip. "I say fuck 'em."

"Hush, keep it down now," Rakesh gritted through clenched ventriloquist teeth. "Voices carry."

For a moment, the party seemed suspended in time. *I've been set up. Lured here under false pretenses.* In JB's addled mind, the only missing element was a bucket of blood teetering precariously on one of the cedar support beams above him, with Gus Beltram clutching the rope's end. JB peered into his empty glass. He was dimly aware that he must be very drunk.

"That's right," JB began again in a voice even louder than the one he'd been using. "I don't care what any of you think. Fuck you all!" Bracing himself, as one did against an oncoming wave, he experienced a tingling in his groin—arousal, and something far worse. The warmth spread before he could stop it, transforming his crisp linen slacks into transparent evidence of his body's betrayal. Around him, the party-going piranhas began to notice, their conversations faltering as they registered what was happening.

"Jesus Christ," Rakesh gasped. "No, no, no, no…"

The moments that followed blurred in a cascade of motion. JB only dimly aware that Rakesh was guiding—no, forcibly steering—him toward the exit. What registered with brutal clarity was Gus's crooked smile, a vicious smirk that tracked JB's trajectory across the room like a predator savoring wounded prey.

"I'm not leaving," JB snarled, his fingers gripping the doorframe with desperate tenacity. He twisted back, confronting the guests with their botched glassy eyes, their tangerine, scaly skin, and their bloated fish lips. The photographer who had been waved away earlier now raised his camera, the flash exploding like lightning.

Gus erupted in laughter, a sound both shrill and calculated. He raised a hand to obscure his mouth, overcrowded with bleached teeth gleaming like a shark's grin.

"I'm onto you, Mr. Utters," JB hurled the words, even as Rakesh's insistent grip pulled him out the door. "Watch your ass!"

* * *

JB sat slumped in his armchair, fading in and out of consciousness, while Mike paced the living room floor. "How could you embarrass me like that?"

He attempted to stand up, but his body was restrained. When his bleary eyes found no such restraints, he was bewildered. "Where's Rakesh?"

"He had to take Andy home." Exasperation shimmered off of Mike in hot waves. "Apparently, he was very drunk too."

The question swelled within him—the one JB dreaded asking, but had to—when he noticed his pants had been replaced with a towel. "What happened?"

Mike stood over him, appearing mostly in shadow as JB experienced the odd sensation of having been shrunk into a tiny version of himself. "You wet yourself."

All this time, JB had assumed he'd merely made some off-color remark, insulted the Beltrams' bad taste, or implied Gus was gay. If what Mike said was true, the situation was far worse than he could comprehend at this moment, yet he found himself delighting in its perverse absurdity. "Well, I wasn't having a good time anyway."

When Mike bent forward, his watery blue eyes shone like mirrors, reflecting JB's face aglow with alcohol and doubt. "I'm not sure if you're still drunk or you're being an asshole, but tomorrow, when you're sober, you'll realize the enormity of damage you've done." Standing upright, Mike inhaled sharply. "What kills me is that you had the audacity to criticize me for spending time with Dan, dismissing my friendship with him as some midlife crisis. You accused me of going out of my way to humiliate myself and my family." Mike turned to walk away, but paused, chuckled mockingly. "Well, congratulations. If humiliating this family was a competition, consider yourself the grand prize winner."

Mike waited, as if expecting a response, but JB had nothing to say. The silence stretched between them, filled only by the sound of the silver clock ticking in JB's study.

Mike huffed in frustration. As his footsteps faded away, JB closed his eyes. He felt weary and still profoundly drunk. The room spun, and he gripped the chair's armrests to steady himself.

His only recollection of those final moments at the party, other than Gus's cheeks blooming like carnations as Rakesh dragged him out of the house, was a curious sense of arousal.

Tomorrow would bring phone calls, texts, maybe photographs in gossip columns. The life he'd constructed so carefully would be scrutinized.

But tonight, in the wreckage of his own making, JB felt something he hadn't experienced in months: completely, utterly present in his own body.

Chapter Five

"Dad!" Emilio pleaded. "Can we go look for sneakers now?"

JB barely heard him. Across the crowded dining room of Tutto il Giorno, he watched an elderly woman at a corner table drop her newspaper with a sharp gasp. Her husband leaned forward, squinting at the front page before his mouth fell open.

"Dad, what are you looking at?"

JB's stomach clenched as he spotted a copy of *Sag Harbor Express* abandoned on a nearby chair. He could make out only part of the headline: SAG HARBOR MURDER...

"Stay here," he told Emilio, rising quickly to retrieve the paper. His hands trembled slightly as he unfolded it.

Sag Harbor Murder Prison Confession

RIVERHEAD—Police have been passed details of a disturbing double homicide after Richard-Jay Santiago confessed to his cellmate. The witness came forward with detailed information alleging Santiago bragged about killing Thomas Fitzsimmons and James Friend in their Sag Harbor home last summer.

JB's vision blurred as he read the rest. Santiago. The houseguest Jamie had mentioned. The partner deal gone wrong. His legs felt unsteady as he returned to the table.

"Dad? What's wrong?"

JB wondered how many of their friends had read the news. He imagined Gus and Winnie Beltram reading the article simultaneously at the breakfast table, scones fresh out of the oven. If only he could've seen their faces once they learned JB hadn't killed Jamie and Tom after all.

"Is that the couple Pop was hooking up with last summer?"

JB gripped his son's arm. "What did you say?"

"Dad, you're hurting me!"

JB released his grip, eyes scanning the other tables to see if anyone was staring. Still feeling hungover, JB braved the public because he'd promised Emilio new sneakers. A promise he made before he'd used the Beltrams' shimmering solarium as a urinal. Mike, while declining the invitation to brunch, suggested that JB shield his bloodshot eyes behind his sunglasses. Except now, he wanted to look directly into his son's eyes. "Why would you say such a thing?"

"'Cause it's the truth." Emilio snatched his father's bacon.

"Who told you that?"

"Dad, I'm not stupid. You don't think I know what's going on between you and Pop? I hear him talking on the phone with his *friends*. He says things you'd never say to a friend, Dad."

JB's mouth hung open. "Listen to me. Things aren't always as they appear."

Emilio rolled his head. "Dad...you guys don't even sleep in the same bedroom anymore."

JB folded the newspaper to focus on his son. "We should have talked with you about this sooner, but your father and I went through a difficult period after my diagnosis. I suppose we didn't want to alarm you, but it made sense, at the time, for us to sleep in separate rooms."

"Is everything all right with you?"

JB saw the worry in his son's eyes. "I'm fine...seriously. That's the truth."

"Then why don't you and Pop sleep in the same room? And why does Pop date other men?"

JB's throat tightened. How could he explain what he didn't fully under-stand himself? That love and betrayal could coexist? That people hurt the ones they love most when they're terrified?

"Sometimes when grown-ups get scared, they make mistakes," JB said finally. "Your father was scared when I got sick, and we both handled it badly. But we're trying to figure things out."

Emilio studied his father's face with unsettling intensity. "Do you still love him?"

"Yes." The answer came without hesitation, which surprised JB more than it should have.

"Does he still love you?"

"I think so. But love gets complicated when people are hurting."

Emilio nodded. "Yeah, I know a thing or two about hurting."

* * *

After dropping Emilio at his friend Evan's house, JB drove home with the newspaper burning a hole in the passenger seat. He found Mike asleep on the sofa, still in his bathrobe from the night before. Even unconscious, Mike looked troubled—his brow furrowed, one hand clutching the sofa cushion as if anchoring himself against some internal storm.

"Wake up." JB held out the newspaper. "Read this."

Mike shot him a curious glance. He took the newspaper and scanned the article, his expression shifting subtly. JB observed Mike's eyes move across the page, searching for any tell, any microexpressions that might reveal what his husband truly knew about Richard-Jay Santiago.

"Interesting." Mike handed the paper back with casual indifference. "I guess you're off the hook for your little murder confession prank."

"Funny how things work out."

JB's cell phone rang. "Did you hear the news?" It was just as JB had assumed; the news of the jailhouse confession was telegraphing its way across the South Fork of Long Island. "Lucky you," Rakesh continued. "This will certainly divert attention away from your performance last night."

"If only that were true." JB cleared his throat. "Still, I'll need to call Winnie and Gus to apologize."

"Is that Rakesh?" Mike rose from the sofa. "Tell that skinny friend of yours no one will forget what you did last night."

"Oh, is that Mike?" Rakesh said in JB's ear. "Tell the whore I said, *Hi*."

"Be nice," JB muttered.

"Well, I must go and spread the good news. Damage control has become my new vocation after my husband and best friend made drunken spectacles of themselves in public."

After Rakesh hung up, JB heard the shower running in Mike's bedroom. He sat in his armchair and read the article again. A new concern emerged: how well had Mike known the killer?

Twenty minutes later, Mike appeared fully dressed in white shorts, a pink button-down shirt, and brand-new white loafers. "Well, I'm off."

"Where are you going all dressed up?"

Mike offered a baffled expression as though he hadn't made a fuss. "I'm meeting Andy for a late lunch."

"Rakesh didn't mention anything about Andy meeting you for lunch. Won't he be hungover?"

"Are you memorizing that article?"

JB put the newspaper aside. "Did you ever meet Santiago?"

"Who?" Mike exhaled impatiently. "Where did I leave my keys?" He entered the kitchen and began opening the cabinets, running his hand along the counter as if some clue were written in braille.

"Jamie and Tom's houseguest. The one who confessed to murdering them. His name is Richard Santiago."

"Richard?" Fake confusion followed by a vaguer recollection drew over his face. "I may have met him once or twice," was all Mike said. He had, by now, become one of those frantic people who searched for keys like they were an antiserum to a poison they'd consumed.

"You were pretty close to Jamie and Tom," JB pressed. "You mean to tell me you only knew Richard in passing?"

Mike rummaged through the magazine rack, avoiding JB's accusatory stare. It was obvious he meant to escape this conversation. "All I know is that he lived off and on in their pool house. I didn't think much of him. He had this scar running through his left eyebrow."

This detail came too quickly, as if Mike had been thinking about Santiago after reading the article. Funny how Mike had never mentioned him. JB could only assume Santiago hadn't interested Mike, which made sense since Jamie and Tom consumed most of his attention.

"Jesus!" Mike shouted. His forehead was slick with sweat. "My keys were on the coffee table the whole time. Why didn't you tell me, JB? You knew I was looking for them."

"How about cocktails later at The American Hotel?" JB offered. "I heard they have a new pianist."

"I don't think so."

"Well, I'll be there around six if you change your mind."

Mike hurried out of the house. JB watched as he backed his Range Rover out of the driveway, gravel crunching under the tires, in a matter of seconds. The performance was over, but questions remained. Mike's too-casual reaction to the news, his detailed knowledge of Santiago, his sudden need to meet Andy—none of it fit together.

JB reached for his phone to call Rakesh, then stopped. Whatever Mike was hiding, exposing him to Rakesh's judgment wouldn't help his marriage. Some investigations would have to wait.

Chapter Six

Days after the news broke about the Sag Harbor murder jailhouse confession, JB invited Angelo and Rakesh to yoga. Afterward, they ate lunch at Lulu's Kitchen on Main Street, sipping Pinot Grigio at a table outside. A Sag Harbor staple, unlike those pretentious little patio-type places that sprang up in town for a season or two, where the consciously young and chic gathered for Bloody Marys and brunch to show off their summer bodies and suntans and be seen and see others.

"Rakesh, you are the most inflexible person I have ever met," JB said.

"I only come for the drinks after," Rakesh replied. "Yoga is torture disguised as exercise. Besides, we all can't have thighs of steel like you."

"I agree with JB," Angelo added. "You should stretch more, Rakesh. Watching you downward dog—I kept thinking you were going to snap in half, stick-figure man."

They scanned the menus through sunglasses, though JB and Rakesh knew it well. By now, JB had fully recovered from his hangover. The day after the Fourth of July party, he'd called the Beltrams to apologize. Neither Winnie nor Gus had responded. For now, JB thought, it was best to let them marinate in their righteous indignation.

"So," Angelo began. "How are things with you and Mike?"

JB kept his eyes on the menu. "Good." The lie felt heavy in the afternoon heat. "How are things with you and Jason?"

"Stressful," Angelo admitted almost immediately as if he hoped JB would ask. "Studying for the bar is taking its toll on our relationship."

"I'll miss seeing him in that police uniform," Rakesh admitted right before he took a gulp of wine.

"Not me. I'm so happy Jason went to law school. I couldn't live thinking that every time he left the house, he might not come back."

"Not to mention how this will change your social standing." Rakesh offered JB a knowing wink. "A doctor *and* a lawyer…you're on your way to becoming quite the power couple."

JB raised his wine glass. "To power couples."

For a while, the three sat, pitching their faces to catch the sun's rays. It was a quiet JB knew wouldn't last as long as Rakesh was present, and there was alcohol involved.

"Speaking of couples," Rakesh started in as if he'd read JB's mind. "Angelo and I are happy to hear you and Mike are doing well. But we're concerned."

JB sipped wine. "Concerned about what?"

"We heard rumblings that Mike may have started sliding back into old habits."

JB slapped the menu down on the table. "I'm not hungry."

"JB, we're your friends," Rakesh said. "I know how much time and energy you've been putting into your relationship with the dinner parties, the visits to the city, and the Broadway shows…we only want to make sure you're all right."

Angelo smiled with unease. "The night of the Fourth of July party, you weren't yourself."

"I—I know." JB struggled to find the words for the feeling he'd experienced right before Rakesh had rushed him out of the Beltrams' home. A sudden sense of urgency mixed with arousal. He'd planned on talking with them about it today, but saw no point now. How could he explain the feeling when he hadn't reconciled it with himself?

"We're here to offer our support." Angelo shot Rakesh a warning glance.

"I know you think this is an ambush," Rakesh continued, ignoring Angelo's signal, "but we're genuinely concerned. If the Fourth of July party was a one-off incident, we can forget all about it. The story will become legendary: 'Were you there the time Professor Pulaski peed his pants at that party?' And everyone, including you, will laugh."

"Professor Pulaski peed his pants." JB chuckled—a giggle that caught in his chest and persisted. "Nice alliteration."

Angelo and Rakesh looked at each other oddly, and soon, they began laughing, too, big chesty laughs that drew attention from nearby tables.

"Gentlemen." Angelo dabbed the tears from his eyes. "Let's take it down a notch before they ask us to leave. I'm still relatively new in town."

Rakesh topped off their drinks. "You'll get used to it. People judge one another out here for wearing red shoes on a Thursday."

It certainly was an unusually odd place to have this conversation, but something had been itching at Rakesh for days. Every conversation, every text was laced with annoyance, and today, he seemed hell-bent on talking.

"Now that we've gotten that out of the way," JB said, hoping to steer the conversation away from his marriage. "Let's nab our server and order some food."

"Before we put a pin in this topic." Rakesh's voice sounded strained, as if he were buttoning tight pants. "There's something else."

JB's stomach dropped. "Get on with it."

Rakesh cast furtive glances at nearby tables, then leaned forward. "Andy saw Mike at The American Hotel lounge the other night. Apparently, he was drunk, hanging all over the new pianist like an organ grinder's monkey."

"Andy said that?"

"Yes—except for my editorial flourish about the monkey," Rakesh admitted. "JB, I could look the other way if it only involved Mike, but think about how he's making you look…not to mention Emilio and your circle of friends."

"Oh, that's what this is about…how my marriage is affecting your social standing."

"My social life is suffering," Rakesh spat, "because Mike is carrying on like Madame Bovary."

JB considered throwing down his napkin, considered telling them to fuck off, considered asking them to come home and deal with whatever it was that he was failing to deal with.

What did Rakesh stand to gain by bringing up the subject of JB's marriage in such a public way?

"And." Rakesh jerked his head, sniffing sharply. "Invites to Gus and Winnie's annual costume party went out, and Andy and I didn't receive one."

"Oh, Winnie and Gus scratched you off their guest list, and it's all because of my open marriage," JB laughed. "That's ridiculous. Lots of couples have open marriages."

"That's true. Lots of couples have an agreement predicated upon mutual respect, not a public flogging and urinary incontinence."

This comment landed so squarely, JB felt sucker punched. He was leaving his body, a survival mechanism perfected during childhood with alcoholic parents—the ability to assess situations with detached precision.

"How often does Andy go out drinking without you? Maybe you should worry about your own marriage."

JB noticed the tendons in Rakesh's neck pulled taut. "He was with clients."

"Gentlemen," Angelo interrupted. "Don't look now, but speaking of the devil."

They turned in unison as Mike crossed the street toward The American Hotel.

"The pianist—Gianni Cuomo—is staying at The American Hotel," Rakesh whispered urgently.

JB forced a smile. *Don't respond*, he begged of himself. His relationship with Mike was something for them to work out privately. Certainly not with friends and most definitely not in public.

"What are you two having?" JB managed, opening his menu with steady hands, though the words blurred together. "I'm suddenly famished."

Chapter Seven

It went without saying that JB thought of nothing else but Gianni Cuomo while driving home after lunch. He refused to jump to any conclusions. If anything was going on between Gianni and Mike, JB knew their affair would come to light soon enough. Mike always proved himself guilty in the end.

When JB arrived home, Mike wasn't at the house. Emilio was in his bedroom listening to music. Buckley was curled up at the foot of the bed.

"Have you heard from Pop?"

"Nope."

"Want to come outside and help me pick vegetables from the garden?"

Emilio cocked his head from side to side, emitting a cracking noise that annoyed JB. "Okay."

They picked tomatoes, basil, and cucuzza. Emilio collected the vegetables in a wicker basket, and JB watered the garden once they were done. Then Emilio stood with his hands on his hips, staring at the cucuzza as if something had occurred to him. "They're so embarrassing."

"What are?"

Emilio offered a dumbfounded expression. "The squash or whatever you call them."

"They're called cucuzza."

"Well, they look like elephant dongs, Dad."

Emilio's comment on the phallic symbolism of the cucuzza got JB wondering how many other people saw them that way, and what did that say about him? JB stared at the long, curved vegetables with sudden self-awareness. Of all the things to cultivate in his garden—of all the symbols his subconscious might choose—why these? Heat rolled up JB's back, a strange mix of embarrassment and recognition. He turned away to focus on his peppers, but the damage was done. Even his garden was betraying him now.

Mike's Range Rover drove up the gravel path. "Looks like Pop's home," JB said. A rental car pulled in behind him.

Emilio's eyes went wide. "Dad, you don't have to do this."

"Do what?"

Emilio's shoulders rose to his ears. "You don't have to play the role of the modern husband—all understanding and evolved about Pop's *friends*."

"Modern husband?" JB repeated. "What are you talking about?"

"Forget it." Emilio turned to walk away.

"JB," Mike called as he got out of the car. "Come say hello."

A man wearing dark linen pants and a black-and-white horizontal striped sweater got out of the rental car.

"JB, I'd like you to meet Gianni Cuomo. Cuomo, you know, like the lake in Italy."

Gianni smiled with unease. "Not exactly."

The bright sun spangled JB's vision. Momentarily blinded, an image of Mike trotting around a ring with Gianni on a leash dazed him. He looked about thirty-five, slight and shorter than Mike, affirming what JB already knew: that aside from JB, Mike leaned toward smaller, more symmetrical men. Men with demeanors that wouldn't conflict with his own.

"Nice to meet you." JB extended his hand, but he retracted it quickly once he realized how filthy it was. "Apologies, I've been gardening."

"Oh, and that's Emilio." Mike motioned to his disinterested-looking son. "Say hi to Mr. Cuomo."

"Hi," Emilio replied before walking into the house.

"How do you like our little town?" JB asked Gianni.

"It's a...how do you say? Lovely."

"Doesn't he have the cutest accent?" Mike cooed.

"Adorable," JB offered. "Let's go inside." Graciousness being JB's forte, he experienced an immediate sense of command over the situation and their skittish guest. "What are you drinking, Gianni?"

"Prosecco, if you have it."

"Be right back."

As JB washed up and fixed drinks in the kitchen, he stole another glance at Gianni through the doorway. What was it about the man that bothered him so much? The meticulously trimmed mustache that seemed both affected and effortless? That linen outfit, which seemed casual yet somehow impeccable. Perhaps it was the accent, melodic and restrained, each word delivered as if it were a precious little gift.

Whatever it was, JB couldn't shake the feeling that Gianni was fundamentally different from Mike's other strays. He shared none of Dan Vega's warm openness, his mocha complexion and glistening dark curls, merely the wrapping on a personality that made everyone feel like his closest friend. Or that couple, who had fallen for Mike in that embarrassingly transparent way, surrounding him at soirées like star-struck fans at a VIP afterparty, hanging on his every word and laughing too loudly at his jokes. No, Gianni kept himself apart, quiet and observant, those amber eyes missing nothing while revealing less.

"JB, where did you go for those drinks?" Mike shouted with a braying, sarcastic chuckle.

JB entered the living room as Mike was giving Gianni a tour of their home, shamelessly boasting about his contribution to the interior design.

The house had been an elongated traditional home built in the '90s, a legacy from JB's deceased parents. JB's father had been eaten alive by alcoholic cirrhosis. Six weeks later, his mother had lain in a hospital full of tubes, brain-dead after sustaining a head injury while intoxicated. JB finally felt safe from the man who'd arbitrarily become enraged, no matter how benign the situation, and his indifferent mother who'd never intervened to protect her son.

Once Mike fully grasped the value of JB's real estate—a coveted slice of the South Fork and a chic loft in Tribeca—he sensed an opportunity and lobbied to redecorate the Sag Harbor home. Months later, JB had entered his newly decorated house, believing he shared the same decor as Britney

Spears. Only his study remained untouched, a small victory he'd fought hard to preserve.

Gazing at Mike and Gianni, JB thought there was nowhere else he'd rather be.

Meanwhile, Mike continued the grand tour. Gianni's expression remained carefully neutral, his eyes taking in the house with the practiced assessment of someone accustomed to evaluating wealth.

Gianni paused before a framed photo of JB receiving his doctorate, studying it with unexpected intensity. "Columbia," he said. "Impressive." Something in his tone made JB wonder if there was more to the comment than simple admiration.

This, JB realized as he distributed flutes filled with sparkling white wine, was the moment he'd been dreading without knowing it was coming. Up until now, Mike had been the sole judge awarding his slavering strays with blue ribbons of his attentiveness, soaking up cheap affections gleaned from their insecurities. But today, the axis of power had shifted. For the first time, Mike wasn't the one bestowing attention—he was desperately seeking it. And from someone who seemed perfectly content to withhold it.

"So, Gianni," JB interrupted, "how do you like staying at The American Hotel?"

Mike paused mid-sip. "How did you know where Gianni's staying?"

"Mike, you forget we live in a small town. People talk."

"It's only temporary." Mike chuckled nervously. "Andy found him a cottage in Noyack. You know the one."

JB did not, but there was no use in arguing about it in front of Gianni. The poor guy looked like he frightened easily.

"I'll start dinner." JB slapped his thigh. "Gianni, do you have any food restrictions?"

There was an awkward beat of silence. The silver clock in JB's study chimed gratingly. Gianni looked at his watch and then peered uneasily at Mike. "I can't stay for dinner." He took a sip of Prosecco. "Thank you for the drink."

"Nice to meet you." JB took the glass from him.

"You're not leaving so soon," Mike said.

JB allowed this scene to play out without him. He returned to the kitchen, wondering if he was the only one who sensed the breeze of suspicion and apprehension swirling around Gianni. A guardedness to camouflage some ulterior motive?

Minutes later, JB heard a car pull out of their driveway.

Mike appeared in the kitchen doorway. "What time is dinner?"

JB sliced cucuzza with a mandolin. "The usual time."

"I'm going to take a shower, then." Mike gave JB a peck on the cheek.

"Did you have a good afternoon?"

"Actually, I did," Mike said with no more enthusiasm than a little boy being asked about his day at school. JB didn't mention that he'd seen Mike earlier walking into The American Hotel.

Why bother?

At dinner, no one mentioned Gianni Cuomo, though his presence lingered like the scent of an annoying cologne. Emilio picked at his food while Mike scrolled through his phone, smiling at messages JB couldn't see. The next night, Mike went out after dinner. And the night after that. Each departure felt like a piece of their family dissolving into the summer heat.

Chapter Eight

The next evening, Rakesh called JB and insisted they meet for a drink at The American Hotel lounge. JB suggested Lulu's, but Rakesh adamantly refused. JB thought he would appear suspicious if he argued, and so he reluctantly agreed.

Gianni was at the piano when they walked into the lounge, but JB didn't make eye contact. They sat at the bar, and Rakesh ordered a round of martinis. "Angelo's joining us. He's running late."

"Late?" JB repeated with light sarcasm. "They fuck like rabbits, don't they?"

"They're young. Remember when you were in your thirties? Fucking was all you thought about." JB glanced at his drink, wondering if he would ever enjoy sex again. He certainly thought about it, but then he wondered if it was the lingering memory of sex like a phantom limb that stirred emotion only in his mind.

The music stopped, and several people applauded. JB noticed that Gianni stepped away from the piano and walked into the restaurant. Angelo entered the lounge at that moment, and Rakesh waved him over. "I saw your buddy, the pianist. Why did you pick this place?"

"The American Hotel lounge is our place," Rakesh argued. "I'm not going somewhere else because of some piano player. Besides, I like the way they make martinis here. Speaking of, let's get you one, Angelo." Rakesh snapped his fingers, and the bartender began mixing a cocktail without even being told.

"So, what do we think of the new pianist?" Angelo asked. "What's his name?"

"Gianni Cuomo," JB said. "Cuomo, like the lake."

"That's not how you pronounce the lake in Italy."

"Enough with all this talk of Gianni, the piano player, from Lake Como," Rakesh huffed. "I have important news to share with you, which is the reason why I asked you both here tonight. Any ideas?"

JB hated Rakesh's propensity for guessing games. "Just tell us."

"I'm a genius." Rakesh wriggled his head. "You will be happy to know we've been invited to Gus and Winnie's annual costume party."

JB hadn't given the Beltrams' snub another thought since Rakesh had complained about their glaring absence from the guest list. He nursed his martini, content to let Rakesh buzz about the details, watching his friend's animated gestures with detached amusement. Rakesh described the pilgrimage to the farmhouse—how he'd approached her majesty with his tail between his legs, kissed her metaphorical ring, and scattered flattery like seeds in hopes of currying enough favor to secure them all invites.

"Even JB and Mike?" Angelo interjected. "How did you manage that?"

"A gift basket of benzos," JB ventured, "and a sizable donation to Winnie's Food Pantry."

"What's wrong with that?" Rakesh replied. "Besides, Winnie loves her benzos."

"Lower your voices," Angelo whispered. In a far corner of the lounge, Gus Beltram sat next to an attractive, olive-skinned man.

Rakesh sat up. "Should I go over and say hello?"

JB stopped him with a flat palm. "You just inhaled a martini. Leave Mr. Utters alone."

Rakesh pouted, thinking. "Okay, maybe you're right."

"More importantly," Angelo added, "who is that silver daddy with him? The way the table light is hitting that profile, he looks like a brooding character in a Caravaggio painting."

JB glanced over his shoulder. The stranger stared back. The man had neoclassical features: dark, wavy hair, flecked with silver; a manicured salt-and-pepper goatee, a prominent nose, and eyes as black as gravel.

The man's eyes locked with JB's for a moment too long to be coincidental. Something passed between them—recognition? Interest? Warning?—before the stranger dipped his head with the slightest hint of acknowledgment and returned his attention to Gus. JB turned away as Rakesh said, "He's probably some television executive. Much more importantly, I suggest we start thinking about costumes immediately before the good ones are all taken. You know Winnie insists we register our costumes to avoid any duplications. This is so exciting. The Beltrams' costume party is going to be the event of the summer."

Chapter Nine

The sunset coloration of turquoise and amber cast a triangle on the floor of JB's study. Emilio stood in the doorway, sighing with frustration. "How long does it take to put on a costume?" He swung his baseball bat so that it made a swooshing sound as it sliced the air. Emilio wore a pinstripe baseball uniform with his lips and one eye painted black in honor of the Baseball Furies. The gang featured in the 1970s cult film, *The Warriors*—a movie he had become obsessed with after watching a scene on TikTok.

The bat, a gift to JB from his father, was a vintage Louisville Slugger. Though JB hated sports, a fact his father knew, he kept the bat as a memento. Proof his father held some feelings toward his only child. At ten years old, Emilio discovered the bat in a box stored in the garage. JB thought it was time to pass along the tradition in hopes that Emilio would do the same one day with his child.

"Pop will be along soon."

Angelo planned on going as Marty McFly and Jason as a begrudging Dr. Emmett Brown from the film *Back to the Future*. Rakesh refused to divulge what he was wearing, which meant he wanted JB to beg, and so, he didn't. JB settled on Julius Caesar and wore his bathing suit and a tank top underneath a long toga with a red cape fastened to his shoulders that scalloped across his back. Mike, on the other hand, couldn't decide. The last anyone heard, Mike had narrowed down his choices to either a sexy state trooper or a gladiator. Both costumes put Mike's long legs on full display.

They were already thirty minutes late when Mike announced, "Okay, I'm ready." He stood in the doorway: tattered cargo shorts, no shirt, scraggy brown wig, dark makeup applied to his jaw to imply a beard.

"What are you supposed to be?" JB asked.

"I'm Tom Hanks in *Castaway*."

Emilio laughed out loud. "You must be kidding? No one will guess that."

Mike's face contracted with irritation. "Of course, they will. I even made Wilson." He presented a volleyball with a smiley face painted in black ink that appeared to have been drawn by a six-year-old.

"I'm sure everyone will know exactly who you are. Even if Emilio and I don't."

"What do you know, *Caesar?* Your costume took zero imagination."

"Let's go," Emilio urged as he ushered his fathers out the door. "I'm starving."

JB stood on the porch for a split second, watching Mike and Emilio get in the car. He felt a sudden intense yearning to stay home as if the night's most difficult tasks lay ahead.

He felt.

Tonight would demand a reckoning he wasn't prepared for.

* * *

The Beltrams' house was near enough to the ocean that the breeze would make being outside comfortable. Waves could be heard crashing on the beach as they drove the winding road. Cars were parked along the grassy incline. East Hampton was a pretentiously unwelcoming place with no sidewalks.

"Wow," Emilio said. "This house is sick."

Globe lights scalloped the entire wraparound porch. A black-and-white checkered walkway led a path to the back yard, where it expanded into a dance floor that appeared like a crossword grid. JB avoided the step and repeat as usual, though he saw Mike's eyes glittering with a maddening blindness as if he were staring directly at an eclipse. A DJ, stationed in the far corner, played cocktail party music. A giant white scaffold was erected over the dance floor. An enormous chandelier hung in the center, and gyrating flashing lights reflected the crystals onto the dance floor like a mirrored disco ball.

A line of servers (all men, of course) dressed in tight black pants and fitted white shirts with no sleeves presented the signature cocktails—guests had a choice of a Winnierita or a Gusjito. JB chose neither. An ice sculpture of a Mardi Gras mask sat in a massive punch bowl in the center of a long table in the Beltrams' living room, where the buffet would be served.

Women embraced the costume party's creative spirit with a vibrant array of attire—decorative eye masks paired with maxi dresses in bright colors, graphic black and white shift dresses, and flowy caftans. In contrast, their heterosexual plus-ones seemed less inspired, resorting to simplistic costume props like novelty turbans, a comical clown nose, or oversized cartoonish eyeglasses.

Only the gay boys, JB assessed, had truly understood the assignment. Their outfits were meticulously crafted and imaginative, ranging from a glittery gold-skinned Icarus, Ziggy Stardust with full glam rock makeup and lightning bolt, Andy Warhol accompanied by Jean-Michel Basquiat, a full ensemble of *Priscilla, Queen of the Desert*, and a perfectly coordinated set of the Village People.

Mike broke away to look for Gianni. JB and Emilio wended their way through the crowd like slalom skiers to greet Angelo and Jason, stationed at the bar. "Emilio, you remember Dr. Perrotta and Mr. Murphy."

"Great costume," Jason remarked. "I love *The Warriors*. It's a classic."

Emilio carried the bat over his shoulders like a yoke and smiled proudly at his father. "My friend Evan sent me a TikTok reel last summer. Now I'm obsessed."

"Just don't lose that bat," JB warned. "My father gave me that bat when I was—"

"A little boy," Emilio shot in with bored indignation. "I know. I know. Don't worry. I won't let it out of my sight."

Andy joined them dressed as a sexy version of King Louis XVI with billowy sleeves, a ruffled collar, and gold swim trunks. "Hey, y'all." He cleared his throat excessively. "Ladies, gentlemen, and nonbinary folk," Andy announced, "may I direct your attention to the driveway on your left." A ripple through the crowd as everyone turned their heads in unison. Silence followed. The DJ began playing, "*Also Sprach Zarathustra Op.30: Einleitung.*"

A figure emerged from the darkness. The outline of a stick figure illuminated by LED lights glowed neon green. "That's the opening to *2001: A Space Odyssey* they're playing," JB said, applauding. The other guests joined in, clapping and cheering, as Rakesh, in his electric costume, entered the party like an alien disembarking a spaceship.

"Oh, my God!" Angelo laughed. "He is so extra."

"The most extra," Andy added.

"Well, if you're going to call me stick-figure man," Rakesh said, "why not embrace it?"

"You're one hell of a good sport." JB gave Rakesh a proud pat on the back. "That's the best costume of the night."

The DJ switched back to cocktail music. The crowd resumed their gossipy conversations. Mike approached with Gianni, who was wearing the black suit he usually wore to work. "Who are you supposed to be?" Mike asked Rakesh.

"The true version of myself," he replied. "And you?"

"Tom Hanks in *Castaway.*"

"Oh, honey." He grabbed Mike's shoulders and turned him around. "If I was going to be stranded with anyone, I'd rather be stranded with him." Rakesh pointed across the dance floor at a man: six feet of built-to-last muscles wearing a tattered pair of cargo shorts and six-pack abs. "Did you change your mind at the last minute? Winnie hates copycats."

Emilio ran up to them. "Pop, did you see that guy over there? He's dressed like Tom…"

"I see him," Mike snapped. He grabbed ahold of Gianni's hand. "Come on. Let's get a drink."

"Don't be rude," admonished JB. "Introduce Gianni to our friends."

Mike dropped his head back and exhaled dramatically. "Everyone, this is

Gianni Cuomo. Gianni, this is everyone."

JB heard Mike slurring. *Could he be drunk so early in the evening?*

Rakesh snapped his fingers. "You're the pianist from The American Hotel lounge."

"Yes, I am." Gianni appeared uncomfortable, particularly since his response elicited several seconds of awkward silence.

Gus and Winnie Beltram came over to greet them. They were dressed as the Great Gatsby and Daisy.

"Gianni, we're so thrilled you could make it," Winnie sang, kissing both his cheeks. "Can I persuade you into playing something later?"

"I don't know."

JB sensed his timidity and wondered if he wasn't used to being in the spotlight. Playing piano in a lounge was akin to white noise for loud drunks.

"Come on, Gianni," Mike pleaded.

"Mike." JB pulled him aside. "Why don't you buy me a drink?"

Mike looked appallingly at JB's hand—firmly wrapped around his arm—as though it were oozing with pus. "Get your own drink."

"I'm warning you," he whispered. "Do not embarrass yourself. Think of Emilio."

"You're warning me?" reproached Mike. "Now that's rich."

A weird sensation caught JB off guard. An urgency that brought with it an awful reminder of what had happened the last time he'd experienced such a sensation on the Fourth of July. Mike wrenched his arm free.

"Guys." Emilio threw his arms across their shoulders. "Let's go inside and get something to eat." JB sensed his son's desire to defuse this situation, but he was too preoccupied with the discomfort in his groin.

The three walked toward the French doors, but Mike staggered away. "Let him go," JB said.

"It's not right," Emilio gritted. "It's not right the way he treats us."

Us.

This was the first time Emilio had ever included himself in their ongoing squabbles. "I understand how you feel." JB reached for Emilio's hand. "It's not right, but it's also not the right time or place. We'll discuss it tomorrow as a family."

JB turned to walk into the house, but Emilio lingered. He glanced back as his son swung the bat, cleaving through the air with such intensity, it could have shattered the ice sculpture. In that moment, JB knew that at fifteen, Emilio understood exactly what his father was enduring—and exactly how powerless they both were to stop it.

JB took a deep breath and forced a smile. "Who's hungry?"

"I am," Emilio replied with resignation, or was it remorse? JB wasn't sure which.

"Emilio." JB's voice took on an insistent paternal tone. "I said, *who's hungry?*"

"I am!" he shouted now with feigned exuberance.

"That's the spirit. I'll meet you at the buffet. I need to use the restroom first."

JB hurried to the powder room. Once inside, he hoisted his toga over his shoulder and pulled down his swim trunks. JB stared down at his unexpected arousal with a mix of pubescent wonder and deep betrayal. *Why now? Why here, of all places?* Was his body finally healing, or was this simply another cruelly timed joke—a momentary resurrection before the inevitable return to reality?

A knock at the door rattled him. "Yes, one minute," but it was too late. The euphoric sense of arousal seeped back into those deep crevices where it had been hibernating since the chemo and radiation. A tumbleweed rolled across the arid desert of his manhood.

When he opened the door, a tall figure dressed in black stood. "Excuse me." The masked stranger removed his sombrero to bow. JB detected an accent. *Spanish? Italian?* Dark makeup applied around his eyes made his irises shine like wet gravel. *Where have I seen those eyes before?*

"After you." JB gestured to allow the masked man to pass. A whiff of espresso and leather rose to JB's nostrils. The cape flapped with dramatic flair as the bathroom door shut behind him.

Winnie arrived then, too, smiling manically. "JB!" she announced as though she hadn't seen him in years. "Are you having fun?"

"Yes, I am. Thank you for inviting me." He wanted to apologize again in person for his behavior at their Fourth of July party, but Winnie was struggling to open the bathroom door.

"Damn it." Then she looked at JB with a smile like glass cracking. "I was hoping not to have to run upstairs. At my age, when you got to go, you got to go. You must understand that now, too?"

JB grimaced with discomfort. "Off you go, then. You don't want to have an accident here in the hallway."

Her eyes flared for a second, and she hurried away.

Winnie appeared harried and somewhat tense, but JB dismissed it as the expected behavior of a perfectionistic host. He toyed briefly with the idea of waiting for Zorro but decided to join Emilio at the buffet instead.

* * *

Winnie got her way, and Gianni played piano while Mike hovered over him, beaming like a stage mom. JB and Emilio sat on the sectional in the solarium and listened. "I shouldn't have come," Emilio said. "This party is lame."

JB leaned forward and nudged his head against his son's. "You know what? The Beltrams have a state-of-the-art theater downstairs. Go watch a movie."

"You don't have to tell me twice." Emilio made a beeline for the basement.

JB had made a terrible decision in agreeing to let his son attend the party, but it was all Emilio had spoken about after they'd received the invite. A chance to debut his Baseball Furies costume before Halloween.

JB ordered a drink at the bar. Without realizing it, the stranger dressed all in black was standing beside him. "I see we meet again."

Zorro cocked his head. "Excuse me?" The man's left eye twitched. "Do I know you?"

Then it occurred to JB that this man didn't possess those shiny, black eyes he remembered standing outside the bathroom, and this Zorro wore a headscarf, not a sombrero. In fact, this man was considerably shorter. The first Zorro moved with the agility of a dancer, each gesture precise and graceful. This second Zorro seemed uncomfortable in his attire—his movements more hesitant, his stance less solid.

Could there be two of them?

Doubtful since Rakesh made it clear Winnie demanded everyone register their costume beforehand. But then again, Mike had changed his mind at the last minute. If there were two versions of Tom Hanks in *Castaway,* why not two Zorros?

"Apologies," JB offered. "I thought you were someone else."

Gianni played two songs. Afterward, he took a bow and wiped his sweaty forehead with a white handkerchief he produced from his back pocket. Mike glanced at his watch and whispered into Gianni's ear—JB was sure—that it was time for Gianni to leave for work.

Winnie herded the guests to the dance floor for the costume-judging portion of the evening. "Come, come, and that means everyone."

The crowd thinned, allowing Gus a clear view of Mike and Gianni standing on the front porch. JB caught Gus's reaction immediately, his lips pursing, his eyes narrowing. The look conveyed the obvious discomfort of a secondhand embarrassment as Mike fussed with Gianni's tie and fixed his hair.

"First the women," Winnie announced into the DJ's microphone, though her naturally booming voice hardly needed amplification. A parade followed, featuring iconic figures like Jackie O in her signature oversized sunglasses, Marilyn Monroe with a white billowing dress, and Katy Perry resplendent in a candy-colored costume. First prize went to a zombie version of Martha Stewart—Winnie's longtime nemesis.

Next, the men—and it appeared, JB noted, they far exceeded the women. Rakesh was joined by a glamorous ringmaster, a sequined devil, the killer clown from the film, *It*, and the artist formerly known as Prince. Everyone cheered vigorously when Rakesh came in first—thankfully, his victory would allay any concerns about him falling out with the Beltrams once and for all.

The music started up. More trays of salmon pinwheels and duck pate crostini were passed, and more Winnieritas and Gusjitos were consumed. JB went to check on Mike, but he was surprised to find that Gianni's rental car was still parked across the street. Rakesh came up behind him. "Let's have a drink to celebrate my victory."

"Congratulations," JB added, still scanning for Mike and Gianni. "I'll meet you at the bar."

Rakesh wrapped his fingers around JB's wrist. "I insist you come with me. You'll want to see this."

"What's wrong? Is it Emilio?"

Rakesh's eyebrows knitted with sad resignation. "Come with me."

JB brushed past him, poking his head in the living room. There he found Mike and Gianni, sitting at the piano bench, locked in a silent gaze. Eyes wide and filled with adoration, each caressing the other's cheek, pantomiming their reflection.

The room seemed to contract around JB, sound receding until all he could hear was the blood rushing in his ears. Mike's hands moved to cradle Gianni's neck—that same gesture he'd once reserved for JB alone, in those early days when touch had been a sacred language shared between them. And then, the inconceivable. They locked lips in a passionate kiss. JB's throat constricted as if physically choking on the truth he'd been swallowing for months. He stepped forward, but someone grabbed ahold of his arm.

It was Rakesh pulling him to the bar. "Let's have a drink and celebrate my big win." As Rakesh guided him away, JB felt the weight of someone's gaze and turned to find Winnie's eyes on him, her expression uncharacteristically pained. For a split second, her carefully constructed hostess mask slipped, revealing something like understanding—or was it pity? Before JB could decide which was worse, she'd already moved on, her social armor back in place.

Rakesh handed JB a Scotch and ordered him to drink it. The whisky scorched like kerosene. "Now laugh like I said something funny." Every muscle and cord and fiber in his long body strained toward understanding, but JB couldn't bring himself to move beyond this crushing embarrassment. That kiss wasn't another mortifying misstep their friends would soon forget. He could see it in their faces. Again, the whispering and pointing.

A photographer who'd been circulating through the party materialized, drawn to the scent of scandal. The camera shutter clicked in rapid succession as the flash cast a garish white spotlight on their kiss. JB's moment of public humiliation preserved forever, probably destined for *Hamptons Magazine's* "Who's Who" section.

For one blazing instant, the cloche lifted, and JB was aghast and humiliated as the steam dissolved, revealing a truth he always knew but refused to accept. That Joseph Byron Pulaski was officially the Sag Harbor cuckold.

Chapter Ten

"Anyone up for a swim?" Winnie called from the French doors.

Rakesh turned to JB. "Did you bring your bathing suit?"

"I'm wearing mine under my toga." JB's eyes were still fixed on Mike and Gianni kissing on the piano bench, which may as well have been a porch swing; they were so entranced. JB pulled his eyes away and smiled at Rakesh. "Let's have a drink first."

Angelo and Jason joined them at the bar. "We're going to change into our swimsuits," Angelo said. "Be right back."

"Two martinis?" Rakesh asked them.

"Jason will have a beer, and I'll have a vodka and cranberry."

"Bridge and tunnel." Rakesh coughed behind his fist. JB erupted in genuine laughter, knowing Rakesh was mocking Angelo's Staten Island roots.

"You're such a bitch, Rakesh." Angelo pulled Jason away.

"You are a world-class bitch," JB said, "and that's why I love you."

Rakesh pressed a glass against JB's lips. "Drink up, old friend."

"Are you trying to get me drunk, Rakesh?" The smile he returned suggested that was precisely his intention. "Where's Andy?"

"Who?" Rakesh draped his hands behind JB's neck. "Can you believe we're almost fifty? Where did the time go?"

JB held him at arm's length, finding drunk Rakesh too sentimental for his taste. "Let's not give the Beltrams' guests any more fodder for their gossip mill." JB glanced toward the piano. Mike and Gianni had disappeared.

When Angelo and Jason returned wearing identical red square-cut swim trunks, JB couldn't help but chuckle. "Well, look at you two."

"What's so funny?" Angelo asked with irritation.

"I'm sorry." JB hated annoying drunks, and tonight he had accepted the role willingly to mask his inner humiliation. "For some reason, I wasn't expecting you to be wearing matching swim trunks."

"I would have thought you two were more the Speedo type," Rakesh chimed in. "With matching hearts on your backsides. Each inscribed with the other's initials."

JB and Rakesh dissolved into hysterics, tears streaming down their faces. Their laughter abruptly halted when Mike and Gianni walked past the bar, now also having changed into their swimwear. JB's gaze fixed on Mike, whose white nylon swimsuit was so sheer that the outline of his groin was visible. Gianni, on the other hand, wore swim trunks three sizes too large. The pair paused briefly, seeming momentarily distracted.

"Going swimming?" JB's question went unanswered. Mike and Gianni turned in unison and proceeded outside as if they hadn't heard him.

"Did Gianni rummage through Gus's resort wear for that tragic bathing suit?" Rakesh asked.

"He probably had to borrow one," JB offered.

"Finish off that drink." Rakesh slapped JB on the back. "I want to go swimming."

Many of the guests were saying their goodbyes, uninterested in getting wet. They lined up in the driveway, awaiting the valets to bring them their cars. The Beltrams' party was clearing out quickly.

Rakesh and JB sat on the pool edge, sipping cocktails. Angelo wrapped his legs around Jason's waist, and the two floated away, kissing. Steam rose from the heated pool. Winnie walked up to them. "Is there anything you boys need?" She had changed into an oversized cream blouse and navy Capri pants. "There's coffee and sandwiches in the kitchen."

Mike pulled himself out of the water. "Do you have anything for a headache?"

"Of course, I do." She laughed exaggeratedly. "Did we just meet?"

Mike and Winnie walked into the house. "That bitch has more prescription drugs in her bathroom than I have in my entire pharmacy," Rakesh muttered.

"Does Gianni seem okay to you?" JB whispered. Gianni sat on the pool's edge, swaying his head in a figure-eight pattern as if he were listening to a song only he could hear.

Andy stumbled over to them. "I don't feel well."

"Oh, pumpkin," Rakesh cooed. "Are you drunk?"

Andy nodded, dimpling, and projectile vomited into a nearby gardenia bush. "Holy shit!" Rakesh ran to Andy's side. "Let's get you home."

JB was amazed at how quickly Rakesh ushered Andy out of the party. This incident with Winnie's gardenia bushes would surely ruin his standing with the Beltrams.

"I'll tell Winnie and Gus you had an emergency," JB shouted, but Rakesh was already out of earshot.

Angelo and Jason floated over. There was no distinction between their bodies, between the water and the air, and JB kept thinking back to when Mike and he were that crazy in love.

"Jason, let's have some coffee," Angelo suggested. "It'll sober us up."

Jason nuzzled his face in the crook of Angelo's neck. "Whatever you say."

They untangled themselves from each other and walked up the steps. They stood hugging, skin glistening and splotchy. Angelo ran his hand through Jason's hair. Both locked in each other's gazes as if they were the only two people in the world.

"JB, why don't you join us?" Angelo suggested.

"I'm waiting for Mike. We'll come inside in a bit."

Angelo's eyes skittered to where Gianni was clinging to the side of the pool. "Don't be long."

"Yes, Doctor."

JB parked himself in a corner. A jet shot warm water against his back. The music had died down. There was no one on the back porch. Everyone had gone inside, drinking coffee in the hopes of sobering up before driving home. JB closed his eyes for a moment. When he opened them, he saw Gianni moving toward him, hands gripping the pool's edge in a crisscross pattern as he made his way closer.

"So, no work tonight?" JB mustered to ask.

"No." Gianni snorted. "Too much drinking. Plus, Mike gave me a pill."

"What kind of pill?"

"I don't know. He said it would relax me." Gianni made his way toward JB, wet and jittery like a dog after a bath. "You don't like me. Do you?"

Here we go. Time for the stray to check in with the husband.

"I don't care enough to dislike you," JB replied.

"I like you," Gianni went on, inching closer. "More than I like Mike."

First, an odd question followed by an even odder disclosure.

JB remained silent. Because after all, what was the point? Gianni had admitted to overindulging in alcohol and whatever pill Mike had given him. Normally, conversations with Mike's strays bored JB. Worst of all were the intoxicated ones, and Gianni seemed particularly shitfaced. But JB was inebriated enough to pursue this conversation with a bit of grit he rarely displayed toward people who he couldn't care less about.

"You like *me* more than you like Mike?" JB clarified. He hadn't meant to sound so abrupt, but the strangeness of Gianni's behavior implied something more premeditated, as though being alone with him had been Gianni's plan all along.

"You want to see how much I like you?" Gianni continued his approach. With each step, he emerged from the water until it was obvious to JB that Gianni was aroused.

Unbidden, the image of his cucuzza plant surfaced in JB's mind.

"See how much?" Gianni's voice curled up coyly at the end like a gift wrap ribbon.

The swagger Gianni displayed seemed so out of character from the timid pianist JB had come to know. This was someone else, and that deception infuriated him. What hubris Gianni possessed in believing JB was so desperately unhappy that a cunning pianist's organ would easily seduce him. It occurred to him suddenly…something his father used to say: *In the Hamptons, interlopers are as ubiquitous as deer ticks. The only way to remove one is to apply steady, even pressure on the head and pull.*

All the agony and injustice. All the illness and betrayal came roaring back as JB stared at Gianni's smug smile—an expression that seemed to mock every last shred of dignity JB had left. Scaring off this pianist was not the solution; Mike would only find a new stray. JB knew with bone-deep certainty that his life had become a recurring nightmare, an endless parade of humiliation. The insanity of his situation pressed like a vice against his temples.

When his friends probed his relationship, seeking to understand why he tolerated Mike's infidelities, JB would weave protective lies, his excuses a fragile armor against their concerned glances. But now, watching Gianni's lip curl with contemptuous pleasure, something shifted. His old self—the compliant, broken cuckold—began to dissolve, and in its place, a cold, razor-edge resolve emerged.

JB scanned the yard—no lingering guests, no DJ packing up equipment—it was the two of them alone. He pulled himself out of the pool, sitting on the edge at the corner. "Okay, why don't you show me?" JB's eyes glanced down at his own groin before darting up to catch the leering look of lust on Gianni's face.

Of course, JB was no heart-doodling fool. He knew full well that Gianni had no carnal yearning for him. *You only want what you can't have.* Or, as JB suspected, you only want the one who has the money.

Around them, all was silent but for the low hum of the pool filter. "Go ahead," JB taunted. "Show me how much you like me. No one will know."

Gianni lowered himself between JB's legs. All bent-kneed and supplicant, primed for pleasure. JB knew this was insane, but the other had been different. He'd built up a resistance to them. An accumulation of antibodies that until now had suppressed any contagion of jealousy. What was JB to do with this man pooled between his legs, Gianni's ears grazing his thighs, huffing hot breaths against JB's swim trunks? If this was how Gianni treated men, he didn't deserve to live.

Would it be murder, or had Gianni's actions sealed his fate?

This is it, he thought. *It ends tonight.*

JB grabbed a heft of Gianni's hair to immobilize him.

Love for his family had become as dense as the Bible. But with each of Mike's indiscretions, the pages of their life had become thick and wet and rank from the sweaty bodies and salty loins of sexual betrayal.

There was hardly a ripple in the water when JB locked his legs around Gianni's neck, intertwining them at the ankles. Gianni's eyes fixed on JB's— a fast, tense flash of surprise, and then came the fear. The pool filter's hum masked Gianni's struggles as his face turned crimson. His features were warped with panic. All the veins in his neck engorged and pulsated. Gianni struggled to free himself from JB's grip, slapping and clawing at JB's legs. As his thighs tightened around Gianni's neck, JB experienced a terrible surge of power—not just over this man, but over the helplessness that had defined his life since his cancer diagnosis.

Now JB was the one grinning.

He slipped back into the pool, pulling Gianni's head below the surface, silencing him. If anyone had come outside, they would have thought JB was lost in thought; his upper body was so composed, so Zen.

No one would have thought that underneath the surface, a man was drowning.

Silence descended. JB gazed upward, into the vast darkness that had consumed his life this past year—a void as empty as the vows Mike had shattered. Moonlight fractured across the pool's surface, transforming the water into shards of silver glass. How many nights had JB retreated to the bedroom above the garage, an exile in his own home, while Mike entertained men in his bedroom? Their bedroom—once a refuge, now a war zone.

Despite beating cancer—a victory that should have felt like redemption— he had lost count of the times he'd fantasized about bursting through the bedroom door, grabbing one of Mike's mutts by the scruff, and hurling them into the street. Too many times. Too late now.

A realization razed through him like a blade. Would murder bring him peace, or was it merely a Pyrrhic victory for cuckolded men everywhere?

JB knew the brutal truth: it would obliterate Emilio's future, and that was a line he would never cross. Not after surviving the toxic legacy of his own father's cruelty. An image of what he looked like at this moment. It was exactly how his father transformed in those explosive instances—cold, detached. The weight of generational violence balanced on the fulcrum of this choice. Being Emilio's father was his greatest achievement—the one pure thing he'd managed in this world. He would not transform into the monster who almost destroyed his life, not over one of Mike's disposable lovers—especially not over someone as insignificant as Gianni Cuomo.

In that piercing moment of clarity, JB unclenched his legs. Gianni resurfaced, eyes blinking and bewildered, mouth gaping like a fish out of water. Uncertain whether JB's actions were calculated or a twisted joke.

"You're crazy!" Gianni said, heaving water.

JB waved an ineffectual hand. A gesture meant to underscore how little he regarded the Italian piano player.

Suddenly, as though the surrounding sounds were amplified, JB heard conversation coming from the kitchen, the hum of insects in the seagrass mixed with the wheeze of Gianni's breath as he expelled water. JB looked around and saw no one. But then, by the pool house, a shadow broke away from the surrounding darkness. Two lambent black eyes emerged, suspended in the nothingness. JB's heart lurched. *Is it real*, he wondered, or the residual maddening blindness that had overcome him? *No*, he thought. *It's only a deer.*

Walking toward the French doors, he tugged at his groin. The fury had left him feeling aroused. One last quick adjustment before he stepped inside the house, leaving Gianni still coughing and heaving in the swimming pool.

They were standing in the kitchen. Winnie noticed JB first. "Oh, dear. Let me get you a towel."

JB stood dripping in the doorway. "Where's Mike?"

"He was napping next to Emilio when I went to use the bathroom downstairs," Angelo replied, "but he was gone by the time I came out. Not sure where he went."

"I should find my family. It's time we head out."

Winnie handed JB an oversized towel. "How about a sandwich first?"

"Thank you." As JB entered the kitchen, he felt his body move with mechanical precision—reach for a towel, accept the sandwich, smile politely—while his mind replayed the event that took place back at the pool, that moment when he'd nearly crossed an irrevocable line.

"Is Gianni still in the pool?" Winnie asked.

"I would love some coffee," JB said.

Angelo perked up and poured him a cup. JB leaned against the sink, eating a sandwich and sipping coffee. What a quintessential Hamptons party: the hosts attending to the lingering guests, waiting for them to depart. Plying the stragglers with coffee and end-of-night sandwiches. Everyone was relaxed and tired. A review of the night retold incorrectly.

Great party.

I had so much fun.

The costumes were amazing.

Wow, you truly pulled off the party of the summer, Winnie!

The kitchen conversation floated around JB like dialogue from a television show he was only half-watching—words without meaning, gestures without purpose.

Mike appeared, saying, "What did I do to deserve this awful headache?"

"Would you like another pill, dear?"

"Winnie, you're an angel." She hurried out of the room as if she'd forgotten to turn off the stove.

"Have something to eat," Gus urged with a mouthful of pastrami. "Food will clear up that headache." Mike nodded and sat at the island, eating a ham and cheese sandwich.

"Is Emilio sleeping?" JB asked.

"Last I checked," Mike replied somewhat dismissively, "he was watching television downstairs."

"Can I interest you gentlemen in a shot of Limoncello?" Gus proposed naughtily.

"Limoncello," Angelo repeated, "I haven't had that in years."

"Go ahead, babe," Jason urged. "I'm driving."

JB waved his hand. "None for me."

Gus's eyes veered wide and turned excitedly over to Mike. "Well, okay. I don't want to insult the host."

Gus trotted off and returned moments later with a tall, thin bottle filled with canary yellow fluid. Angelo, the consummate teacher's pet, began opening the cabinets and searching for glasses. "No, no, my dear boy." Gus wagged a finger. He opened the freezer and produced frosted shot glasses. "There's only one way to drink Limoncello properly. That's ice cold and with a sprig of mint." Gus set the glasses on the island and poured three shots. With an impish grin, he asked JB, "Are you sure you don't want one?"

"Some other time."

Gus swatted his response away like a fly and leered at Jason. "Come on. Have a taste."

Jason smiled and reached his arm around his boyfriend's waist. "I'll sip some of Angelo's if you don't mind."

Gus handed out drinks. "*Salute*, boys!"

The three shot their drinks and set the glasses down hard on the island. Winnie returned, having changed her outfit again. Now she wore a blue-and-white caftan. In her hand, she rattled a pill bottle like a maraca. "Is that the sound of angel's wings I hear?" Mike camped.

Winnie placed a pill on his palm like a priest administering communion. "Anyone else?"

JB decided now was the time to leave. The party was taking a turn that didn't sit right with him. "Mike, I'm going to fetch Emilio. We should get going."

"Alright, Mr. Party Pooper," he groused. "Where's Gianni?"

When his question went unanswered, Mike walked to the French doors and opened them. A balmy breeze coiled in. Winnie glided across the room, caftan luffing at the hem, to shut the doors.

Mike's scream shattered the kitchen's casual atmosphere. "Somebody help!" The words came ragged and constricted, as if an invisible cord had been pulled tight around Mike's throat. "Somebody, help me!"

Chapter Eleven

The lifeless body floated face down in the pool, fingers splayed wide in the calm water. JB charged ahead of everyone and leaped in. Jason helped him haul Gianni's motionless form onto the deck. The night air, still sticky with champagne and perfume, now carried the metallic tang of chlorinated copper.

Gianni's right temple had swollen into a grotesque bulge. The skin had split open, creating ragged, irregular edges that exposed butter-yellow fat and rosy muscle fibers. Fresh blood pulsated like a crimson stream across pallid skin.

Angelo dropped to his knees to assess Gianni. "He's not breathing! Winnie, call an ambulance." She tottered back inside the house.

"Is he dead?" Mike held up his hand to shield his eyes. "He can't be dead."

Angelo pinched Gianni's nose closed and covered his mouth with his own. JB watched Gianni's chest rise as Angelo breathed into his mouth twice. Pressing two fingers against his carotid, Angelo said, "No pulse." JB watched in horror as Gianni's body juddered under the pressure of Angelo's chest compressions. Two more rescue breaths revealed that Gianni was still pulseless.

"It looks like he hit his head," JB offered. "You think he dove in and hit his head?"

No one replied.

"What's wrong with his neck?" Mike asked, having stolen a glimpse before turning away again. "It's all red."

"He must have hit his head diving," JB insisted. "Maybe he broke his neck."

"Oh God," Mike groaned.

Angelo's forehead was beaded in sweat. After another round of chest compressions and two more rescue breaths, he paused to check for a pulse. "I got nothing."

Winnie returned, breathless. "An ambulance is on its way."

Gus held his forehead. JB could only imagine the thoughts tumbling through his mind: *Maybe this Gianni fella isn't dead. Maybe he's drunk and passed out. What if he is dead? What will that do to our reputation?*

"Let me take over," Jason said to Angelo. He began pumping Gianni's chest in a purposeful rhythm, but the intense concentration on his face was tempered by crisp shakes of his head that displayed his skepticism that Gianni could be revived.

A siren wailed in the distance. The sound sent a physical shiver down JB's spine. *That was quick. Too quick? Had someone called them before Mike found the body?* These thoughts materialized in JB's mind and vanished, impossible to examine in the chaos unfolding around him.

The Beltrams' home, which hours earlier had glittered with festive lights and the jewel tones of elaborate costumes, now stood bathed in the garish strobes of an emergency vehicle—candy apple red, jaundice yellow, and sapphire blue pulsing across the manicured lawn. Two male paramedics, carrying equipment, ran into the backyard. Angelo spoke to one of them as the other attached leads to Gianni's chest and fixed an oxygen mask over his nose and mouth. Once he turned on the monitor, it emitted the piercing wail of a flatline. Electroshock was administered twice. Gianni's body spasmed.

Did I kill Gianni?

The question flooded JB's stomach with cold dread. Sweat pricked his scalp. He could still feel the pulsating sensation of Gianni's neck between his thighs. But Gianni had been alive—gasping, heaving—when JB walked away. Hadn't he? JB couldn't be sure anymore what was real and what his mind had constructed to protect him.

The single beep from the monitor caused everyone to flinch. "Looks like we got a pulse."

JB's eyes locked on Gianni's face as everyone else's did. A collective sigh of relief washed over them. Except for JB, who thought, *What if Gianni lives?* How was he going to explain he'd almost strangled him to death?

The paramedics hauled Gianni into the ambulance. Once again, the siren sent splinters of electricity down JB's spine as it sped away.

"The police are here," Gus announced.

Jason introduced himself. JB overheard their monotone conversation, using words he'd only heard watching crime shows on television. Winnie whispered to Gus. His neck muscles tensed. Everyone had broken off into smaller groups. Only Mike stood alone, staring at the pool, arms wrapped tightly around his body like he wore an invisible straitjacket. "Are you okay?" JB asked him.

"Get away from me!" Mike bolted toward the French doors, tripped, and fell on the steps. JB ran to help him up, but Mike slapped his hand away. "Don't touch me!" He wept on the Beltrams' porch stairs as the policemen observed with keen interest.

Winnie bent over Mike. "Would you like another pill, dear?"

"No," Angelo insisted harshly. "No, he doesn't want another pill. He's had enough. Everyone has had enough."

JB sensed some deeper fold of truth in his words. A period, punctuating the end of the long run-on sentence that had been the Beltrams' costume party.

The two officers explained that everyone would need to be questioned before anyone was allowed to leave. "Can someone turn on the lights!" one of the officers asked.

Instantly, the Beltrams' backyard was bathed in a blinding white light, erasing any memory of the shadowy, fantasy world they had been part of hours earlier. JB blinked at the floating retinal moths. How ridiculous they looked, standing on the checkered dance floor in swim trunks and what remained of their costume makeup. An odd cast of characters in a Fellini film. Stripped bare of their frivolity, they were once again who they truly were—adults behaving like children.

An officer walked around the pool. "Do any of you know how to turn off the filter?" Gus proceeded toward the unit, smartly camouflaged by plastic foliage. The distant hum of the filter was silenced like the last groan of a dying man.

***

Everything changed when the police announced that Gianni Cuomo had died en route to the hospital. Mike collapsed like a marionette with cut strings. Funny, JB thought, with his weeping watery blue eyes, Mike made himself the victim.

While the police officers explained what would happen next, JB wondered if anyone else saw through Mike's charade. Such audacity. Playing the role of the grieving widow while his actual husband was standing nearby, alive. If anything, Mike's reaction to Gianni's death only pushed the needle of suspicion further in JB's direction.

Two homicide detectives emerged from the Beltrams' house: an imposing male dressed in navy, handsome with a muscular frame and buzzed dark hair. His partner followed right behind him, eyes absorbing every detail.

"Looks like it was some party." There was an edge of sarcasm in her voice. "Which one of you people lives here?"

"We do," Gus replied as he gestured toward Winnie. "The name is Beltram."

The woman identified herself as Detective Betty D'Amico. She was a foot shorter than her partner but with the confidence of a giant.

Jason moved toward them. "Sean? Sean Sullivan? Is that you?"

"Jason Murphy," Detective Sullivan returned. "What are you doing here?"

"What am I doing here? What are you doing here?" Jason extended his hand, but Sullivan bear-hugged him instead.

"You two know each other?" D'Amico and Angelo asked simultaneously.

"Yeah," Sullivan chuckled. "It's been like what…ten years?"

"More than that." Jason's cheeks flushed. "We were in the academy together."

What an awkward situation. As if this party couldn't get any more interesting.

He watched Angelo's face contract with unease as he pondered whether Sullivan and Jason had been classmates or fuck buddies or both.

D'Amico wandered around the pool's edge. She squatted to look below the surface. "Did anyone see what happened?"

Everyone shook their heads in unison.

Angelo started in first. "My name is Dr. Perrotta. I noted a gash over Gianni's right temple. He may have dove in and knocked himself unconscious. That would explain how he drowned."

"Detective Sullivan," D'Amico shouted. "Can you break away from Officer Murphy for a minute?"

"I'm no longer on the force," Jason clarified.

"Jason recently graduated from law school," Angelo added.

"Law school!" Sullivan punched Jason in the shoulder. "I always knew you were going to be more than a cop."

"I still have to pass the bar." Jason's face remained flushed, an intense red JB was sure had to scald his skin.

"Let's begin with the Beltrams." D'Amico reached into her pocket for an elastic tie to pull her hair into a ponytail. "As for everyone else, I'll need you to come inside so forensics can do their job."

Sullivan glanced at Jason, JB noted, and they were locked momentarily in each other's gaze. For a second, a flare of reluctant desire flickered in Sullivan's eyes.

"I'll let you get back to work." Jason walked sheepishly to Angelo's side.

"How exactly do you know Detective Sullivan?" Angelo asked through a rictus smile.

"Let's talk about this later?"

"What did you do to him?" Mike charged toward JB, hands trembling, tears streaming down his cheeks, anger like poison in his veins, making him sneer and spit and contort his face so he was unrecognizable. "You did this. Didn't you?"

The detectives paused on the porch, listening. "Mike," Jason said. "You don't know that."

"He's drunk and obviously medicated, thanks to our host," Angelo added.

"Shut up," Mike hissed. "You two are only covering for JB because he's your friend, but I know he did it." He jabbed his pointed finger in JB's face.

"I don't care what anyone says because I know you're a murderer."

Emilio appeared on the porch. His Baseball Furies makeup now smeared grotesquely across his young face. "Dad?"

The word hung in the air, weighted with confusion and the first seeds of fear. The sight of his son, still partly a child in his costume, yet old enough to understand exactly what was happening—gutted JB more effectively than any physical blow. Everything he had built for Emilio—safety, stability, a life untouched by the violence that had defined JB's own childhood—teetered on the precipice of destruction.

"Go back inside," JB managed. "I'll explain everything."

"You mean to tell me you've been sleeping this whole time?" Mike grabbed ahold of Emilio's arm, pulling him close. "Have you been drinking?"

"Pop, you're hurting me."

"Tell me the truth," Mike demanded, sniffing sharply.

"Get your hands off my son," JB thundered.

"Enough!" D'Amico shouted, silencing them.

JB was suddenly aware how this looked. A display of rage so out of character would now be all that he was measured by. The trouble was, how out of character was this rage when he'd displayed it twice in one night? The first time, being with Gianni Cuomo when he'd nearly strangled and drowned the piano player, and now, with Mike, in front of his family, friends, and worst of all, two homicide detectives.

"I'm going to need everyone to go inside right now." D'Amico's voice sliced through the night with the finality of a guillotine blade. She swept her gaze across their runny face paint, their privileged fantasies dissolving into foolishness. "The party is officially over."

As they filed inside. JB remained motionless for one heartbeat longer. Beyond the chaos, beyond the lights and sirens, the pool water had finally stilled into a perfect mirror of the night sky above. Peaceful. Undisturbed. As if nothing had happened. As if Gianni Cuomo had never existed at all. Detective Sullivan's hand landed firmly on JB's shoulder, startling him back to reality. "Inside," he said quietly. "Now, please."

Chapter Twelve

Many hours later, as the first hint of dawn glowed on the horizon, they remained holed up in the Beltrams' house. The detectives had been interviewing everyone since two a.m., methodically working through each party guest.

Emilio's spoon clinked rhythmically against the ceramic bowl, each sound amplified in the kitchen's unnatural silence. JB watched him, grateful for this mundane anchor in a world suddenly spinning out of control. The smell of milk and sugary cereal—so innocent, so jarringly normal—turned JB's stomach.

"Seriously," Emilio said. "Like dead, dead?"

Winnie and Gus looked over from the sitting room. JB signaled Emilio to lower his voice. Everyone had gone silent, whispering short sentences and gesturing with their hands. Everyone felt confused, torn, fragmented. Everyone was concerned that law enforcement was cataloging their every movement and word.

"Where's Pop?" Emilio asked.

"He's speaking with the detectives now."

"Will I have to speak to them too?"

JB considered the question, wondering if the detectives would expect to question his son. Of course, JB would try to spare Emilio that experience, but it seemed unlikely he could. "I don't know."

Once Emilio finished eating, JB suggested he watch television, but to text or call no one. Emilio saluted his father and set the bowl in the dishwasher before heading back downstairs. JB eyed the Beltrams as he poured himself another cup of coffee. Winnie yawned into her hand. She appeared beyond weary. Bags had ballooned under her eyes, which stared off into the distance. Gus leaned over and gave her cheek a peck. Winnie responded by reaching under his chin to caress his face. JB watched this exchange with a hollow ache spreading beneath his ribs. When had such tenderness dissolved from his own marriage? He couldn't recall the last time Mike had reached for him with such affection and kindness. Now, there was only accusation and rage.

The Beltrams were the first to speak with the detectives. Jason and Angelo were interviewed next, but separately. A forensic team had invaded the Beltrams' yard, collecting evidence so they could conclude whether Gianni's death was an accident or a homicide.

JB sat at the kitchen table, hands folded so tightly his knuckles blanched white. He consciously relaxed them whenever he caught himself, only to find them clenched again moments later, as if his body was preparing for a fight his mind was still processing.

The image of Zorro outside the powder room surfaced in JB's memory—those dark eyes studying him from behind the mask, the brief but meaningful silence between them. When had that Zorro left the party? And the second one—the shorter one he'd mistaken for the first—where had he disappeared to? JB strained to remember any glimpse of either later in the evening, but his memory was too preoccupied with the passionate exchange between Mike and Gianni for him to have noticed.

JB received a text from Rakesh, the fourth one in a series that had grown progressively impatient and hostile. JB silenced his phone without reading the message. He knew Rakesh was eager to learn every gory detail. Through the kitchen window, JB could see a local news truck had parked outside, its satellite dish extended like an accusatory finger. Reporters had assembled beyond a row of giant green shrubs, their cameras occasionally flashing when someone passed by a window. The Hamptons rumor mill—always efficient—had transformed into a media feeding frenzy with remarkable speed.

JB could recall every moment of that last encounter with Gianni. He played the events over and over, each mental replay more distorted than the last. His pulse quickened as the disparate pieces leading up to Gianni's death snapped into place—like puzzle pieces he desperately wished he could push apart again.

They were alone in the pool; Gianni had come on to him. That memory stood sharp and clear: the sudden shift from timid approach to brazen proposition. JB remembered Gianni positioning himself between his legs, watching the man's persona transform. The brash, self-assured version of Gianni had emerged, a metamorphosis that ignited a white-hot fury deep in JB's core.

After that, the memory blurred like ink bleeding into water. Rage consumed JB—a primal, uncontrollable force. He recalled wrapping his legs around Gianni's neck, squeezing with the mechanical precision of a hydraulic press. And then—a moment of hesitation. He had released Gianni. Released him!

Gianni had surfaced, gasping and heaving, as JB climbed from the pool. Alive. Or so JB had believed in that suspended moment of aftermath.

Gianni dove into the pool and cracked his skull. Probably. No, definitely. That's exactly what happened. The combination of alcohol and pills confused him. That's why he dove into the shallow end. He struck his head, and while he was unconscious, face down in the pool, he drowned. Case closed.

Angelo gave JB's shoulder a little squeeze. "Is there any coffee?"

"You scared me." JB reached to grip his hand.

Angelo wore an oversized T-shirt that read *Chef's Kiss* over his swim trunks. Winnie had given each of them the same T-shirt—a promotional giveaway from an appearance she'd made in Southampton last summer—so they didn't have to wear their costumes while speaking with the police. JB wasn't sure which was worse.

"We look like the Beach Boys," JB remarked.

"Who?" Angelo kidded.

"If you want coffee, you'll have to make it."

Angelo began filling the pot with water. Winnie came in and whispered as if they were in church. "I should be doing that."

"Why don't you relax?" JB insisted. "We can manage."

"I can't relax. There's a news truck outside."

Angelo spooned coffee into the filter, his movements deliberately slow. "I heard they already ran a story on News 12."

"Already!" Winnie sounded alarmed. "Gus is in the bedroom trying to reach our lawyer."

"How do you know about the News 12 story?" JB asked.

"Who do you think told me?" Angelo replied. "The cognoscenti of Sag Harbor."

"Rakesh!" Winnie waddled away hurriedly. "Gus, Gus, we were on the news."

Angelo and JB sat at the kitchen table waiting for the coffee to brew. "I've been ignoring Rakesh," JB confessed.

"I know. He's not speaking to Andy. Said he will never forgive him for making him miss the scandal of the century."

"Speaking of scandals. What's the deal with the hot detective and your man?"

Angelo groaned. "What are the chances that one of the detectives investigating Gianni's death by misadventure is my boyfriend's ex?"

"Death by misadventure?"

"Well, that's what this is," Angelo explained. "An accident. Anyway, what are the chances the investigating detective is Jason's ex?"

"It's a small gay world after all."

Jason appeared, wearing his swim trunks and a *Chef's Kiss* T-shirt. "Oh, good. You made coffee."

Angelo tugged Jason's arm. "Can we go home now?"

"I'd like to stick around until they question JB."

"You don't have to."

"No, I want to." Jason's voice dropped to a whisper, his eyes boring into JB's with unsettling intensity. "Mike is likely telling the detectives right now that you are responsible for Gianni's death."

"That's ridiculous," Angelo argued. "JB couldn't have done it. He was in the kitchen with us."

"JB was the last one to see Gianni alive."

"Do you seriously believe Mike is going to tell the detectives JB murdered Gianni?" Angelo interrupted. "How can they take him seriously when he was obviously drunk and high?"

"Let him speak, Angelo."

Jason squatted between them and put his arms across their shoulders. "The detectives have to consider this a homicide until it's ruled out. When someone claims to know who the murderer is, the detectives must take that accusation seriously."

Mike entered the kitchen then, wearing tattered cargo shorts and a *Chef's Kiss* T-shirt, compliments of Winnie Beltram. He didn't stop to speak with anyone. He paused in the kitchen doorway briefly before heading for the front door. "Looks like the band is breaking up," Angelo said.

"What band?" Jason asked.

"It's a private joke." JB rushed after Mike. A black sedan was parked out front. "Mike, where are you going?"

"Go to hell!" Mike's eyes were puffy, his face wan. JB stood on the front porch and watched Mike get in the Uber until the car drove away.

When JB turned around, Detective Sullivan was standing in the doorway. For a suspended moment, the detective simply studied him. "Mr. Pulaski," he finally said. "We'd like to have a word with you now."

JB savored the sun's warmth for one final moment—the last normal feeling he might have for a long time. He knew that crossing that threshold would split his existence into two distinct lives: the one ending now, and the one about to begin.

Chapter Thirteen

By the time JB met with the detectives in Gus Beltram's study, he was running on fumes. He'd been awake for nearly twenty-four hours, riding a rollercoaster of adrenaline crashes and spikes that left his body feeling simultaneously leaden and hypersensitive.

"Please," Detective Sullivan said, "have a seat."

The bright light of morning cast rays through the window, giving JB a better look at them.

Sullivan, a man in his thirties, had dark hair and blue eyes that missed nothing. The cut of his cheap suit emphasized his broad shoulders and narrow waist. D'Amico, on the other hand, was all grit. Tiny, sharp-edged, and stocky around the middle, she carried herself in a brusque manner to exert authority. A professional hazard of being a diminutive woman in a field dominated by misogynistic men.

D'Amico started right away. "You were the last one to see Mr. Cuomo alive, correct?" No preamble, no easing in—just the accusation thinly veiled as a question.

"Apparently."

"Witnesses say they saw you two in the swimming pool alone," she continued. "What did you talk about?"

JB pushed out his lower lip. "Nothing in particular. Mr. Cuomo was quite drunk at the time. He'd also taken drugs."

"Drugs?" D'Amico repeated. "How do you know?"

"Mr. Cuomo said that Mike had given him one of Winnie's pills to relax him." D'Amico and Sullivan exchanged glances. "I'm assuming by the looks on your faces that neither Winnie nor Mike mentioned the drugs?"

D'Amico smiled. "The toxicology report will confirm that."

"What about you?" Sullivan asked. "Any alcohol? Any of *Winnie's* pills?"

"Alcohol, yes. Drugs, no."

JB purposely referred to Winnie's pills as drugs to underscore his testimony that Gianni and Mike were intoxicated and high most of the evening. It was a good piece of advice Jason had given him.

Sullivan had positioned himself behind the desk where D'Amico sat, monitoring JB's reactions as he answered questions. "How did Mr. Cuomo seem to you?"

"Loopy." JB grimaced. "It was uncomfortable being around him, so I went inside, but he was alive when I left him."

"What made you uncomfortable?" Sullivan followed up.

"English is not Mr. Cuomo's first language. Adding drugs and alcohol to the mix, he was almost completely incoherent. So, I decided the best thing for me to do was to extract myself from the situation."

D'Amico interlaced her fingers. "Can you think of any reason why your husband would accuse you of murdering Mr. Cuomo?"

Seventeen years together, a son between them, and Mike had chosen to blow up his family in the most nuclear fashion. It took a certain degree of courage he hadn't believed Mike possessed. Although Mike had a penchant for dramatic scenes, accusing JB of murder would alienate him further from their friends and draw unwanted scrutiny upon their family. Why Mike would risk that, JB had no idea. "I'm not going to speculate why Mike lied. Only that he was on the same cocktail as Mr. Cuomo, which might explain his confused paranoia."

"Were you jealous of your husband's relationship with Mr. Cuomo?" D'Amico asked. "It had to be humiliating for you to see them carrying on in front of all your friends."

Initially, JB's mind wove around the question of how much honesty would complicate matters for Mike, but in the end, he offered, "My husband and I have an understanding when it comes to our marriage."

D'Amico smirked, leaning forward slightly. "So, you're okay with your husband making out with another man at a party?" Her tone held the particular incredulity of someone who'd already judged what she couldn't understand.

"*Okay?*" JB repeated with a short laugh. "I'd prefer if he didn't, but as I said, Mike and Mr. Cuomo were under the influence of drugs and alcohol."

"So, you have an open relationship?" Sullivan clarified.

"It's more of an unspoken agreement," JB explained, "and before you ask, Mike has had other *friends* like Mr. Cuomo."

"I don't get it." D'Amico winced. "No judgment, but that type of arrangement wouldn't fly with me."

JB interlaced his fingers in his lap, the only outward sign of the tension coursing through him. "My husband and I have been together for seventeen years. We adopted a son. We're a family. Life changes. Relationships evolve if they're meant to survive. While our choice may confuse some people, we're still committed to living as a family."

"Any chance your husband fell in love with Mr. Cuomo?" D'Amico asked.

Certainly, Mike had carried on at the party as though he and Gianni were in love, but Mike's dramatic reaction to Gianni's death seemed performative. What nagged at him was why. "You'll have to ask Mike that question."

"I think that's all for now." D'Amico stood. "Before you go, may I ask you to take off your T-shirt?" D'Amico's request came with practiced neutrality. JB hesitated for a fraction of a second—long enough for both detectives to register it—before pulling the shirt over his head. The study's cool air raised goosebumps across his exposed skin as he stood with arms outstretched. D'Amico circled him slowly, her eyes methodically scanning every inch of his torso, assessing, cataloging.

The silence stretched until it seemed to fill the room with its weight.

"How did you get those scratches?" D'Amico pointed to the red excoriations on the outer surface of his knees, her finger hovering above the skin without touching. JB experienced a sudden wrench of panic that must have registered in his eyes, because Sullivan's impassive expression turned wary.

"Mosquitos," JB managed. "I guess that's what I get for wearing a toga outside in the summer."

JB chuckled; the detectives did not.

In that moment, JB knew with absolute certainty that his flippant remark came across as a frantic attempt to swat away their suspicion. But like all hungry insects drawn to blood, every averted glance and every nervous snicker only nourished their growing skepticism.

Chapter Fourteen

JB drove Emilio home around two that afternoon, the silence between them dense and suffocating. Every few minutes, JB glanced at his son's profile—the tightened jaw, the hollow eyes still rimmed with smudged makeup from his Baseball Furies costume—searching for something to say that wouldn't make things worse. By the time they pulled into the driveway, that silence had calcified into something immovable.

Mike was sprawled on the couch when they entered, a half-empty bottle of vodka on the coffee table, a tumbler balanced precariously on his chest. He didn't even lift his gaze when the door opened, didn't acknowledge their presence—not even Emilio's. That deliberate disregard for their son cut JB more deeply than Mike's cowardly departure from the Beltrams' without them. Emilio stormed into his room and slammed the door.

JB stood over Mike, observing the dirt on his hands, the fresh scratches on his legs. "What happened to you?"

"Fuck off."

"Keep your voice down," JB whispered. "You made quite a spectacle of yourself last night. Let's not have a repeat performance for the neighbors today."

"No!" Mike roared, surging upright, vodka sloshing from his tumbler onto the hardwood floor. "I will not be muzzled by you."

He glared with such a penetrating stare that chills inched down JB's arms. There was something different in Mike's eyes—not just anger or grief, but a cold, calculated hatred.

JB's cell phone rang. "Hello?"

"Finally," Rakesh said. "I've been climbing the walls. How are you?"

"Not good." JB headed outside to speak in private. "Mike accused me of murdering Gianni Cuomo. It was an Oscar-worthy performance."

"I heard it was awful. Where are you?"

"Home with Mike."

"The two of you under the same roof?" Rakesh clarified. "That doesn't bode well with Mike's accusation of murder, my friend. If I'd thought Andy was a killer, home alone with him would be the last place you'd find me."

JB stopped mid-conversation, words dying in his throat. Across the garden, his cucuzza plants lay destroyed, their pale flesh scattered across the dark soil. Crushed tomatoes had left red streaks. Split cucumbers and uprooted carrots jutted from the earth at odd angles. Where yesterday had stood his meticulously tended sanctuary now lay a garden in ruin.

"JB, are you there?"

He shook his head. "May I call you back?"

"There's something I need to tell you first," Rakesh said with some urgency. "I don't want to add more negativity to an already awful situation, but you should know the Beltrams have issued a statement."

JB unlatched the garden gate, surveying the damage. He asked himself over and over what had come over Mike to do such a thing.

"What kind of statement?" JB asked, though there was a part of him that didn't want to know.

"Not that it matters, you know, but the Beltrams insinuated that the death of Gianni Cuomo was the result of foul play."

"Foul play?"

It was stupid of the Beltrams to make a statement to the press during an ongoing investigation. The detectives had asked that no one speak to reporters, but JB didn't have to ask Rakesh why the Beltrams did anyway.

"You know Gus," Rakesh said. "By insinuating foul play, instead of an accident, the Beltrams are protecting themselves from any liability."

"Well, hopefully, no one will read it."

"Darling, this was on television."

Media whores.

JB would never consider commenting to the press when it was possible Gianni's family hadn't been informed yet of his death. JB glanced into the house. He saw Mike lying on the living room couch, his arm bent over his eyes as if he were sobbing. JB wondered if Mike would follow suit and speak with reporters. A chill crawled up his back, thinking about it.

"It's a defensive move," Rakesh went on. "The police haven't said anything about foul play. Angelo said Jason called it death by misadventure, which, if you ask me, sounds pretty awesome. That's the way I want to drop dead."

"Only you could joke at a time like this."

"I'm walking on sunshine," Rakesh sang. "But don't worry. It's not like anyone is going to listen to a TV chef and her closeted husband. I'm worried about Mike. People are already talking about the way he behaved last night."

"People are talking?" How Rakesh loved to bolster his gossipy claims by using a hypothetical court of opinion whose jurors lived exclusively inside his head. But this time, JB heard a gavel knock of truth in his statement.

"You have to admit Mike and Gianni were acting peculiar," Rakesh continued. "Staring into each other's eyes like they were rolling on ecstasy."

"What did Winnie give them?"

"I'm not sure. Xanax, maybe."

"We'll find out once the toxicology report comes back."

"You know there'll be an autopsy."

JB's knees suddenly felt weak. He leaned against the garden gate to steady himself. The scratches on his knees, Gianni had caused them. Would they find his skin under Gianni's nails?

"If there's anything Andy and I can do to help you, JB—I mean, with Mike, let us know. We're here for you."

Funny how their friends were choosing sides, each writing their own narrative. Sure, it had been uncomfortable when Mike had flirted with Dan Vega and that couple at parties. Back then, everyone had perfected the art of ignoring the situation, smiling and shrugging it away. But now that Gianni Cuomo was dead, there was nothing to smile or shrug at.

Another Sag Harbor murder.

How long before the media resurrected the story of Jamie Friend and Tom

Fitzsimmons? Their murder had nearly destroyed JB's sanity, especially given Mike's relationship with them. Fortunately, the lurid details of the affair never came to light in the media. JB fretted that this time they might not be so lucky. What were the chances that some ambitious reporter might connect Mike with all three victims? It seemed not just possible, but inevitable.

Staring at the garden, JB could envision Mike's tense shoulders as he violently hacked at the vegetation, could almost hear the howl of his husband's rage echoing across the mangled plants.

And then, like the click of a gate latch, a gruesome thought creaked open in JB's mind. The same hands that had violently dismembered his beloved garden—could they have done the same elsewhere?

Chapter Fifteen

Days later, JB felt no compunction when it came to Gianni's death. He searched the corners of his conscience where guilt should have taken root, but found only an unsettling void.

He threw himself into restoring the garden despite the summer's waning days. After clearing the ravaged vegetables, he planted flowers in their place—a defiant burst of life amid the fallow ground. Only a single portion of the cucuzza plant had survived, fecund and bearing squash—its resilience both a comfort and a reminder of what had been lost.

That afternoon, JB entered the house after one. Mike lay on the sofa, drinking vodka. Emilio ate a sandwich, not prepared by Mike, in the kitchen. "Why don't we go for a drive after I shower?" JB suggested.

Emilio stared sullenly at his food. "I don't know."

"What's wrong?"

Emilio dropped his head back and sighed. "There's this girl I was seeing from school."

"And?"

"Her parents won't let her talk to me on account of the murder."

The death of a piano player at the home of a celebrity TV chef had been national news. It didn't surprise JB to learn that this girl's family had heard it. What concerned JB now was what life would be like for his son once he returned to school. Would he be ridiculed? Emilio had brilliantly navigated the rocky terrain of explaining his two gay dads so well that some of the other students envied him. To explain away the rumor of a crime of passion involving those same two gay dads was another story altogether.

JB sat across from Emilio. "I did not kill Gianni Cuomo."

"I didn't say you did, jeez."

"I know you didn't," JB said, touching his arm, "but I want you to hear it from me."

Mike walked into the kitchen. "Don't lie to him, JB." He laughed bitterly and stared at Emilio with an expression that held not even an ounce of anything that could be called paternal.

Emilio punched the side of his head over and over. "Stop it," JB shouted.

Abruptly, the boy stood up, knocking the stool to the floor, and ran out of the kitchen.

"Goddamn it, Mike," JB spoke harshly but in a low voice. "I don't care what you say to me, or our friends, just don't drag Emilio into your drunken conspiracy theories."

"You won't get away with it."

"Why don't you take a shower and sober up."

"The whole town is talking about you," Mike warned. "There's gonna be an uprising, you wait!"

"Led by you, no doubt." JB opened the refrigerator, surveying what he could make with what little groceries they had. Since Gianni's death, Mike and JB had avoided making public appearances unless completely necessary. The grocery store, being a necessity, had become a minefield for gossipers. He found pork chops in the freezer and set them on the counter to thaw.

"Go on," Mike hissed. "Pretend like nothing happened. Make dinner. You're good at that, making dinner and pretending like nothing happened. Just you wait." Mike turned and stumbled back into the living room.

JB gripped the edge of the marble island with such intensity that it frightened him. The pressure felt insurmountable, and he knew it would only get worse before it got better. JB took a deep breath and decided he'd make pork chops on the grill along with coleslaw and tomato salad. He had to maintain some semblance of order.

He decided then, at dinner, he would inform Emilio and Mike that they were moving back to Manhattan. JB had to get his son as far away from Sag Harbor as possible. Mike could join them, but JB suspected he wouldn't.

As he started for the barbecue, his cell phone rang. "I need to speak to you and Mike." The worrisome tone of Jason's voice alarmed him. "Can I come by now? It's urgent."

* * *

"Did you know Gianni Cuomo was married to a woman?" Jason asked.

"What are you talking about?" Mike stood up, wavering briefly, then sat down hard. Mike had continued drinking despite JB's urging to stop. His eyes were glassy with dark circles hammocking them.

"I spoke with a friend earlier," Jason went on. "He said Gianni has a wife and two children in Palermo, Italy."

"A friend?" JB repeated mockingly. "Detective Sullivan…that friend?"

"Yes, that friend." Jason let his sarcasm pass without comment.

"That's not possible," Mike said with indignance. "There's no way Gianni was straight. I can attest to that."

JB shifted uncomfortably. "Go on, Jason."

"Gianni played piano at the Blue Whale on Fire Island last summer. Apparently, he had quite the reputation." Jason goggled his eyes. "Have you heard the expression, gay for pay?"

"Gianni Cuomo was a hustler?" JB clarified.

Jason nodded. "The owner of the Blue Whale confirmed that Gianni had shacked up with a couple who essentially took him in for the summer. I don't know all the details, but it ended badly. They sued Gianni for theft and extortion."

"Theft and extortion!" Mike repeated. "What are you talking about?" Mike stood up again. His knees wobbled.

"I'm telling you this before the news gets out…the press will have a field day. Imagine what they'll write once they find out about Gianni and his…"

"His what!" Mike snapped.

"Sit down," JB ordered. "Sit down and shut up."

"I will not," Mike shouted. "Did you start this rumor, JB? Jesus, will you stop at nothing?"

"This is no rumor," Jason insisted. "Gianni's wife, Daria, is on her way to Sag Harbor to claim his body."

"I don't want to hear this!" Mike stormed into his bedroom and slammed the door.

JB walked Jason outside to speak with him alone. "I'm sorry about Mike," JB began. "He's not handling this well."

"Get yourself a lawyer."

It took a moment for JB to respond. He was so taken aback, not knowing what to say. JB was forced to contemplate the possibility that the situation his family found themselves in now had sprung from his own fair hand. The frustration he'd experienced for allowing Mike certain liberties in the past, inconsiderate of his own son's well-being, and the catapult into cancer wasn't exactly all his fault. But he couldn't excuse himself, either.

"A lawyer?" JB found his voice, grasping at Jason's words. "Wouldn't that be tantamount to an admission of guilt?"

"You've been watching too much *Law & Order*. There's a good chance the police will bring you in for questioning once the preliminary autopsy results come back."

"More intel from your *friend*?"

"No. Just fifteen years of law enforcement experience."

"I'll decide to retain a lawyer when the time comes," JB insisted. "If it comes at all."

Jason took a deep breath. "Is there any chance they might find your DNA under Gianni's fingernails?"

"Why would they find my DNA?" JB feigned confusion, but his stomach somersaulted.

Jason's eyes traveled deliberately to JB's legs, lingering on the knees where the scratches—now healing into pale pink lines—remained visible. "Those marks on your legs..." His words hung in the air, thick with suspicion. "Could they have come from Gianni?"

There was simply nowhere else for JB to go but to continue his lie. "Those scratches were not inflicted by Gianni Cuomo," JB replied with as much conviction as he could muster. "They're mosquito bite scratches."

"I don't know all the facts. They don't gel, but I wouldn't be surprised if the police ask you to come down to the station for questioning. If they do, take my advice, bring a lawyer."

JB saw Jason, staring, woefully, expectantly, waiting for his response. "Who else besides Mike thinks I murdered Gianni?"

"Gus Beltram," Jason said without hesitation. "You went around town bragging that you were responsible for the deaths of Jamie Friend and Tom Fitzsimmons."

"That was a joke."

"A joke no one found funny."

"Besides, that murderer confessed," JB added. "Anyway, if I had killed Gianni, wouldn't I have been covered in his blood? He had a gash on his head."

"Gus said you entered the house soaking wet," Jason explained. "You could have rinsed off in the pool. Plus, Gus stated that you were the first one to jump into the water to rescue Gianni. Gus believes you pulled Gianni out to contaminate yourself with his blood in case the police found any on you at all."

"Apparently, I'm not the only one watching too much *Law and Order*."

"I'm advising you as a friend." Serious blue eyes darted from side to side as Jason spoke. JB thought he was under surveillance. Was there more Jason wasn't sharing with him? JB realized with intense focus that he hadn't the full story or where to look for it. And now it was time for JB to turn the tables.

"Well, let me give you some advice, *friend*," JB said. "Angelo means the world to me. He saved my life, and I would hate for him to get hurt."

"You have nothing to worry about."

JB peered down at Jason, taking in his startled, befuddled expression with barely suppressed suspicion. "I saw the way Detective Sullivan looked at you. I know what I saw."

Jason gave a wan smile. "Get yourself a lawyer, JB."

JB returned to the house and fixed himself a double Scotch. After drinking it in one gulp, he retreated to his study until he had calmed himself sufficiently to start dinner.

* * *

JB was talkative and engaging as they ate, but neither Mike nor Emilio added much to the conversation. "I think we should move back to the city."

Mike perked up. "When?"

"I was thinking maybe…tomorrow."

"We're not staying here until Labor Day?" Emilio asked with obvious disappointment. "Who wants to be in the city in August? It's so friggin' hot."

JB experienced a sudden pang of empathy for Emilio. Gianni's death had detonated a final blow to an already challenging summer, but it was for the best. It was both necessary and vital to distance his son from the town gossip and ridicule.

"I need to finish my fall syllabus before classes start," JB explained. "It's easier for me to work in the city."

"I think that's a great idea," Mike offered. "I, of course, will not be joining you two."

"Dad, please," Emilio begged. "I don't want to go. Not yet."

"Emilio, it's for the best." JB despised the sound of his voice. It reminded him of his father whenever they'd argued. His tone had always been absolute and final. "We can go to the movies and museums. We can go bike riding in Central Park. Oh, I know…we can go to DUMBO and eat pizza at that place you love."

"No!" Emilio shouted with his hands pressed against his ears. "You're only doing this because of Gianni Cuomo."

"That's not true, Emilio." But even as he spoke those words, he heard not an ounce of truth in them. "We can still come back on weekends." But JB had no plans to return until after the investigation was over, and everyone had forgotten that he was a suspect in the death of an Italian piano player. A real-life Casanova who allegedly extorted money from a gay couple last summer.

"I hate Gianni Cuomo!" Emilio slammed both hands down on the table.

"I'm glad he's dead."

The house phone rang. JB got up to answer it. "Hello?"

"Mr. Pulaski?" The voice on the line carried the unmistakable flat vowels of Brooklyn.

"Yes, who's this?" JB asked, though the tightening in his chest told him he already knew.

"Detective D'Amico," she replied, the official tone leaving no room for warmth. "We'd like you to come in for questioning tomorrow. Let's say around one?"

JB glanced at the table. Emilio and Mike stared apprehensively as if JB were listening to a kidnapper's ransom instructions. "One works for me. See you then."

Emilio piped in. "Who was that?"

"It was Dr. Perrotta," JB lied. "We're having lunch tomorrow."

"Angelo Perrotta, huh?" Mike asked dubiously. "You didn't recognize his voice."

JB grinned. "It was a bad connection."

"So, we're not moving back to the city tomorrow?" Emilio asked.

"Tomorrow's too soon." JB poured wine with an unsteady hand. "I was only thinking out loud."

And with that, JB shut his mouth tight for the rest of the meal. The family dinner—his desperate attempt at normalcy—suddenly felt like the last meal of a condemned man. Beneath the table, his knee began to tremor—the ground beneath him quavering.

One o'clock. The hour when his hard-won happy life would finally collapse under the weight of one fateful night by a swimming pool.

Chapter Sixteen

Clean-shaven and sullen, JB drank coffee in his study. Aside from the sunlight streaming in through the window, the room was dark, which was how he preferred it. Even after the renovation, his study was as it had always been, featuring wide plank floors, heavy drapes, and a leather armchair. Since his cancer diagnosis, JB spent long hours alone in his study.

The silver clock ticked with metronome precision, counting down the minutes until his appointment with the detectives. JB stared out the window at the perfect view of the garden he'd restored after Mike had ransacked it.

"Why are you dressed up?" JB saw Mike in the doorway out of the corner of his eye.

JB swiveled to face him. "The detectives asked me to come down to the station. I'm telling you only because you're sure to find out. I ask that you not tell Emilio. Not yet."

Mike leaned against the doorjamb and folded his arms. "I can do that."

"Did you know Gianni Cuomo was a hustler?"

Mike's features hardened into familiar contempt, but his eyes betrayed a flicker of wounded pride. "Gianni was not a hustler."

JB's eyes drifted to the papers stacked neatly on his desk. "I reviewed our bank statements last night. It seems you've been withdrawing large sums of money…larger than usual." Mike opened his mouth to speak, but JB held up his hand to mute him. "Ordinarily, I wouldn't have noticed." JB let out a snort. "That's not true. Ordinarily, I wouldn't have cared. You always treated yourself well, but now that I know Gianni Cuomo was a man who swindled older gay men of their money, I have to ask you again: did you know Gianni was a hustler?"

"I don't know what I ever saw in you," Mike gritted, his tone thick with venom and something that might have been woundedness. "You're a pompous, disgusting human being."

"So, you didn't know Gianni had a family in Italy?"

"Of course, I didn't know."

JB rummaged through the stack of papers. "Phone records show that you made several calls to Italy. Do you know anyone in Italy, Mike?" JB fanned the phone bills out on his desk. He had highlighted several calls with the country code +39. "As you can see, they're all to the same number."

"I never made any calls to that number," Mike replied with emphasis, but JB could hear the crack in his voice. Could see the pained expression emerging behind Mike's veil of indignation. Perhaps he didn't know Gianni had a family in Palermo, and all those calls to Italy were something he never thought to question if Gianni asked to use his phone. But one thing JB was certain of: learning Gianni was a hustler had cut Mike so deeply he was unable to disguise the pain.

"Why don't you call now and see who answers?" JB said.

"Why would I?" Mike replied tremulously, his lower lip quivering.

"Because you know who will answer." JB grinned with satisfaction. "What do you think the detectives will say when I tell them about the money and the phone records?"

"Go ahead. You're the one they called in for questioning."

JB felt a degree of admiration for Mike's cunning. Confronted with the news about Gianni's family, the phone calls to Italy and the bank withdrawals appeared not to ruffle him as much as JB had hoped.

"I did not kill Gianni Cuomo," JB said. "That's a rumor you started. Have you any proof other than your unsubstantiated drunk and drugged memory?"

Mike's eyes gleamed as if he had been waiting to show his winning hand. "You were alone with him in the pool that night. You were the last one to see him alive. Call it what you want…circumstantial…sure, but once Gianni's wife arrives, she'll confirm what I told the police, that Gianni would have never dived into a pool, because he can't swim."

JB stood up and took a menacing step toward Mike. "People make stupid choices when they're high. What were you two on that night?"

"None of your business."

Mike turned to leave, but JB grabbed his arm. "Take this." JB thrust cash into Mike's hand. "You're on an allowance now."

"What do you mean, allowance?"

"I've frozen your credit and debit cards," he explained tartly. "Obviously, you can't be trusted. I'm only looking out for my son. Wouldn't want his silly father to spend his inheritance on hustlers to feed his pathetic, aging ego."

JB exited his study, closing the door behind him. The crash of a lamp against the wall was the last thing he heard before exiting the house.

* * *

The police station was a red brick building off Main Street. Detective Sullivan escorted JB to an office where Detective D'Amico sat at a desk. "Mr. Pulaski, thank you for coming," she said. "Please have a seat."

JB sat across from her. The overhead fluorescent light buzzed faintly, casting harsh shadows that emphasized every stress line in D'Amico's face.

"We have some additional questions," she continued. "The preliminary autopsy report has been filed. The ME cannot rule out a homicide."

"Seriously?"

"The cause of death was listed as drowning, but the ME noted petechial hemorrhages of the conjunctiva. Those are ruptured blood vessels in the whites of Mr. Cuomo's eyes that are consistent with strangulation, and there was bruising around his neck."

"Couldn't those injuries be consistent with a diving accident?"

D'Amico shook her head. "Not likely." She proffered a photo from the autopsy. It showed a close-up of Gianni's head injury. A gash about two inches long with bruising on either side. "The Beltrams' pool is made of gunite. If Mr. Cuomo had hit the bottom with enough intensity to crack his skull"—she punched her palm—"the medical examiner said he would have found remnants of concrete and sand in the scalp wound."

"And?"

"There were none," she explained. "See here?" She tapped the photo repeatedly. "These tiny flecks. They're splinters of wood. So, I asked myself, why would a man found drowned in a pool have wood splinters in his head wound if the pool is made of gunite?"

JB offered a befuddled shrug.

D'Amico stood up. "My first thought was that Mr. Cuomo had stumbled into the bushes to pee and snagged a few branches in his hair, but the way the ME described the splintering…" JB found his gaze fixed on the photo, on the raw edges of Gianni's wound. Something tightened in JB's chest. "…and the way the fibers are embedded in his gash," D'Amico continued, either oblivious to or deliberately ignoring JB's reaction, "it seems likelier that someone had struck him with a wooden object, which rendered him unconscious, and that's why he drowned."

"Struck him with what?" JB asked. "A log?"

"That was my first assumption too, but the wood splinters identified are not consistent with the firewood or any of the vegetation found on the Beltrams' property."

"So, you didn't find a weapon?" JB clarified.

"Not yet." D'Amico sat down again. She opened a folder and produced several more photos. "The Beltrams had hired a professional photographer. He graciously provided these three." JB sat up to view them. The first was a photo of JB, Angelo, and Rakesh posing for the camera after Rakesh had won first place for best costume. The second showed JB and Rakesh at the bar. In the background, Mike and Gianni sat at the piano, locked in a trancelike gaze. The last was a group photo. JB remembered posing for it because it had been taken early in the evening, hours before Gianni's death. "This is your son?" She indicated Emilio.

"You know it is."

"Nice boy." Turning to Sullivan, she asked, "Wasn't he?"

"Very polite," Sullivan replied.

"What does my son have to do with this?"

"The wood splinters found in Mr. Cuomo's gash were identified as lacquered ash."

The room tilted sideways. JB's eyes dropped to the photo again, drawn as if by magnetic force to the image of Emilio. There, amongst his friends and family—dressed in costumes—Emilio gripped the Louisville Slugger.

JB forced himself to look up, meeting D'Amico's expectant gaze with a carefully composed expression of confusion. "I'm not following you."

"That's a Louisville Slugger, right?"

JB sat perfectly still, trapped in the crosshairs of D'Amico's rifle. This whole time, she had been breadcrumbing him with morsels of information so that JB would arrive at the same conclusion—that she suspected the baseball bat was the murder weapon—without having to tell him herself. "Yes, it is."

"My understanding is that it's somewhat of an heirloom."

The way JB saw it, there was no need to go round and round the bases. The Louisville Slugger, he knew, was an antique made from white ash that had been dipped in lacquer. There was no point in pretending he didn't know this when it was clear the detectives did. "Yes, it is," JB confirmed. "My father gave it to me when I was eleven."

"We'd like to see your son's baseball bat," D'Amico spoke in a small but steely tone.

"Is that what this is all about?" JB shrugged off the request with ease. "Why didn't you ask me to bring it with me today?"

D'Amico smiled. "The facts of this case are evolving minute to minute. We only just learned about the fibers."

It occurred to JB that perhaps the detectives were toying with him for reasons that weren't yet apparent. Did they know something he didn't?

"I can go get the bat now if you like," JB offered, his voice neutral and guarded.

Turning to Sullivan, she said, "I told you he'd cooperate."

The Louisville Slugger is in Emilio's closet. Intact. Pristine. It can't be the murder weapon.

JB whispered this to himself without the faintest susurration of anything even remotely like doubt. For a moment, he considered saying this to the detectives, but didn't. There was something in the way this compact woman had glanced at her hulky partner seconds earlier that unnerved JB. What had they discussed before his arrival?

"Well, if there's nothing else." JB stood up. "I'll go get the bat."

D'Amico rose from her chair again. "As a matter of fact, there's one more thing."

"And what would that be?"

D'Amico grinned. "We'd like you to volunteer a sample of your DNA?"

There was only one answer any innocent man would give—although it might fundamentally change the way he was perceived if his sample matched the one recovered from under Gianni Cuomo's nails.

"Okay." JB heard the strain in his own voice, felt his carefully affable expression fracture at the edges. The room seemed airless, the walls pressing inward. For a suspended moment, he saw himself as they must see him—a potential killer negotiating the terms of his cooperation. "You can take the DNA sample," he finally said, measuring each word, "when I return with the bat."

As he stood to leave, JB knew with absolute certainty that the bat would be exactly where it should be—in Emilio's closet, untouched since the party.

He had to believe this because the alternative was unthinkable.

Chapter Seventeen

JB drove the shortest route home, his grip strangling the steering wheel as he careened down the winding road. The Thuja Green Giants, pitch pines, and oak trees blurred into a verdant smear at the edges of his vision. His heart hammered against his ribs as he called Emilio's number for the third time. "Goddammit," he muttered when it went directly to voicemail again. "It's your father," he said, struggling to keep the panic from his voice. "Call me back immediately."

JB replayed an event from the night of the party: Emilio's face had contorted with rage after Mike had stormed away from them. The bat had cut through the air with such ferocious intensity—an arc of lacquered ash that whistled as it sliced the night. The force behind that swing could have rendered anyone comatose, could have split the flesh from the bone with the merciless impact of a wrecking ball. But Emilio wasn't violent. He was sweet and kind. He was gentle and forgiving. There had to be another reason for the ME to have found lacquered white ash in Gianni's head wound.

It took less than fifteen minutes to reach the house. Mike's car wasn't in the driveway, and neither was Emilio's bike, which he typically discarded on the front lawn like a felled animal. JB parked the car and bolted for the door, but it was locked. He fumbled for the keys, praying the bat was in Emilio's closet, pristine and bloodless, just as JB had delivered it to him. The Louisville Slugger his father gave him at age eleven, the same one he gifted to Emilio when he turned ten—it had to be there!

The key wouldn't fit in the lock.

Mike can do whatever he wants to me. He had already been made a fool when Mike had exposed their marriage to ridicule in a desperate attempt to feed his own vanity. JB had volunteered to remain in the firing line of Mike's relentless brigade of humiliation until he overstepped a boundary that had not yet been defined. Emilio's future was a red line not to be crossed.

There it was. The key that opened the door.

"Hello? Hello?"

His voice sounded flat in the empty house. JB ran directly to Emilio's room, hoping he'd find him still in bed, staring at his iPad. He pushed open the door. Emilio's bed was neatly made, the room bathed in the orange glow of the afternoon sun. He threw open the closet door.

Where is it?

JB tossed sneakers and slides over his shoulder, rummaging through the closet until it was empty. Clothes piled in a heap, his breathing shallow and erratic. "It has to be here," he shouted, whirling around, heart spasming in his chest. His gaze ricocheted from corner to corner, cataloguing and dismissing hiding places. The bed. It had to be under the bed! JB yanked the covers off with one violent motion, then shoved the mattress askew, dropping to his knees to peer into the shadowed space beneath the frame. Nothing but a forgotten sock and clumps of Buckley's fur, mocking him with their mundane innocence.

Where is it?

JB dialed Emilio's cell, cursing when it went straight to voicemail again. "Emilio, this is your father. Call me right away, son. I'm looking for the bat. Where is it?" His fingers frantically texted, but there was no response.

He crumpled to the floor, heaving with an enormity of panic he hadn't experienced before, not even when he'd been diagnosed with cancer. JB's mix of loathing for his husband and anxiety for his son sat like a jagged lump in his throat. For several long seconds, he glared at his phone, willing Emilio to respond, but he never replied. Next, JB checked Mike's closet, the garage, the pool house, and the garbage cans, but he found no bat.

Lacquered white ash. D'Amico's description of Gianni's wound echoed in his head like a foghorn.

He recalled Gianni's dead body on the Beltrams' checkered dance floor. He willed himself somehow—compelled to see it again with clarity. There was a gash. Skin split open and bleeding like raw sirloin. And JB saw, from his new perspective, that the wound bristled with tiny splinters of wood. After the detectives questioned them, JB drove Emilio home. Did he have the bat with him then? JB couldn't recall. What if he'd left it in the Beltrams' basement? He dialed their house phone, but the answering machine picked up. "Hi, it's JB," he began shakily. "I know you're both still recovering from this awful tragedy, but I'm looking for Emilio's baseball bat. I can't explain now, but there's a chance he may have left it in your basement. I'm coming over to look for it."

He stormed through the front door, but JB stopped dead in his tracks. Emilio turned the corner, pedaling the bike with frantic urgency. The boy was moving too fast, taking the turn with reckless abandon. He leapt off the still-moving bike, letting it crash into the hedges, its front wheel spinning uselessly in the air. Time compressed as he took in his son's face—red, crumpled, tear-streaked. It was the same expression he'd worn as a toddler during his most overwhelming tantrums, a face too young to contain such adult anguish. "Dad," Emilio sobbed, the word fracturing in his throat. "I'm sorry. I'm so sorry."

JB whisked his son inside, sat him on the sofa, and held his hands. "Son, you have to tell me the truth." Emilio threw his body forward, weeping. JB pulled him upright and locked eyes. "Where is it?"

Emilio couldn't begin to say the words. "I…I…don't know"—Emilio stared guiltily back at JB—"I don't know where the bat is."

At first, JB didn't believe him, but when he examined Emilio's painful, twisted face, any last grain of doubt vanished. JB saw what he'd always known—Emilio was kind and good. Most of all, he was innocent. Why had he allowed himself to fall into the rabbit hole of suspicion D'Amico had created? That was something he'd deal with another time. For now, he had to find the bat. "So, you don't know where the bat is?" JB clarified.

"I'm sorry, Dad," Emilio bawled. "I know how much that bat means to you, but I don't know where it is. I'm so sorry."

JB gathered his son into his arms, his own tears breaking free—not tears of grief or fear but overwhelming relief that washed through him like a cleansing tide. His son was innocent. The conviction settled into his bones with absolute certainty. How could he have ever doubted his innocence? "Listen to me." JB tilted his son's chin up, forcing eye contact. "I don't care about the bat itself. I only need to know where it is."

"I don't know." Emilio wept, pressing his head against his father's chest.

JB pulled away, gripping Emilio's shoulders. "You have to get ahold of yourself. Try, son. Try to remember when you saw it last?"

Emilio's gaze rose to meet JB's. "I had it at the party."

JB nodded frantically. "Yes, I know. You showed it to everyone. When was the last time you saw it at the Beltrams' costume party?"

Emilio rubbed his forehead exhaustedly. "I had it with me downstairs while I was watching television."

"Well, that's where it has to be."

"No," Emilio whined. "The next day, when I realized I didn't have it, I went to the Beltrams'. They said they hadn't seen it. They wouldn't even let me in the house to look around."

"Gus and Winnie wouldn't let you in their house?"

Emilio shook his head. "Mr. Beltram was clear that our family wasn't welcome in their house ever again."

JB had been swept up in a maelstrom of all-consuming guilt and fear, convinced against all reason that his son was somehow involved in Gianni's death. The possibility had driven him to the edge of madness, every thought twisted by doubt and dread.

But now the truth crystallized with brutal clarity. The Beltrams had barred his child from searching for his bat. The Beltrams, who had spewed toxic accusations at the press. The Beltrams, whose pristine pool had been the scene of a murder.

JB stood, his decision hardening. Gus Beltram had made a critical mistake. He'd underestimated a father's love.

Chapter Eighteen

JB pounded on the Beltrams' door as though it were Gus's face. When no one answered, he turned the knob and found it unlocked. The door swung open. Winnie stood at the kitchen island twenty feet away. Sunlight glinted off the butcher knife in her right hand, the blade gleaming as she sliced through something red and raw on the cutting board. "Oh, hello, JB." Her voice dripped with artificial sweetness.

"May I come in?"

Winnie picked up a dish towel and cleaned the blade. "It appears you already are."

"I knocked, but when no one answered, I tried the door."

"It's the Hamptons," she said, smiling. "Who locks their door?"

JB imagined how many photos Winnie had posed for where she'd learned to perfect the art of smiling with little genuine enthusiasm.

"How can I help you?" Winnie's unflappable demeanor had a disorienting effect on JB; he couldn't remember why he'd burst into her house. He saw not one shred of evidence that would indicate this home had hosted a costume party that had ended in murder.

"The night of the party," JB began. "My son was dressed in a baseball costume. He was carrying a bat."

"Oh, is that what this is all about?" Her conversational tone somehow emphasized her growing impatience.

"Why wouldn't you let my son in your house to look for it the other day?"

"Isn't it obvious?" she replied with extravagant sarcasm. "You realize we hosted a party where someone was murdered. Gus and I hadn't slept for over twenty-four hours, traumatized by this horrific crime, and then, Armando shows up on our doorstep in a panic."

"Emilio," JB corrected, somewhat snidely. "My son's name is *Emilio*."

"I don't appreciate your tone." She shifted her grip on the knife, her fingers tightening around the handle as she turned to face him fully. The blade caught the light again—a flash of silver that momentarily blinded him. "Pardon my candor, but we weren't about to let the son of a suspected murderer into our house."

"I did not kill Gianni Cuomo," he said, his voice steady despite his shaky hands. "Now, may I please go downstairs and look for my son's bat?"

"I'm afraid I can't allow that." A voice sliced through the kitchen from the hall. Gus Beltram stepped into view. He'd been in the study, listening the entire time.

"Oh, hi Gus," JB said, his tone shifting to feigned casualness. "Hiding in the closet. I should have guessed."

"That's enough!" Winnie's palm cracked against the marble countertop.

"It's alright, dear." Gus raised his hand to quiet her. "I know what you and your *friend* call me behind my back, JB. Word gets around town. Unfortunately, that has nothing to do with why we can't let you search our house."

"Is that right?" Standing there in the Beltrams' immaculate kitchen—all gleaming surfaces and sharp edges—JB experienced a perverse thrill in learning that Gus knew what Rakesh and he thought about him. To expose someone to a truth about themselves was like holding up a mirror and handing them a flashlight.

In those tense moments, JB calculated his odds. He could ignore Gus and Winnie and barrel downstairs without their permission. What would they do? Tackle him? Call the—

A sharp knock at the front door froze everyone in place. "I'll get that." Gus's grin was as thin as a paper cut, a bloodless slice across his face. He moved toward the entryway, each footfall a possible countdown to JB's undoing. Blood rushed in his ears as he watched helplessly—trapped between Winnie's knife and whatever waited beyond that door—as Gus reached for the handle with grand theatrical flair.

"Come in, Detectives," Gus announced.

JB squinted through his narrowed lids. "You called the police?"

"You said you were on your way here," Gus replied. "We were only protecting ourselves."

"And left the door unlocked to entrap me." JB had completely underestimated this situation. He appeared more suspicious now than before—that was the worst part.

"We'd like you to follow us to the station." Sullivan's eyes pleaded with him to cooperate. JB had no choice.

"Thank you, detectives." Gus escorted them out.

"Wait a second." Winnie presented D'Amico with two squares wrapped in wax paper. "I made white chocolate chunk blondies. Take them for later."

Gus and Winnie stood in the doorway as though they were saying goodbye to dinner guests. Gus even gave Winnie a peck on the cheek. *What a photo op.* Except no reporters or paparazzi were waiting in the bushes. By now, the media cared as much about the death of a foreign piano player as they did for a dead deer found on the side of the road.

* * *

The detectives upgraded JB to an interrogation room. Everything was institutional gray beneath fluorescent lights that buzzed like trapped insects. The Formica table—scarred by years of nervous fingernails and desperate fists—was surrounded by three metal chairs that creaked with every shift of weight. A one-way mirror dominated one wall, its reflective surface offering JB nothing but his own haggard face while concealing whoever might be watching from beyond. He slumped in his chair while D'Amico sat opposite him, hands neatly folded on the tabletop. From the corner, Sullivan loomed over them, sipping coffee and studying him silently.

"So, the bat wasn't in your son's closet?" D'Amico asked.

"No, he doesn't have the bat, which is why I went to the Beltrams'. Emilio believes he left it downstairs."

Sullivan pulled a chair up to the table and sat on it backward. His arms hung over the top rail, accentuating the bulge of his biceps. "So, you decided to break into the Beltrams' house to look for it."

"The door was open."

"Unlocked," D'Amico corrected. "The door was unlocked but not open. You opened it."

JB felt the impulse to shout that what he'd done was not breaking and entering, a knee-jerk reaction to defend himself, but a little voice inside his head encouraged him not to speak too quickly. JB took a few deep diaphragmatic breaths. "When my son realized he'd left the bat at the Beltrams' house, he went over there to look for it, but they wouldn't let him in."

"And so, you decided to take matters into your own hands?" D'Amico interjected. "That's why you broke into the Beltrams' house."

"Why are you wasting time? You know I didn't break into the Beltrams' house. Are you trying to trip me up? Catch me in a lie? Get a warrant and search the Beltrams' house."

"We searched their house the night of Gianni Cuomo's death," Sullivan explained. "No murder weapon was found."

The slap of disappointment stung JB's cheek. "I know you don't think my son killed Gianni Cuomo. Mike and Winnie already provided you with his alibi." JB paused to clear his throat. "Which means you think I did it."

JB should have listened to Jason—and hired a lawyer. He wondered how many innocent people made the same mistake and spoke with the police voluntarily to avoid suspicion, only to cast a wider shadow of doubt. *What a fool I've been.* The detectives knew all along that the bat had been the murder weapon. It was obvious they'd lured JB here to question him about it earlier, knowing too well it had been missing once the Beltrams informed them that Emilio had come looking for it the day after the murder.

JB recalled his conversation earlier with Mike, the phone records, and cash withdrawals. The memory of his massacred garden still blazed in his memory. "Detectives, have you accounted for the whereabouts of everyone who remained at the party from the time I left Gianni Cuomo in the pool alive until Mike discovered him floating in it dead?"

"Mostly everyone," D'Amico said.

"Mostly, but not everyone." JB stood up then. Sullivan rose with him. "I'd like to leave now. Unless you plan on arresting me."

* * *

Stepping into the hall, JB experienced a vertiginous sensation like exiting a steam room. Drained and exhausted, he couldn't wait to get outside. The air felt warm on his cheeks as he pushed open the door. There was so much for him to consider, but right now, more than anything, he wanted to be home.

In the parking lot, a couple dressed in black walked toward him. JB recognized the tall gentleman as the man who was having drinks with Gus Beltram two weeks earlier. The salt-and-pepper hair. The goatee trimmed to perfection. Eyes as dark as gravel.

Where else have I seen those eyes before?

Accompanying him was a plump, diminutive woman wearing a black dress with lace sleeves and oversized black shades. Her hair was pulled back, her face down. She clutched at the man's arm as he escorted her into the police station. JB couldn't wrench his gaze away from the man, who nodded in recognition as they passed. He watched them enter the building. As he turned away, the stranger stole one last glance.

What connection did this man have to Gus Beltram? And who was this woman he was escorting into the police station? Then, the realization hit JB with stunning force—this had to be Daria Cuomo, Gianni's widow, accompanied by someone who clearly knew her well.

Although JB suspected it had to be Gianni's wife, he reminded himself again of the situation at hand. Right now, he was a person of interest, and the bat his son had been carrying the night of the Beltrams' party was likely the murder weapon. What he knew was that Rakesh and Andy had left the party early. Angelo and Jason had been in the kitchen with Gus and Winnie from the time they'd left him alone with Gianni until the exact moment

Mike had discovered him floating face down in the pool. He recalled Angelo saying he'd seen Mike napping in the basement with Emilio on his way to use the bathroom, but that Mike wasn't there when he came out.

The pieces clicked together with terrifying precision, like tumblers in a lock he never wanted to open. The question now was, where had Mike gone during those crucial minutes?

Chapter Nineteen

The house was dimly lit as JB entered. Two candles flickered on the dining room table—an unexpected touch that immediately set his nerves on edge. The only other light source came from the kitchen, where he heard someone moving about with deliberate care. "Hello?" he called, his hand still on the doorknob, ready for a quick retreat. After his interrogation at the police station and the realization that had dawned on him in the parking lot, every domestic sound now carried sinister potential.

"You're home." Mike appeared in the kitchen doorway, wearing the canvas apron JB had bought him when he'd begun cooking classes several years back. Classes Mike abandoned once he'd realized cooking took precision, attention—and above all, hard work.

Mike was clean-shaven, his blond hair combed neatly to the side—a stark transformation from the disheveled, vodka-soaked figure of the past few days. He wore a baby-blue polo that accentuated his eyes. It was the Mike of before—before cancer, before Gianni, before suspicion had invaded their home like an infestation.

Mike kissed JB's cheek. "Care for a cocktail?" He smelled of tomato leaf and basil.

"Who are you, and what have you done with Mike?"

"Shut up." Mike swatted playfully at JB and turned to fix him a Scotch.

The table had been set with the Tiffany dinnerware they used only on holidays, the Laguiole en Aubrac flatware JB's mother had left him after she died, and the Baccarat crystal. A table that would have made Winnie Beltram proud. "Where's Emilio?"

"He's sleeping over at Alan's house tonight."

"Evan," JB corrected. "Don't you know our son's friend's name?"

Mike forced a smile and set the glass of Scotch in front of JB. "Let's not fight tonight."

JB sipped, allowing Mike to believe he was accepting the olive branch he'd extended.

But JB had his own agenda.

"Are those garlic knots?" JB asked as Mike set a basket of chewy, buttery baked dough topped with minced garlic in front of him.

"Your favorite." Mike held up his wine glass. "Cheers."

"What are we celebrating? A cease-fire?"

"I got a job today," Mike announced. "I'm going to sell real estate again at Lawson's."

"With Andy?"

"Don't roll your eyes. Andy has done well out here. Sure, he had some setbacks last year."

"According to Rakesh, Andy has become a world-class drunk."

Mike squeezed his eyes in disbelief. "Andy just lost his mother."

"You hated selling real estate."

"Girl's gotta make money somehow now that you've cut me off."

JB didn't take the bait. The Scotch was kicking in. JB considered the last time Mike had worked. He'd had so many jobs: personal trainer, real estate broker, artist. For a brief time, he was a stay-at-home dad, but that didn't last long. Ultimately, JB had to hire a nanny. To anyone viewing in from the outside, Mike was spoiled. He was using JB, but that was not how JB saw it. In his eyes, they were married, and like his parents' marriage, his mother didn't work. Why should JB expect Mike to?

"I wish you all the best." JB clinked Mike's glass. Underneath, he was thinking that it would be only a matter of days before Mike found an excuse not to work: a headache, lost keys, emergency laser hair removal. Anything to avoid wasting hours at an open house waiting for prospective buyers. Mike lacked the bite of a salesman. He had no grit. Only the talent to bitch. "You didn't ask me how my interview went with the police?"

Mike served chicken piccata he had ordered from a local Italian restaurant. "Oh, yes, I forgot. How'd it go?"

"Interesting." JB cut into the chicken breast. "By the way, do you know where Emilio's bat is?"

Mike's fingers tighten around the stem of his wine glass. "I haven't seen it, why?"

"The police believe it might be the murder weapon," he said with deliberate blandness. Mike gulped his wine, nearly spilling some on his polo. "Are you sure you haven't seen it?"

Mike gave a short laugh. "Yes, I'm sure."

"I don't believe you."

"You can't help yourself." Mike picked up his plate and stood up.

"Where are you going? We haven't finished eating this lovely meal you bought."

Mike walked into the kitchen and dropped his dish and utensils into the sink. JB followed him, holding the Scotch steady, not spilling an ounce. "If you chipped that dish, I'm taking it out of your first commission."

"I see what you're trying to do, but it won't work."

"Where is the bat, Mike?" JB's voice dropped to a menacing whisper as he moved closer, invading Mike's space, eliminating any retreat. Their faces were inches apart, close enough for JB to see the tiny capillaries in Mike's eyes, to smell the wine on his breath, to notice the slight tremor in his lower lip. "Answer me," he demanded after several seconds of suffocating silence. "You owe me that much after everything I've given you."

"Given me?" Mike's voice cracked.

JB winced at his own words, the petty barb unlike him—a deviation from the man he'd prided himself on being. Yet this time, the lapse felt justified, almost necessary. He hadn't wanted to succumb to anger, but Mike had been methodically unraveling their family's fabric, thread by deliberate thread, pulling at loose ends until the entire tapestry of their life had unspooled.

Mike stared into the sink, his shoulders rigid with tension. JB sensed a subtle defeat emanating from him. This evening, with its stilted conversation and unspoken accusation, hadn't unfolded according to whatever script Mike had written in his head.

"What are you doing? What were you hoping to achieve this evening with a romantic Italian dinner for two and this happy homemaker persona you cooked up?"

"You're so cruel. Even when I try to be nice, you don't appreciate it. You acted this way the entire time you were sick, pushing me away when all I wanted was to be near you."

JB was stunned. He felt ashamed and furtive—as if realizing Mike had endured the same brutal months of chemo and radiation, the two of them suffering in parallel yet somehow alone. It had changed them both, in different ways. They had become what JB had feared: another version of his parents. Twisted and hardened, their affection growing cold like the garlic knots on the dining room table.

But then JB remembered how quickly Mike had diverged from him, finding comfort in the arms of that couple. "What about Jamie and Tom?"

"They were a distraction since you had completely shut me out. You even moved out of our bedroom."

"I only moved out so you…"

"I never asked you to."

JB's heart lurched. "But I thought…"

"I know what you thought," Mike shouted. "And I slept in our bedroom alone. Night after night I told myself, 'He's going through the biggest challenge of his life.' I reminded myself that the Pulaskis don't talk about their feelings. 'Just let him work through this alone,' I'd think, 'if that's what he wants.' But you never once asked me what I wanted. What I needed. You came first. You always do!"

Mike tore off the apron and charged into his bedroom.

JB stood in the center of the living room, staring at the apron discarded like a jilted lover on the floor. He thought about knocking on Mike's bedroom door to apologize, but a spark of memory flared up in JB's mind. The man he'd met in that bar on Christmas—the one who had seemed like a giant storefront window displaying the picture-perfect life he'd dreamed of—had shattered. What remained was a stranger among the shards, someone who'd lost himself to that couple last summer.

And yet, JB felt the same way now as he did back then. To leave Mike would have been like amputating his arm. He still wasn't prepared to self-mutilate.

Not yet.

Not until he knew the truth about Mike's involvement in Gianni's death. Not for himself, not for Mike, not even for the seventeen years they'd shared. For Emilio. Their son deserved to know whether his father was a victim or a murderer. And JB wouldn't rest until he uncovered the answer, no matter how much blood spilled from the wound of discovery.

Chapter Twenty

The next morning, JB texted Angelo and asked if he could stop by his office.

After spiraling into an abyss the night before—convinced he was married to a murderer—JB woke determined to regain control of his life, particularly regarding Emilio. He took an early hot yoga class, got his hair cut, ordered a chai tea at Provisions, and dressed for his appointment in a crisp, short-sleeved canary yellow shirt and beige khakis. Despite this carefully assembled normalcy, he couldn't ignore the sour, vinegary warning churning inside him.

Angelo's office was small, clean, and musty—the lingering scent of an old water leak hung in the air. "How are you holding up?"

JB let out a bitter laugh. "As best as anyone who is being investigated for murder. Plus, Mike and I are at each other's necks. I don't know how much longer we can live together. It's too much for Emilio."

Angelo wheeled his stool closer to JB. "You're not a murderer. No one believes you are."

"Tell that to the police."

Angelo leaned back to assess him. "Well, you look good."

"On the outside, maybe, but I have evil inside me. I just squash that part of me so no one can see it."

"Whatever it is you're doing, keep it up. Now, what can I do for you?"

JB hesitated. "It's probably nothing, but recently, I've been having what can only be described as spontaneous erections."

Angelo gaped. "You know how many men in your situation wish they had that very problem?"

JB glanced away anxiously as if someone were listening. He went on to explain the details surrounding the few instances where he'd felt simultaneously aroused and on the verge of incontinence. "Could this in any way be related to a recurrence of my cancer?"

"I doubt it. Between the chemo and radiation, your body went into shock. It's normal not to get erections afterward. In fact," Angelo lowered his voice, "most men never recover their ability to gain or maintain an erection. For you to experience spontaneous erections associated with some heightened form of emotion..." He paused, studying JB's face. "It's not just a good sign. It's remarkable."

"You know me. I don't fret about my health, but I worry about Emilio. Now more than ever." He turned to look away, choking back the unexpected swell of emotion. "I keep thinking, what would happen if I wasn't around?"

"You're not going anywhere." Angelo squeezed JB's knee, giving it a quick shake. "I'm not happy to hear things between you and Mike aren't going well. Why don't I draw some blood? The results will put your mind at ease. One less thing for you to worry about."

As Angelo typed his notes, JB sat, thinking this was a relief. "How are you enjoying working out east?"

"It's fine." JB noted a shift in his demeanor.

"What's going on?"

"It's Jason—" Angelo paused, unable to continue. "This whole Detective Sullivan thing has me rattled."

JB shot him a look of wild disbelief. "Why?"

"I can't talk about it right now." Angelo fell into an indignant silence—yet JB had a sudden recollection of Jason and Sullivan staring into each other's eyes the night of Gianni's death.

"I understand." JB hugged him. "You have patients to think about. Why don't we get together after work? Does Rakesh know?"

Angelo shrugged, sullen. "Knowing Rakesh, he probably knew before me."

"Let's talk later. In the meantime, don't let this eat at you. Jason loves you."

* * *

JB pulled into the driveway only to discover Mike's car was parked in front of the garage. *So much for going back to work.* Inside, he heard Mike, laughing that obsequious, shrill laugh he reserved for flirting at parties.

"JB," Mike said with surprise. "I wasn't expecting you. Come and meet Gianluca."

"Call me Luca." His smiling face brightened as he shook JB's hand. "So, we finally meet."

"Yes, finally."

Luca's voice was deep with an indeterminate accent. It dripped with a good upbringing, summers spent in Capri, winters skiing in the Dolomites, boarding school with British teachers. He smelled like mint and varnished wood. He had sculpted features and those shiny black eyes. It felt like meeting a celebrity JB had only seen in films.

"Finally?" Mike repeated. "Do you two know each other?"

"No," JB said quickly as Luca replied, "Yes."

Mike looked at JB. Then at Luca. Then at JB again. "Well, which is it?"

"Two ships passing in the night," Luca replied casually.

"Two ships?" Mike repeated with mounting frustration. "Am I missing something here?"

"We've seen each other in town a few times," JB explained. "You were at the Beltrams' costume party."

Luca nodded.

"You were?" This revelation threw Mike off. "You know Gus and Winnie Beltram?"

"Zorro," JB continued.

"So much for my disguise," Luca chuckled, and then he waved his arm as though he were brandishing a sword.

"Your eyes give you away," JB went on. "I recognize people by their eyes."

Mike cleared his throat. JB could tell he was unhappy not being the center of attention. "Luca is in town scouting homes for his wealthy boss," Mike offered to remind them he was still in the room. "Andy said I knew the

Hamptons better than anyone, so I'm showing Luca around."

The Italian and JB stood in the silence of no one having asked Mike for those details. And yet, it seemed odd to JB that Andy had passed a lucrative opportunity to someone as undeserving as Mike. "Where have you taken Luca so far?"

"A few places in Amagansett. We're off to East Hampton next." Mike rambled on about the neighborhood. As usual, he was pretending to know more than he did. "We're also looking for a place for Luca to rent since he's staying at The American Hotel and hates it."

"Oh, is that where you two met?"

"No," Mike said facetiously. "Finish your drink, Luca. We should head out soon."

Luca took one last sip. "Would you care to join us?"

Mike spun around. "What?"

"Thank you, but I'm having drinks with friends."

Luca indicated with a pout that he was disappointed. "I hope to see you again soon, now that we've met officially."

"Good luck house hunting." When JB shook his enormous hand, furred on the back with dark hairs, it sent a trill of electricity through his body. "You'll love it out here once you get settled into a proper place, not a hotel."

"I'll have you over for dinner." Luca glanced at Mike. "Both of you, of course."

Mike tried to pretend he was interested, tried hard, but as usual, JB noticed, he had become annoyed. "Come on." Mike reached for Luca's arm to pull him outside. "It's getting overcast."

When JB looked up, there wasn't a cloud in the sky.

JB watched Mike's car disappear down the gravel drive, Luca's profile visible in the passenger seat.

All the connections he'd been puzzling over suddenly felt more urgent. Luca knew the Beltrams well enough to attend their exclusive costume party. He knew Gianni well enough to escort his grieving widow to the police station. Yet he'd presented himself to Mike as nothing more than a potential real estate client—a plausible coincidence that had somehow inserted him directly into their family's chaos.

Most troubling of all was the timing. Luca had materialized in their lives as the murder investigation intensified. If Luca was connected to both Gianni and the Beltrams, what did that mean for Mike, who now sat beside him, oblivious to whatever game was being played?

Chapter Twenty-One

They were in Rakesh's den, sipping martinis on an oversized chartreuse sectional. A square wood coffee table etched with Moroccan-style carvings was situated on top of a red-and-black Turkish rug. *Too many bright satin throw pillows*, but that was classic Rakesh—too much was never enough. Knick-knacks, tchotchkes, and figurines he collected from every corner of the world were proudly on display in his home or else carefully packed in his garage. For what purpose, JB had no idea.

"Well, then, what's the problem?" Rakesh asked Angelo. "You two love each other, you still enjoy having sex with one another, and you're young. So, Jason's ex-boyfriend happens to be super-hot."

Angelo gave a withering look and glanced at his watch. "I'm leaving."

"Sit down." Rakesh took a sip of his martini.

JB tugged at Angelo's hand. "What's really troubling you?"

"I'm so confused. You met Detective Sullivan. He's Clark Kent."

"But they broke up," JB reasoned. "Jason wants you, not Clark Kent."

Angelo shook his head. "What confuses me is that sex with Jason has been great, or so I thought. We're versatile, but for the most part, Jason is a top. After meeting Sullivan, I couldn't help but think maybe he's not, and I've made him take on that role, and then I thought, maybe I'm not enough."

Rakesh offered a dramatic sigh of frustration, to which JB quickly silenced him by holding up his hand. "Haven't you experimented with different types of men?" JB asked. "Do you think every man I dated resembled Mike?"

"God knows I tried all types," Rakesh interjected. "Please, I chased JB for years. Now I'm with Andy. The two couldn't be more different. So, years ago, Jason was into Superman. That doesn't mean he wants that now. Besides, why do you assume Clark Kent is a top? I've known plenty of big, muscular guys who throw their legs in the air higher than the Rockettes."

"I don't know why this ex-boyfriend has me doubting myself," Angelo conceded. "They say we rarely see the ones we love for who they truly are. Maybe I'm not seeing Jason for who he truly is?"

"Oh, please," Rakesh groused. "Pity party. Table for one. If you ask me, you're being awfully whiny."

JB glowered at Rakesh. "Angelo, listen to me. Relationships ebb and flow. It's not always like it is in the beginning. You have doubts now, but it's not like Jason has given you any reason to mistrust him. Has he?"

"No, he hasn't."

"Maybe you're the one who finds Clark Kent sexy?" Rakesh ventured. "Have you been fantasizing about what it would be like to be Lois Lane?"

"Me? That's some IMAX-level projection."

Rakesh rose to his feet with a slight wobble. His tan caftan created a striking silhouette, enhancing his sudden metamorphosis from opinionated friend to impassioned spiritual leader preparing to unveil some profound—if not slurred—truth. "If you ask me," he declared, jabbing a finger skyward, "gay men have surrendered to heteronormative constructs for far too long." He began pacing, the caftan swirling dramatically around his ankles. "Gay marriage. Gaybies. Gay divorce." Each concept punctuated with increasing volume. "And perhaps most troubling of all…" he paused for dramatic effect, "monogamy."

"How many martinis have you had?" JB stood up to take Rakesh's cocktail since he was spilling most of it on the rug. It was then he noticed the bruises on Rakesh's forearms. "Where did you get those?"

"Wrestling shoplifters," Rakesh replied. "JB, think about it?" he continued. "You and Mike have an agreement. An insane one, but an agreement nonetheless."

"Don't drag me into this. I'm no role model."

"Angelo," Rakesh went on. "I love you, so I'm going to spare you the trouble of learning this on your own. Do yourself a favor and have a three-way. Let Superman and Jason spit-roast you."

"Spit roast?" Angelo repeated. "What am I, a pig?"

"Yes," Rakesh exclaimed. "Let them spit-roast you. Do it now while you're still spit-roast worthy. Live your life, and if it doesn't work out…well, guess what? There's always another younger, cuter man who wants to be a doctor's wife. But if you choose not to take my advice, then please, stop *whining* and start *fighting* for your man."

It shouldn't have surprised JB how brutally honest Rakesh was being with Angelo. He had a habit of speaking his mind. Certainly, he had no conscious ability to edit his words. What surprised JB most was that he agreed with almost everything Rakesh had said. It got him thinking about his relationship with Mike.

For years, he was the top. It hadn't occurred to him that Mike might have wanted more versatility in the bedroom. He wondered if Mike was exploring the boundaries of his sexuality through these affairs now that JB was unable to perform, instead of viewing them as conquests to boost his greedy vanity. It was as if Mike were a man who'd happily given his youth to an older husband and now, at midlife himself, was desperate to reclaim the youth he'd squandered.

As for all the good things JB provided, as for the security, comfort, and love—Mike had smashed them to bits in a span of twelve months. Perhaps he didn't know what he was doing; perhaps it was a kind of neurosis that came with growing old gay. Perhaps he was telegraphing to the world that he was burning down a house he no longer wanted to live in with JB.

Seventeen years and the joy of love had faded once the cancer came, and the cheating had begun—not simply Mike's flirtatious dancing at parties but humiliating public affairs. A cruel taunt that Mike was getting what JB could no longer provide him.

I survived cancer. I survived the most aggressive assault my body has ever faced. I can live without Mike.

They should have separated sooner. Each betrayal clicked in his mind like slides from a grim presentation: Jamie and Tom, inviting his husband into their bed while JB battled cancer. Dan Vega, whom Mike had paraded around town like a purebred. And now, Gianni Cuomo, whose death had somehow transformed Mike from cheater to grieving lover. The slideshow of humiliations ended, leaving JB with a single, undeniable truth: he had been in remission from cancer for months, but still suffered from a malignancy named Mike.

It was time to amputate—not slowly, not with hesitation, but with the brute efficiency of a battlefield medic excising an exsanguinating limb. This realization flooded his system with something that felt like adrenaline mixed with relief.

There is more to life than this. I deserve better.

Listening to Rakesh preach and provoke Angelo, looking like a bruised Buddhist monk, wearing a designer caftan, JB decided he would ask Mike for a separation. He'd made up his mind. The story Mike had told the other night hadn't rung true to him then. The one where he portrayed himself as the pitiful husband pleading to play a part in his cold husband's one-man play as he fought cancer on his own. The truth was that Mike had become a cheat and a liar. Now he saw through that veil of deceit without any doubt. Mike had conjured up his sad backstory only to get in JB's good graces once he'd cut him off financially. And he might have succeeded, had Rakesh not shown him the light.

"Yes!" JB shouted, not realizing he'd spoken aloud until both men turned to stare at him.

"So, you agree?" Rakesh arched an eyebrow.

"Yes, I agree." JB nodded eagerly, a surge of energy coursing through him that he hadn't felt since before his diagnosis. "Not with everything, but certainly with the part about fighting—for what you want, for what you deserve." He looked at Angelo. "That's Jason, if he's what you truly want."

Rakesh leaned forward and clinked JB's glass, eyes narrowing with amused curiosity. "Seems like my speech has awakened the beast. Nice to have you back, old pal."

"Yes." JB raised his glass in a toast that felt like a declaration of war. "It's good to be back."

JB took a deep breath, feeling his entire body align with his decision. The path ahead would be difficult—separation, likely divorce, the impact on Emilio—but for the first time in months, he felt himself emerging from a long hibernation, blinking in the dazzling light of clarity.

Chapter Twenty-Two

JB woke up the next morning and ambled through the house. He noticed Mike's car wasn't parked outside. There was a note taped to the refrigerator, informing him that Mike was going to be out all day and that Emilio was spending the afternoon with Evan, which he'd underlined twice to show JB he remembered the name of their son's best friend.

JB smiled, declaring this a day of self-indulgence. He fixed a pot of coffee, poured a mug, and grabbed a yogurt from the refrigerator. He threw on his old Columbia University T-shirt that Mike hated and a pair of cargo shorts with a frayed hem. He drove into town, knowing he would raise eyebrows at how he'd decided to present himself in public. JB bought supplies to replant his vegetable garden again, this time with vegetables, not flowers, reclaiming the plot of land that Mike had spitefully destroyed.

Hours later, with the August sun beating overhead, JB knelt in the earth that had once nurtured his beloved vegetables. The dirt felt warm and alive between his fingers as he dug holes for tomatoes, cucumbers, and carrots. He didn't care if they grew or how late it was in the season. His only care was the statement this made—a declaration of independence written in seedlings and soil.

Well past noon, JB entered the house, lacquered in sweat that glistened on his skin like a fresh coat of varnish. He poured a glass of ice water and drank it with desperate thirst when the sound of tires crunching over the gravel driveway pulled him from his moment of relief. JB moved to the window and discovered Luca parking a cherry-red Fiat convertible.

JB stepped onto the front porch, shielding his eyes from the midday glare. Luca exuded an effortless style that belonged to another era entirely: hair slicked back, dark Ray-Bans, and a crisp linen shirt over white slacks.

"Mike isn't home," JB explained.

"Did I catch you at a bad time?"

It was then JB became acutely aware of his appearance—the same tattered, sweat-stained clothes now soiled with earth, knees dark with dirt. "I was in the middle of gardening."

"How lovely." Luca's eyes lit with genuine interest as he proceeded toward the backyard. "Now I know why you didn't answer the phone."

JB followed, brow furrowing. "You called the house phone? Why didn't you call Mike's cell?"

Luca glanced over his shoulder and deliberately lowered his sunglasses to peer over the rims. "Because I was trying to reach you."

"Me?" Confusion bloomed, followed by a whisper of flattery, before his expression hardened into an accusing scowl. "What are you doing here? I mean, really?"

Luca squatted beside a flower bed, his trousers stretching across formidable thighs that bulged like ripe fruit. He held a dahlia between his fingers and brought it to his nose. "Only a garden can show you the beauty that is life."

Something didn't sit right with JB. Luca waxing poetically about flowers and flirting seemed more than a tad off. Was Luca going to pretend JB hadn't seen him having a drink with Gus Beltram or escorting that woman into the police station? But if that was the way he wanted to play it, JB was ready to roll the dice.

"I'm replanting vegetables." JB squatted next to Luca, their knees barely touching.

"Deer?"

"No, something crueler than ravenous deer."

In the quiet of that charged moment, unresolved secrets existed between them like invisible threads, and pretense was on full display. Luca held JB's gaze with the intensity of someone who stares recklessly at you while driving. JB found himself cataloging the details: silver strands threading through Luca's black hair, the prominent, rosy-tinted bridge of his nose, and the unbuttoned linen shirt revealing his tanned skin flecked with dark hairs leading to the shadowed cleft of his chest.

Maybe it was the relentless August sun bearing down; maybe it was his middle-aged madness, his fear that life was shorter than he'd imagined, having been dealt the blow of cancer. Inching closer, JB breathed Luca's scent—salt water and espresso. JB felt tired and frustrated with a sort of gnawing discomfort that he could not name, out of kilter because he could not identify the sensation of having it.

Next, JB did something that surprised even himself. He leaned forward and pressed his lips to Luca's, acting on an impulse that seemed to originate from somewhere deeper than rational thought. The kiss was full but gentle, exploratory—a question mark suspended between them. This, then, was the sensation JB could not identify—this hunger that had been dormant for so long, now awakening with alarming intensity. Luca responded with practiced expertise, putting one hand behind JB's neck and the other cradling his cheek, holding him with unexpected tenderness as he kissed him deeply. It was the kind of fantastic affection JB needed. The kind he craved.

JB, hearing gravel spitting up in the driveway, pulled away. Their faces parted, but lingered close, as if trapped in a magnetic field. Luca grinned salaciously. Once JB heard the car door slam, he shot to his feet. Mike was walking up the front porch when he stopped suddenly to drop his sunglasses down the bridge of his nose. It took Mike a couple of seconds to fully comprehend what he was seeing.

"Luca?" Mike moved toward them. "Did we have an appointment?"

"No," he replied casually. "I was in the neighborhood and thought I'd drop by to see if you had any homes to show me."

Mike maintained his suspicious expression, though JB could see him struggling to suppress it. "Why didn't you call my cell?"

JB closed his eyes, still tasting Luca's lips.

"I'm afraid I came here under false pretenses," Luca admitted, glancing at JB and then at Mike.

"What's going on?" Mike chuckled, the sound forced.

JB froze at that moment, not knowing which he was enjoying more, watching Mike in the throes of jealousy or the expectation of what Luca might say next.

"I was hoping you were free for lunch," Luca said.

Mike stepped closer, heading unnervingly with a confrontational glare. "Lunch?"

"I know this is forward of me, but I decided this morning to invite myself over to your house for lunch, but only if you allow me to cook."

Mike shot a look at JB, who shrugged, seemingly just as surprised. "Well, I don't know. JB, do we have anything for Luca to make?"

"Do you have anything?" Luca waved an arm across the garden. "Look at *che bella cucuzza.*"

"Squash." Mike grinned. "Can't wait to see what you cook up with them. Let's go inside. I'll fix us a drink."

Mike whipped around and headed into the house. Luca followed, caressing JB's cheek like the petal of a dahlia as he passed him.

* * *

JB took a quick shower and changed into light blue linen shorts and a button-down pink shirt. He combed his hair as he assessed himself in the mirror. Still surprised by his aggressiveness toward Luca, he wondered how long it would take for Mike to sense the sexual tension between them.

What have I gotten myself into?

He rolled up his sleeves as he stood in the kitchen doorway. Luca had donned one of JB's black chef's aprons, the one with the leather straps. He imagined what Luca would look like wearing nothing else. Mike hovered, sipping a martini as Luca thinly sliced cucuzza with a mandolin and fried them in olive oil.

"Smells delicious," JB said, announcing his presence. "I'll set the table."

"No, please, come here," Luca beckoned. "Mike tells me you're the cook in the family. I want to show you how many ways you can prepare cucuzza."

"Mike, would you mind?"

"Setting the table? Yes, I would mind."

"I could use another drink, Mike," Luca said as he removed crisp slices of cucuzza from the frying pan and set them on a paper towel. "Fix us all a drink." Mike huffed and made a dramatic exit.

A stray not fawning over Mike—had JB stepped into an alternate universe? Luca had set himself squarely in the middle of his marriage, but JB knew Mike never backed down from a challenge.

"You're playing a dangerous game," JB muttered.

"I'm not playing a game." Luca focused on the cucuzza. "I'm making lunch."

JB chuckled at the absurdity of it all. He knew Mike didn't find any of this funny, and yet, he found it hilarious. The odd series of events that had occurred that afternoon left JB feeling bewildered and incandescent. "What exactly do you think you're doing?"

Luca turned around. His dark eyes gleamed with that familiar mischief. "I told you. I'm making lunch."

JB leaned against the counter, both dreading and anticipating the meal ahead. The emotional terrain had shifted beneath his feet, and he felt off-balance, caught between guilt and exhilaration. Luca had thrown him, he couldn't deny it, and he felt strangely aware that he'd brought it on himself with that kiss.

Yet there was something unnervingly exciting about this dangerous game unfolding in his own kitchen. Luca represented everything Mike's previous conquests had not—mature, confident, substantial—not one of Mike's runts yapping for attention, but a man of equal footing to JB himself. *Where is this going?* And more troublingly: why did part of him want to find out, despite all the warning signs?

"I come bearing gifts." Mike's voice preceded him into the doorway, where he appeared, balancing two perfectly chilled martinis, each garnished with a twist of lemon rind.

"*Finalmente!*" Luca exclaimed, quickly wiping his hands on his apron before taking them. He leaned forward, pressing a lingering kiss to each of

Mike's cheeks. *"Mille grazie."*

Mike grinned at JB as if he'd scored a critical point in a game only the two of them understood.

* * *

Luca insisted JB sit at the head of the dining room table. "It is your house, no?"

JB beamed. Out of the corner of his eye, he caught Mike rolling his.

Luca prepared a casserole made with squash, heavy cream, Parmesan, mozzarella, and fried pancetta. He also made a dipping sauce from yogurt, sour cream, and chopped chives for the fried cucuzza chips.

"You're a genius," JB remarked after tasting both. Mike poured another round of martinis, but Luca asked for a glass of wine instead.

"I love to cook," Luca said. "Especially for friends."

"Speaking of cooking and friends," Mike started in. "How do you know Gus and Winnie Beltram?"

Luca finished chewing. "I told you already. My client met them abroad. They discussed financing a restaurant, but it didn't work out. They remained friends, and my client suggested I look them up once I arrived in the Hamptons."

"Winnie and Gus have always been so gracious to us. Isn't that right, JB?"

JB debated whether to engage in this trivial conversation when it was clear Mike had poked this stick at the same disinterested bear before.

"Well, if you won't tell us who your client is," Mike continued. "I'm sure I can get it out of Winnie after a few drinks."

Luca dabbed a napkin to his lips. "You might embarrass her by bringing it up."

"Embarrass?" Mike gaped. "Now, I have to know the story."

Luca lifted his wineglass and sat back. "The reason why the restaurant never came to be is because Winnie Beltram is not...a chef."

Mike jerked his head. "What do you mean, she's not a chef?"

Luca took a sip. "She's a self-taught cook. Not that there is anything wrong with that, but my client wasn't about to finance a chain of restaurants with a menu created by a housewife."

"I'll have you know that Winnie Beltram ran a very successful specialty food shop and catering business," Mike said.

"True, but unfortunately, that is the end of the story for someone like her. My client is risk-adverse. He likes a sure thing, and I agree. That's why I asked Andy to have you show me houses instead of him."

"You hear that, JB?" A rosy flush spread across Mike's features. "Luca requested me himself."

"I am sitting right here. Now, can we stop interrogating our guest?" Luca offered JB a thankful expression.

A cell phone rang, loud and sharp. Mike flinched. "Damn it! Where did I leave my phone?" He darted for the kitchen.

Luca set down his glass and put his hand on JB's. "I enjoyed our kiss earlier."

JB blinked, pulling his hand away. Now, in the quiet, awkward space between him and the Italian, JB felt obliged to explain. "About that."

"Damn it!" Mike stomped back in. "I forgot I have a showing in Wainscott."

"Wainscott?" JB repeated. "Are you all right to drive?"

Mike waved a dismissive hand. "Sorry to rush off." He kissed Luca on both cheeks. "Lunch was fabulous. I'll call you later. Maybe we can have a drink together at the hotel?"

Mike's invitation lingered like cigarette smoke wafting in the still air before Luca finally responded, "I have an appointment later. Why don't you call when you have something to show me?"

All business. Mike must be fuming.

"Sure." Mike's smile was toothy and forced. "That's what I meant by having drinks. It was so we could discuss a plan to see houses." Mike's phone buzzed again. He glanced at it. "Shit. It's Andy. He must be pissed." Mike turned and headed out the door without saying another word. "My keys," he shouted from the front porch. "Where are my keys?" Mike returned, eyes flitting about the room like a mother looking for her lost child. "JB, help me!"

"Where did you see them last?"

Mike glared with annoyance. "If I knew that, they wouldn't be lost."

"Your poor planning is not my emergency." JB went quiet, seemingly embarrassed by his outburst.

"Could they be in your car?" Luca offered.

Mike's face lit up with the kind of expression associated with running into an old friend at a party. He bolted back outside. Within seconds, the engine roared, and Mike barreled out of the driveway.

Luca turned to JB. "Shall we have another drink?"

"That's a great idea." JB reached for the bottle. He poured a glass of wine for Luca. "You know what? I think I'll have another martini."

"Good." Luca followed JB into the kitchen. "I thought you might be afraid I was trying to get you drunk."

JB poured two shots of vodka into the shaker and added ice. "Are you?"

"I cannot lie. I am." Luca stood in the doorway, arms braced against the frame above his head. His biceps flexed so that JB did a double-take. Again, Luca had unnerved him. Indeed, his attention had been devoted exclusively to JB since the moment Mike had introduced them, but why?

JB firmed his jaw and offered a taut smile. "Listen, this has been awfully flattering, but I'm not Mike. You want something from me, and it's not sex. God knows you could have your pick of the many attractive, younger, unattached men here in Sag Harbor. All you have to do is go back to your hotel and have a drink at the bar."

JB watched Luca's eyes ski down the front of his shirt, stopping somewhere around his waist. "Is that what you want me to do?"

"What I want you to do is tell me what you're doing here. I saw you the other day with that woman. I assume she's not your rich client?"

The silence that followed was brief but dense—like the hush before a thunderclap. Luca's smile faltered, then disappeared entirely. He stepped closer. The seductive playfulness drained from his features, replaced by something colder.

"Her name is Daria. Daria Nicoletta Cuomo."

"Cuomo?" The name landed like a stone dropping into still water, sending ripples of confirmation through JB's body. "She's Gianni's widow."

Luca's lips curled into a smirk—not playful now, but knowing and dangerous—that made JB certain he was on the right track. "What if I told you she is?"

"I'd say we're finally having a real conversation."

Without warning, Luca turned his big, handsome face to JB and kissed him with calculated intensity that felt like both a distraction and a claim. JB remained motionless, neither responding nor pulling away, his mind racing to decode this new tactic. The kiss lasted only moments, but time stretched and warped around them.

When they separated, Luca's gaze was searing—hypnotist's eyes— attempting to penetrate something deep within JB. Luca took JB's hand and placed it on his chest. A steady, strong heartbeat pulsed beneath JB's palm.

"The link of fate connects us," Luca murmured. "Ever since the first time I saw you, I can't stop thinking about you. Are you happy I came today?" His thumb traced a line along JB's clavicle before he nudged it against the notch above his sternum.

Instinct told JB not to answer. This wasn't real. Real people didn't say such things unless they had ulterior motives. He pulled his hand away, feeling the ghost of Luca's heartbeat still tingling against his palm.

"I think I'm coming down with a terrible headache." JB took a step back.

Luca observed him with unnerving focus. His eyes methodically memorized JB's face as if studying an owner's manual. He seemed determined to quickly decipher the instructions that would allow him to operate the complex machinery of JB's thoughts and desires.

"Will I see you again?" Luca's voice grew softer now, almost vulnerable, though JB couldn't tell if it was genuine or another performance.

JB leaned against the kitchen counter, arms folded across his chest. "Does Mike know about Daria?"

"No." Luca offered a grin that didn't reach his eyes. "I want you to know my feelings toward you have nothing to do with Daria. I hope you believe me?"

JB studied him, noting the barely perceptible tension in Luca's shoulders, the way his fingers twitched slightly at his sides. It was like catching a poker player's tell. Luca was playing it carefully, and now so would he.

"I believe there is the truth," JB said slowly, "and then, there is another truth hiding behind it. My concern here is that I have lots of questions. Unfortunately, I don't think you'll be honest with me."

Luca appeared troubled with the direction the conversation had taken. "Please, go ahead. Ask me anything."

JB shook his head. "Some other time."

"Would you like me to go?"

"I think that's a good idea."

JB stood motionless in the kitchen doorway, arms still crossed over his chest, watching Luca's retreating figure. He remained there, silent and still, staring after him until Luca got in his

car and drove away. Only when the sound of the engine had faded completely did JB release the breath he hadn't realized he was holding.

Afterward, JB sat in his study trying to piece together a narrative that would explain Luca's connection to Gianni's widow and his sudden, unexpected appearance in his life. Not to mention his ties with the Beltrams. But even before Gianni's murder, Luca's presence at The American Hotel lounge, exchanging alluring glances, had made JB forget, briefly, the knot of resentment his marital ties had formed in his gut.

But there was something about Luca that nagged at JB. His absolute confidence, his shameless flirtation, provided a tincture of pure excitement JB couldn't deny, but the undertow of mystery swirling beneath the surface was as intriguing as it was unsettling.

As JB sat in the gathering shadows of his study, the possible answers arranged themselves like chess pieces on a board. Surely, Gianni had told Luca all about JB's crumbling marriage. After Gianni's death, Gus Beltram could have told Luca that JB was the prime suspect. Why else would he have requested Mike if not to uncover Gianni's murderer? That seemed the likeliest reason. Had the unexpected encounter in the police station parking lot prompted the need for a more aggressive approach? All these seemingly harmless flirtations now took on a calculated cast—not the spontaneous chemistry between two men, but a plot to get closer to him and Mike.

To expose the truth by exploiting the very cracks already fracturing their marriage. Was today Luca's first strategic step in some larger game?

JB wasn't sure.

But as he replayed the memory of that kiss—the taste and texture of it still lingering on his lips—he confronted an uncomfortable truth: part of him didn't care what game Luca was playing, as long as he could stay in it a little longer.

Chapter Twenty-Three

Days after lunch, JB still couldn't decipher Luca. He'd encountered him two more times—once when Luca accompanied Mike to retrieve forgotten keys for a Pine Street cottage, and again when Luca picked up Mike for a Montauk waterfront property viewing. Both times, JB maintained a polite distance, deliberately avoiding any moment alone with him. Mike, meanwhile, seemed blind to everything except Luca's attentiveness.

But JB faced more pressing concerns than deciphering Luca's motives. The shadow of suspicion lengthened around him daily: police now openly considered him a person of interest in Gianni Cuomo's murder, and the Louisville Slugger—that family heirloom his son had proudly carried to the Beltrams' costume party, now identified as possibly being the murder weapon—had vanished. These two facts twisted together in the minds of investigators, forming a noose of circumstantial evidence that tightened with each passing day around JB's neck.

His friends, however, wouldn't allow his retreat—particularly Rakesh, who insisted that true innocence demanded living unburdened by suspicion. "Hiding only draws more attention to you and your family," Rakesh had argued. Despite his misgivings, JB agreed to join his friends at James and John's Saturday afternoon pool party.

Turning into the gravel driveway, guests were greeted by a long row of Spartan juniper standing like silent sentinels. The roundabout was flanked by wax myrtle and a flowering eastern redbud, its pink blossoms vibrant against the deepening afternoon sky.

Three young men wearing nothing but yellow Speedos and pink plastic visors welcomed guests, their oiled bodies gleaming in the late summer's languorous vibrancy. After air-kissing the hosts and ordering a cocktail, JB coiled through the throngs of shirtless and hairless men with their dewy, tanned skin and not an ounce of body fat. James and John were known to stock their parties with very young, very pretty gay boys with no discernible ties to the Hamptons. Vulnerable and desperate like frothing hopefuls at a Nickelodeon casting call. Lecherous older queens swam around them, hiding their bellies beneath billowy blouses, teeth bared. A living diorama of the gay predatory hierarchy.

Alone, sipping Scotch amongst the forced conviviality, JB looked like a man lost at Grand Central Station. Across the pool, Luca was speaking with Rakesh. He didn't meet JB's gaze, and when Rakesh excused himself to join JB, Luca turned and walked in the other direction.

"I see you met the Italian," JB said. "What were you two talking about?"

"He was showing me the steps to the *tarantella.* Did you know it means 'the dance of the spider' in Italian?"

"Ha-ha."

"Luca did most of the talking. Something about Lawson's firm helping him find a house for his wealthy client. I was only half paying attention, what with all the eye candy. I think James and John have outdone themselves this year."

JB noted that Mike had entered the party and made his way directly toward Luca. It was deliberate, and for the benefit of their friends as well as for his ego. Mike had been focusing a great deal of attention on Luca. Like a fighter who'd lost round one, Mike was hell-bent on a round-two knockout. JB never told Mike that Luca knew Gianni's widow. For now, he was keen to observe this match from afar.

"I see Mike has bounced back," Rakesh said. "My, he does run the spectrum. Luca seems too aged for him."

"Luca is far from old. Someone needs corrective lenses."

Rakesh's head shuddered dramatically, hand clutching his throat like manicured talons reaching for an imaginary string of pearls. "Defensive much?"

JB laughed casually. "I only meant that Luca is probably our age and very attractive."

JB glanced away, catching Luca's eye. Mike followed Luca's line of sight until they were both now staring at him. JB nodded with a benign, courteous smile he reserved for people that didn't interest him. Rakesh, JB saw, observed this too, and his face indicated that he was attempting to piece together a puzzle, and even though the loops and sockets didn't fit, that was inconsequential.

"Excuse me"—Rakesh zigzagged a finger across JB's face—"has a certain stuffy sociology professor suddenly developed a hankering for a Mediterranean hunk?"

"Oh, please," JB said dismissively, but there was no winnowing away from Rakesh once he'd locked his eagle eyes on unsuspecting prey.

"*Mmm.* This is delicious. What a tasty morsel you've presented me with today."

"Speaking of tasty morsels…where is Andy?"

"Andy and I are not exactly seeing eye to eye lately." Rakesh appeared unable to choke back the emotions that bubbled up.

JB sensed the tension roping them like a lasso. He grabbed ahold of Rakesh's arm and pulled him away. Behind the junipers, JB knew, James and John had created a secret garden. A haven amid a haven that was the most special place on their property. JB guided his friend there and sat him down on the wooden bench. "Tell me everything."

"A few weeks ago, I got a call from Lawson, the big man himself, informing me that Andy showed up at work drunk."

A cocktail or two at lunch was commonplace out east. For Lawson to call Rakesh had JB wondering how intoxicated Andy was and if this wasn't the first time.

"I knew Andy had been drinking more than usual," Rakesh spoke in a hushed voice, "but it's the summer. Christ, JB, we all drink a lot in the Hamptons. You can practically smell the gin in the air."

JB took an impatient breath. "Stop making excuses for Andy. Lawson didn't call you because he had a martini at lunch."

"Andy couldn't come today because he's already passed out drunk in bed."

JB wondered how he'd missed the warning signs. True, Andy had projectile vomited at the Beltrams' costume party, but JB thought everyone deserved an embarrassing drunken pass at a Hamptons event.

"The loss of a parent can do a number on a person."

"This isn't grief," Rakesh replied sharply. "Andy's been struggling with something for a while now. I don't know what it is, but it began last summer. I can't help but think it coincided with his brother's arrest."

"But you said they aren't close."

"That's what I thought, but I discovered they'd been communicating. I have a feeling RJ was pressuring Andy for help when he got arrested, and he's badgering Andy for money now that their mother has passed away." Rakesh offered a bitter laugh. "Like she had anything to leave her sons."

"I'm so sorry." JB wrapped his arms around Rakesh and pulled him close. Rakesh rested his head against JB's chest and sighed exhaustedly. A glint of something unexpected flashed across Rakesh's face as his friend glanced at his mouth. Something wanton, something longing—a raw vulnerability that seemed foreign on Rakesh's usually guarded features. Before he could process what was happening, Rakesh leaned forward, and JB felt his friend's full lips press against his own.

JB pulled away, his hands firm on Rakesh's shoulders. "What are you doing?"

Rakesh squeezed his eyes shut, his face contorting with embarrassment and regret. "Sorry, old friend. Moment of weakness." He straightened his posture, attempting to reclaim his dignity. "Andy and I haven't been intimate in a very, very long time."

"Why didn't you tell me sooner?"

"Oh, I don't know. Maybe it was the cancer, the philandering husband, and oh yeah, the murder."

"I've been a real shit friend. Haven't I?" Once again, JB hugged him. "If there is anything you need, just ask me." Rakesh stiffened up and didn't respond. JB pulled back and stared pointedly at Rakesh's welling eyes.

"Promise?"

"Cross my heart."

"Let's return to this dreadful party. I don't want anyone to snap a photo of us and post it on social media. I can see it now: 'Murder suspect found canoodling in the bushes with the local pharmacist.'"

"Fuck them. Fuck all of them." Rakesh laughed while wiping his cheeks. "Isn't that what some stuffy sociology professor said once at a party right before he peed his pants?"

JB dropped his head back, laughing. "I'll never live that down."

"Not as long as I live and breathe." They walked in the front entrance. James and John greeted them like they'd just arrived. Rakesh pulled JB to the bar where they ordered drinks.

Angelo hurried up to them, bursting like a carbonated beverage. "Grab your drinks and follow me."

JB saw his eyes were protruding. "What's the matter?"

Angelo held up his hand to shush him. "Come with me, doctor's orders."

He led them upstairs to a glass-enclosed second-story addition James and John called the treehouse. There, Angelo introduced them to two older men who looked up from their conversation with bright, expectant faces.

"Rakesh and JB," Angelo began. "I'd like to introduce you to my new friends, Alfie and Dale."

The two men were clearly a long-established couple—JB could see it in their synchronized movements as they both stood to greet them. In their sixties, well-maintained, with the kind of effortless style that came from wealth. They had an energy about them, the chattiness of folks who genuinely enjoyed meeting new people.

"Welcome, welcome," Alfie said warmly, shaking JB's hand with both of his. "Angelo's been mysterious about why you wanted to hear our little sob story."

"Not so little," Dale added with a rueful laugh. "Though I suppose it depends on your perspective."

They settled back into their chairs, and JB noticed how they unconsciously mirrored each other's posture—the way couples do after decades together.

"We were telling Angelo about our run-in with the Big GC," Alfie said.

"The Big GC is Gianni Cuomo," JB clarified.

"That's what everyone called him on Fire Island," Dale explained. "Big personality, big…well, let's say he lived up to the nickname in multiple ways."

"Oh, stop," Alfie said, swatting at him playfully. "We're trying to be helpful here."

Angelo gestured for them to continue. "Tell them about last summer."

"Right," Alfie said, settling in. "We met the Big GC at the Blue Whale—he was their piano player. Talented, I'll give him that. Could play anything you requested."

"Very low key," Dale added. "We started going there regularly to hear him play."

"And maybe to flirt a little," Alfie admitted with a self-deprecating smile. "Two old queens still trying to turn heads."

"Speak for yourself," Dale shot back. "I'm timeless."

Despite their banter, JB could see something more serious brewing beneath the surface.

"Anyway," Alfie continued, "we got to know him pretty well. Invited him to some parties, introduced him around. He seemed like he was struggling financially, so we tried to help out where we could."

Dale's expression darkened slightly. "That's when things got interesting."

"Interesting is one word for it," Alfie said. "We started getting these anonymous photos in the mail. Pictures of us in… let's call them private moments."

"Blackmail photos?" Rakesh asked.

"Amateur hour blackmail," Dale confirmed. "It was insulting. Like he thought we were closeted politicians or something."

"So we invited him over for dinner," Alfie said. "Sat him down with a nice bottle of Barolo and basically said, 'Honey, if you need money, ask. But this cloak-and-dagger nonsense is beneath all of us.'"

"He actually seemed relieved," Dale added. "Apologized, said he was desperate, didn't know what else to do. We felt sorry for him."

"That's when he got us," Alfie said, and now the humor was completely gone from his voice. "While we were being understanding about his pathetic blackmail scheme, he was systematically robbing us blind."

"Systematic?" Dale repeated sarcastically. "It was more like a bad plot lifted from some dusty episode of *Matlock* about two bumbling con artists."

The room grew quiet. JB could see the real pain in both men's faces.

"Art, jewelry, cash," Dale said. "Stuff we'd collected over thirty years together. Things that meant something to us."

"How much?" JB asked gently.

"Over fifty thousand dollars," Alfie replied. "But it wasn't just the money. Some of those pieces… they were irreplaceable."

Dale reached over and squeezed his partner's hand. "We sued, obviously. But by then he'd already fled to Sicily, and now we'll never see a dime since somebody bumped him off."

Alfie's phone chimed. He glanced at it and showed Dale, who nodded. "Our date has arrived."

"Thank God for the invention of social networks," Dale said. "Back in the day, we had to schlep to bars for boys. Now it's like Amazon: one-click ordering and same-day delivery."

"Here," Alfie said, handing them each a business card. "If you need to know anything else about the Big GC's methods, give us a call. We're happy to help if it means someone finally gets justice."

"You're staying out east?" JB asked.

"Permanently, actually," Dale replied. "After the last hurricane destroyed our Fire Island place, we decided it was time for a change of scenery."

"Found a wonderful house through a local broker," Alfie added. "Mike. Absolute gem of a man. He went above and beyond for us."

JB's expression grew serious. "Mike Fogarty?"

"Of course you know him," Dale said with genuine pleasure. "What a sweetheart he is. First house he showed us, we knew it was the one."

Alfie blew air kisses. "Well, TTNT."

Rakesh shrugged. "Excuse me?"

"*Tootles till next time,*" they sang before trotting off.

The three friends stood in the treehouse like statues after a hurricane;

Alfie and Dale's story clung to them like debris. Rakesh cleared his throat. "Do you think Mike knew they were the same couple that Gianni stole from last year on Fire Island?"

"How would Mike even know to ask?" Angelo reasoned.

"Look how easily the story came up now, and we're strangers," Rakesh explained. "Imagine the long conversations Mike had with those two, showing them houses?"

JB sensed his friends' eyes on him as he replayed the events of the past few weeks in his mind. He began to wonder whether Mike was aware that Gianni had extorted money from Alfie and Dale. If he had known, why hadn't he brought it up? After all, if Mike had sold a house, it would have been physically impossible for him not to gloat about it.

"I need a drink," JB said.

"Great idea." Rakesh steered them to the bar. "Where is Jason?"

"Home studying."

JB half listened, fuming as he wrestled with the thought of how Mike could have kept such a secret and why. Although his friends tried to engage him in conversation, JB felt a heavy ache in his stomach, like an anchor weighed down with betrayal and shock. It was true what Angelo had said the other night at Rakesh's house: We rarely see the ones we love for who they truly are. But it was obvious now that JB was no longer in love.

"Scotch, JB?"

He flinched slightly when Rakesh handed him a drink. The dull ache in his gut began to ease as he took a sip. "I'm not surprised Mike didn't tell me. It's not like we're on speaking terms."

Then, JB heard Mike's voice in the adjoining room. He moved closer to observe him encircled by an eager audience as Mike made an elaborate gesture, bracing himself against a younger man's shoulder. In one swift movement, Mike's entire body language transformed, his back hunching, shoulders drooping forward, head tilting at that particular angle that JB recognized with horrifying clarity was meant to mimic him. Mike's fingers raked through his hair until it stood at odd angles, his face contorting into that self-conscious, uneven smile JB sometimes caught in reflective surfaces.

"I'm a professor, dear boy," Mike intoned, voice pitched lower and infused with an exaggerated academic pomposity. "Now fetch me a Scotch before I piss my pants."

This wasn't simply mockery—it was betrayal disguised as entertainment, years of shared vulnerability weaponized for cheap laughs.

In an instant, Mike lost the pose and reverted to his old self, hanging on the younger man and laughing. For a brief moment, cruelty flashed across Mike's face—an expression JB didn't want to see but couldn't forget. If too much knowledge was dangerous, ignoring it was far worse. JB forced himself to watch this spectacle before him. After enduring Alfie and Dale—listening to their exaggerated words, punctuated by countless exclamation points and sentences riddled with double entendres—he descended deeper into the depths of Mike's betrayal.

Mike offered a curt bow, clearly applauding himself for his triumph. All eyes were fixed on him as he stood at the forefront of a semicircle of treacherous friends, celebrating his victory. He had proven to everyone, including his cuckolded husband, that despite being cut off financially, Mike hadn't just survived; he had persevered.

JB was horrified. JB was mesmerized. JB was embarrassed in ways he couldn't fully articulate, but as usual, he showed no signs of vulnerability for the ravenous party-goers to prey upon.

His friends, JB realized, who loved and supported him, saw the situation clearly. Saw the smile he'd hammered to his face, though it tugged with tension under the nails of his forced conviviality.

"What are we doing for Labor Day?" Angelo asked with an awkward laugh.

"I'm going home!" JB announced. "Not for Labor Day. I mean, I'm going home right now."

Rakesh grabbed his arm. "Don't go. If you go, he wins."

JB offered a pleasant smile, but deep down he was seething. "There is no winning. Only degrees of losing."

Gay marriage—it instantly seemed so stupid an idea. From somewhere high above the clouds, JB observed himself walking to his car until he began a plummeting descent. There was no air to breathe. His mind nosedived, trying to grab onto anything that might explain why Mike hadn't told him he'd sold a house, or why Mike had thought it was funny to mock him in public as he spiraled to the ground.

JB fumbled with his car keys. *Breathe.* He pitched his face toward the sun, closing his eyes, he stared at the burning orange behind his lids. His breath slowed down until finally, he was more or less himself again.

"Leaving so soon?"

The voice cut through JB's spiral of humiliation and rage. He didn't want to talk to anyone, but especially not to him. Turning, he found Luca standing there, radiating more energy than mere flesh and blood should contain.

For long, tense seconds, neither man spoke. The distant laughter and music from the party faded into white noise as they regarded each other in silence.

"Are you okay?" Luca finally asked.

JB caught a whiff of pine and sunscreen mingled with something more primal beneath. He saw a flicker of something unidentifiable in Luca's eyes—concern? Desire? Calculation? His body responded with a surge of heat that had nothing to do with the summer sun. In that moment, with Mike's mockery still burning in his ears JB saw with absolute certainty what would happen next. The realization was both terrifying and exhilarating—a cliff edge he'd been approaching these past twelve months without realizing it.

"I'll follow you back to your hotel."

Luca gave a choked laugh. "Are you serious?"

JB let out a heavy breath. "Tell me your room number before I change my mind?"

* * *

The American Hotel loomed ahead as JB pulled into an empty parking spot and hurried into the lobby. Luca threw the door open and pulled him inside. The room was small: dark wood paneling, drab carpet, and a patchwork quilt of an American flag lay on the bed.

Luca began peeling off his own clothes. JB's pulse galloped—he'd never been with anyone other than Mike. The room felt heavy with mildew and anticipation. When Luca guided him toward the bed, JB turned away, but Luca gently cradled his face, bringing their gazes together.

"Look at me," Luca whispered.

He pulled JB's shirt off his head and removed his shorts. JB felt defenseless yet ravenous as Luca loomed above him, emboldened and hungry. "I'm afraid I might not be able to perform," JB started to say.

Luca's lips curved into a knowing smile. "I see you've conquered your fear."

With a grace that belied his strength, Luca lifted JB's legs in one fluid motion, strong hands wrapping around his thighs with reverent appreciation. "It should be required for you to register your legs as deadly weapons," he murmured as he pressed his lips to the sensitive flesh of JB's inner thighs.

The apprehension returned, barreling toward him. "I don't usually do this," JB stammered.

A mischievous smile grew on Luca's face as he tore open a condom wrapper with his teeth. "Trust me."

And somehow, JB had always wanted this, ever since they'd first locked eyes in the lounge downstairs. JB rationalized that experiencing this with someone who wasn't Mike made the act even more forbidden, more visceral.

JB's eyes, fixed and blazing, held Luca's gaze for a long moment. "Go ahead," he whispered.

"You are so sexy," Luca groaned.

Euphoria swept through JB's body. The perfection of Luca's slow, sensual rhythm had him wondering why he'd never sought this pleasure before from Mike. This unfamiliar sensation overwhelmed him—the friction, the heat, the weight of a man thrusting inside him with intensity. Luca quickened his pace. Sweat dripped from his forehead onto JB's lips. The briny taste only intensified the mounting pleasure. JB squeezed his eyes shut, unsure how to quiet his brain. It had been so long since he and Mike had been intimate. And not once in all those years had JB felt this feverish impulse to surrender control, to lose himself in the scent, taste, and touch of another person.

Luca released a moan that echoed through the stale air of the small hotel room. After a final shudder, Luca collapsed onto JB's chest, panting and slick with sweat. They kissed languidly, drifting in a euphoric haze. "What about you?" Luca whispered. "Did you not enjoy it too?"

JB pulled Luca closer, their cheeks pressed together. "I did enjoy it. I enjoyed it very much."

The truth, JB knew as he lay in the afterglow, was that he'd slept with Luca not out of spite—though that would have been the simpler explanation. No, this was about proving to himself that he had moved on, that his marriage was over with no possibility for return. The act itself had been both a declaration of independence and a funeral for a relationship that had been dying for months.

JB smiled inwardly, surprised by the absence of guilt. In its place was something lighter—relief, perhaps, or the peculiar peace that comes with finality. His arm and leg draped over Luca's torso, clinging to him like a piece of clay that had molded perfectly in the space between them. Whether Luca was trustworthy remained an open question, but in this moment, that seemed less important than the fact that JB had finally broken free from the prison of his failed marriage.

That familiar sensation of being completely present in his own body he'd experienced the night of the Beltrams' Fourth of July party had returned, but transformed—no longer a reminder of his humiliation, but the intoxicating awareness of his own agency.

Chapter Twenty-Four

J B drove home despite Luca's insistence to stay. "Let's take a shower, eat in the restaurant, and come back to my room," Luca had urged. "We'll make love all night." As delicious a thrill his invitation sounded, JB had unfinished business with Mike.

It's over. He was no longer happy—*they* were no longer happy, all three of them trapped in the gilded cages of their beautiful Hamptons home and stunning Tribeca apartment. Their family had corroded from within, damaged beyond any hope of restoration. If anything, by sleeping with Luca, JB had hurled himself in the opposite direction of a path moving toward reconciliation. Now, there was no turning back. But first, JB wanted to know why Mike hadn't told him he'd sold a home to Alfie and Dale and whether Mike knew all about Gianni's entangled relationship with them.

JB ruminated about it obsessively until he turned into the driveway. A rental car was parked alongside Mike's SUV. JB opened the front door and heard voices. The outline of a woman came into view as he approached. JB recognized her as Gianni Cuomo's widow.

Daria Nicoletta Cuomo.

She sat on the edge of the sofa, hands clutching an embroidered handkerchief, dabbing her large, pale-blue eyes, glassy and red from weeping. "JB," Mike huffed with frustration as though his sudden presence had interrupted their conversation. "Mrs. Cuomo, this is my husband."

She nodded, sniffling.

"Mrs. Cuomo," JB spoke in a low voice. "My condolences for your loss."

Without her dark sunglasses, JB could see Daria's small, elegant features clearly for the first time. She was older than he'd expected—fine lines webbed her translucent skin, and deeper creases framed her mouth. *"Grazie,"* she managed finally.

On the coffee table, Mike had offered her a glass of wine, which she hadn't touched. Mike's glass, on the other hand, was empty. "Mrs. Cuomo called me earlier," Mike began to explain. "She's returning to Italy this evening and wanted to meet me."

"I want you to have this." Mrs. Cuomo opened her purse and withdrew a gold chain displaying a medal of a man holding a walking stick and carrying a child on his shoulders. "St. Christopher is the patron saint of safe travels. Gianni told me how kind you were, that you watched over him, and let him call me on your phone. That's how I found you. I still have your number."

Mike stared awkwardly at the medal in his hands as if it were furred with mold. "I can't accept this."

"Please, you must." Her face twisted with pain and a terrible, lost grief. "I know all about my husband." She paused, and that wistfulness in her eyes coiled into the room almost palpably. "I know what happened last summer. Those men threatened us. When Gianni said he was returning to America, I said, *No!*"

JB pinched the bridge of his nose. He couldn't block the image of Gianni with Alfie and Dale, the three of them cavorting on Fire Island while his wife took care of their children in Italy.

"Your relationship with your husband is none of our business," JB said, though Mrs. Cuomo had piqued his interest. Was it the way she looked in his direction without making eye contact? This visit felt strange, almost staged. If Mrs. Cuomo truly knew all about her husband, she had to know the nature of his relationship with Mike.

"Gianni promised he'd never do anything like that again." Mrs. Cuomo pounded her knee with surprising force for such a delicate-looking woman. "He promised!" She raised a trembling fist toward the ceiling. "But I knew he couldn't be trusted." She choked up then, emotion exploding through her. The transformation was jarring—one moment collected, the next moment shattered. "That's why I sent my brother, Luca, to watch over him," she continued, each word emerging as if torn from her throat, "but even he couldn't save my Gianni."

"Luca is your brother?" JB asked.

The words hung in the air like smoke, acrid and impossible to wave away.

"Yes." Her eyes flitted from JB to Mike. "Do you know him?"

JB nodded, unable to speak—struck by the memory of lying in a postcoital lassitude with Luca only a short while ago. *What a fool I've been.* This was exactly what Luca had wanted all along: to worm his way into his marriage. And to think that JB believed he'd had the upper hand, rejecting Luca's advances after he'd made them lunch, only to throw himself at Luca's feet earlier at the party because, in the end, he was no better than Mike.

"Yes, we've met him." Mike glanced at JB.

"*Allora*, I must go now." Mrs. Cuomo uncrossed her ankles and stood up. "Please, accept the medal and wear it in good health. It will keep you safe."

Mike escorted her outside. JB walked into the kitchen to fix himself a Scotch, but stopped short. He stared at the bottle on the counter but thought, *No, I need to think clearly.*

Why hadn't Luca told JB he was Gianni's brother-in-law? Was it to get closer to him? Surely, Luca knew Gianni and Mike had been carrying on an affair. Had Luca seduced him only to learn more about their relationship with his brother-in-law, or did he truly have feelings for JB? If only Gianni's widow hadn't told him what her relationship was with Luca, maybe he could have subsisted in this fantasy where he'd been swept up in a seduction with a handsome Italian. Instead, he felt trapped in an endless nightmare of odd mistrust, deceit, and paranoia.

Mike entered the house and immediately refilled his glass with wine. "You ran out of the party pretty quickly."

With a grunt, JB propelled himself toward Mike. "Are you out of your mind, letting that woman in our house?"

Confusion flickered across Mike's features. "At the party, Luca said that Gianni's wife wanted to thank me in person."

"Are you so vain that you would believe the wife of a man you were having an affair with wanted to come over here and thank you? For what? Fucking her husband?"

"You heard her."

"You don't know this woman. Her husband was murdered!"

JB allowed the silence to build between them as a one-sided conversation took place in his mind. After he'd spoken with Dale and Alfie at the party, JB had rehearsed a million questions he'd planned on asking Mike, but none of them seemed as important to him now, other than: Why had Luca kept his relationship with Gianni from him? And why had Mrs. Cuomo come over here to reward Mike—her husband's lover—with a goddamn medal?

JB ended the conversation in his head and proceeded with his initial plan to interrogate Mike. "I guess congratulations are in order."

Mike picked up his phone to check his messages. "What are you talking about?"

"I met a couple at the party today."

Mike shrugged as if to indicate he couldn't care less.

"Why didn't you tell me you sold a house to Dale and Alfie?"

"Oh, that." Mike drank back his wine and walked into the kitchen for a refill.

"Did you know Gianni stole from those two men last year on Fire Island? Did you know who they were while you were traipsing around town showing them homes?"

"Keep your voice down," Mike whispered. "Emilio is in the other room."

JB's head jerked toward his son's bedroom. "You mean to tell me that Emilio has been here the entire time you were being awarded man of the year by your ex-lover's widow?"

"She wanted to thank me!"

The rage coursed through JB's arms, staring at Mike, was its own slender form of hell. JB walked to his son's bedroom door and knocked. There was no answer—not even the usual teenage grunt of acknowledgment. "Emilio?"

Silence.

JB knocked again while opening the door. An ominous sense of foreboding enveloped him like a gray mist, thickening with each step he took into the room. The sight that greeted him froze his blood.

Emilio lay slumped against his headboard, his iPad casting an eerie blue glow across his face, illuminating a vacant expression that wasn't sleep—wasn't anything JB had ever seen before on his son's face.

"Emilio!" JB shook his son's shoulders, the boy's head lolling sickeningly. "Emilio!"

But his son's eyes were upturned, showing only whites. A thin line of drool oozed from his slack lips, glistening in the iPad's cold light.

Mike appeared in the doorway. "What's the matter?"

"Call an ambulance. Something's wrong with Emilio!"

Chapter Twenty-Five

JB stood outside the waiting room doors, his body physically present while his mind replayed the past hour's events: the medics clearing Emilio's airway, the metallic snick of the intubation equipment, his son's body jerking as they worked; the ambulance siren wailing as they raced to Stony Brook Hospital, each minute stretching into an eternity; the emergency room staff descending upon Emilio's stretcher like a well-choreographed swarm, whisking him away through double doors that swung shut in JB's face with terrible finality.

What to do now but wait? He paced the small area before the doors, muscles coiled with the need to act—to do something, anything—while being forced into the most unnatural state for a parent: complete helplessness.

He prayed Emilio's doctor would bound through the waiting room doors at any moment, announcing his son was alive and well. Alive and well, he prayed.

Mike sat a few safe seats away. They hadn't spoken a word the entire time they'd followed behind the ambulance in their car. Rakesh had begun texting him soon after they'd arrived in the ER, but JB refused to do anything other than stare at those doors. Mike's phone had begun to ding as well, a series of alerts to them both, which JB continued to ignore.

"Oh, my God. JB, you need to see this."

"Don't speak to me."

JB kept his eyes fixed on the waiting room doors until the danger—if indeed there was danger—was resolved.

When JB's phone rang, he hesitated for the tiniest fraction of a second before answering. "I can't talk right now."

Rakesh guffawed with delighted mockery. "Oh, honey, make the time. You are not going to believe this."

"I'm serious." JB's voice was tight with caution. "It's Emilio…" The mere mention of his son's name razed through an emotional dam, releasing a flood of sobbing.

"What's wrong with Emilio?"

JB squeezed back the tears because if his father had taught him anything, it had been to never show the cracks. Never allow sadness to soften your austerity. He took a deep breath, puffed out his cheeks, and exhaled. "Emilio overdosed. We're at the hospital now."

"I'll be right there."

"No," JB replied. "I'll call you after we speak with the doctors."

"You shouldn't be alone."

"I'm not alone. What did you want to tell me?"

"JB, you need to see this." Mike had uncoupled himself from his phone to show JB what all the fuss was about. JB stared confusedly at the screen while simultaneously listening to Rakesh explain that explicit photos of Gus Beltram had been leaked online.

"The closeted prick is sucking dick." Rakesh's description captured the image better than the actual photo itself. Nipples McGillicuddy on his knees, his lips hungrily wrapped around the Big GC.

In the cool, sanitized waiting room, JB couldn't speak. Gus might be a pretentious, self-hating homophobe who'd found a woman to love him, willingly turning a blind eye, but even men like him didn't deserve the onerous fate that awaited him.

Throughout his life, JB possessed an uncanny ability to detect the darker aspects of human nature, along with the survival instinct to distance himself whenever he met their presence. This explained why he never questioned Gus's sexuality: the matter simply didn't command his interest. He had, of course, heard the whispers and had anticipated this revelation would eventually surface. Now that it had, he felt nothing but pity. The smooth-sailing Beltram ship hadn't only run aground—it had erupted in flames and plummeted to the depths of Hampton Bays.

"Your son is awake," the doctor announced. "You can see him now."

"I have to go," JB said to Rakesh before hanging up. "Is he all right, doctor?"

"He's very lucky. We found benzodiazepines in his urine toxicology. Do either of you know how he could have gotten his hands on them?"

JB shook his head and expectantly glanced at Mike, who shrugged. "We don't keep any narcotics or sedatives in the house."

"For now, he's on one-to-one observation until the psychiatrist evaluates him."

A mixture of apprehension, fear, and excitement swirled in JB's gut. "Can we take him home after the psychiatric evaluation? I'd rather he not stay overnight in a hospital."

The doctor scrutinized him. "Your son's overdose is considered a suicide attempt until proven otherwise. He's not going anywhere tonight."

JB stared at his shoes. "I see."

The doctor pulled back the curtain. Emilio was sitting up in bed, appearing exhausted. Eyes swollen. Lips chapped. His dark curls, slicked to one side damp from sweat. A nurse held a straw to his lips as he sipped water from a cup.

"Dad," Emilio croaked, his voice scraping like sandpaper. His eyes, usually so bright and confident, now darted anxiously between JB and the medical staff. "I didn't do what they say I did. Swear to God." His words tumbled out with desperate urgency. "I didn't try to kill myself. You have to believe me."

JB met Emilio's gaze, searching for his son beneath the pallor and fear. "No one is saying you did anything."

But Emilio wasn't looking at him anymore. His focus had shifted to where Mike stood. The change was immediate and electric—Emilio's body tensing like a cornered animal.

"You did this to me!" The words erupted from Emilio's throat as a primal shriek, his finger jabbing accusingly toward Mike. The monitor beside his bed began beeping more rapidly, tracking his surging heart rate.

JB could feel the heat of embarrassment blazing across his face, mingled with confusion and dread. The medical staff exchanged glances, their professional demeanors slipping enough to reveal concern.

"Me?" Mike's response was laced with both defensive outrage and something worse—a note of sarcastic disbelief that made JB's stomach turn.

"Get him away from me!" Emilio began clawing at the guardrails, attempting to climb out of the stretcher. JB and the nurse attempted to restrain him. "He wants to kill me!"

"That's not true," Mike shouted.

JB's guts were in knots, wincing at the shrieking coming from his son's mouth. Emilio continued thrashing, hitting the IV pole. Another nurse entered to assist them. JB fought to restrain his son's wrists, staring into his eyes, but only seeing a terrifying surge of panic.

"No one is going to hurt you," JB insisted, but Emilio was lost in the frenzy of fear, kicking his long, coltlike legs and knocking one of the nurses back. "Mike!" JB shouted. "Get out of here!"

Chapter Twenty-Six

Hours later, JB drummed his fingers against the steering wheel as he navigated the winding roads, the manicured golf course stretching to his right and the shimmering bay to his left. How could he live amid such beauty yet feel the world had become a desolate wasteland?

Once assured of his son's safety, JB reached several critical decisions, foremost among them that Mike needed to leave their home. The finality of this verdict sent an almost physical jolt through JB's body. He decided to continue supporting his husband financially, despite knowing that Mike's commission must have been substantial. Tonight wasn't the time for financial disputes. Separation was the priority—Emilio's psychiatrist agreed. But first, JB needed to shed these clothes—perhaps burn them—now contaminated with Luca's scent, which clung to the fabric like a revolting stink.

The front door to the house was ajar when JB pulled into the driveway. The trunk of Mike's SUV was unlatched. Something didn't feel right. JB chewed his bottom lip. He stepped inside the house. The stillness unnerved him. In the kitchen, JB found three overstuffed garbage bags. Mike's packed suitcases sat outside his bedroom door.

"You're home." Mike's eyes fixed on JB as if he'd never seen him before. As if they were strangers. The intensity of the silence stretched out between them. Oddly, neither attempted to fill the void, only existing within that silence, and JB didn't know what to make of it at first. Mike didn't appear like himself. Something felt off, and that's when it hit him.

Mike wasn't drunk.

"How's Emilio?" Mike's mouth twitched with hesitancy.

"The doctor says he's going to be all right."

"I had nothing to do with it." Mike's steely gaze crackled with intensity.

"I want to believe that," JB said, but he couldn't forget his son's violent reaction to seeing Mike in the emergency room. The terror in Emilio's eyes—he'd felt threatened at the sight of Mike; there was no denying it. It was unthinkable, the awful accusation Emilio had made. And yet, the on-call psychiatrist had expressed doubt, suggesting that Emilio's story didn't add up but that she hoped with a little rest, he would gain some clarity.

"I'm moving out." Mike's hands were trembling slightly—the first visible sign he was falling apart that JB had seen in him since this nightmare began.

"I think that's for the best."

Mike flinched with surprise at JB's immediate acquiescence. "I've stopped drinking. In fact, I poured all the booze down the drain."

"I see."

Mike's face cracked then—for a moment—revealing something raw and desperate. "I don't care if you don't believe me." He proceeded to carry the garbage bags outside and dumped them into the trash bins. Mike had stopped drinking many times in the past, only to start up a few days later. Never once had he sought out help or attended an Alcoholics Anonymous meeting. When Mike returned, JB was standing in the dining room with his arms crossed over his chest. "Where will you stay?"

A flicker of embarrassment skittered across Mike's face. "With friends."

Friends, huh?

"You'll keep me updated on Emilio's progress?"

"I will."

Mike seemed almost too resolute. It felt more like he was escaping something rather than making a decision that was best for his family. A calculated move to show he was in control, that Emilio's well-being meant more to him than his own, but JB had his doubts.

"For what it's worth," Mike said, picking up his suitcases, "I still love you. I never stopped."

You have a funny way of showing it, JB thought, because he remembered too well those nights Mike had entertained men in their old bedroom. It had been so open, so cliché, and so indiscreet that it seemed as if Mike had wanted to taunt him.

"I guess this is goodbye." Mike lingered for a second. His eyes welled, making them go swimmy and watery.

"Wait." JB started toward Mike but stopped short. This was a trap. The night Rakesh had lectured Angelo on relationships, JB had decided his marriage was over. Unfortunately, he'd gotten swept up in the thrall of Luca's seduction. But with the memory of Mike mocking him at the party still fresh in his mind, JB felt like a man selecting the right knife from the butcher's block. It was time to amputate his arm—self-mutilation as self-preservation.

"I fucked Luca."

Mike's face flushed violently, but his eyes revealed something beyond anger—a comprehension, as if some terrible theory had been confirmed. "Lucky you."

"Luck had nothing to do with it." JB's mouth slid into a spiteful grin, though something inside him withered at his own cruelty. A terrible silence rose between them. JB had imagined this moment would bring catharsis—the savage pleasure of inflicting a wound equal to those he'd endured. Instead, he felt a sickening lurch of recognition. He'd become exactly what he despised in Mike: someone who weaponized their spouse's vulnerabilities for self-gratification.

"Touché." Mike didn't sound particularly wounded. It was as if he'd been playing some elaborate game whose rules JB had only now discovered.

When the lights from Mike's car were no longer visible, JB felt nothing. Only vindication, not for himself, but for his son. And beneath that, a hollow space where love had once resided—a vacancy that felt less like freedom than like loss.

* * *

The following day, JB contacted the detectives and requested to meet with them in person.

"I'm sorry to hear about your boy," Detective D'Amico said.

She took notes at her desk as Sullivan stood nearby. "The reason I'm here," JB began, "is because my son insists this wasn't a suicide attempt, and I believe him."

"What do you think happened?"

JB vigorously rubbed his temples. "Emilio believes my husband, Mike, drugged him."

D'Amico glanced at her partner. "That's a pretty serious accusation," Sullivan said.

JB leaned forward, elbows on the desk. "Detectives, yesterday I attended a party and met the couple who accused Gianni Cuomo of blackmail and robbery last summer on Fire Island. They told quite the story. Without knowing who I was, they informed me that the realtor who sold them their Sag Harbor home was Mike."

D'Amico shrugged. "So?"

"This morning, when I visited my son, in the psych ward..." JB's voice cracked. He held a fist to his mouth, found his footing. "I asked Emilio about the night Gianni Cuomo died. He recalls falling asleep in the Beltrams' basement. He said that he was suddenly very tired, like he'd felt yesterday. He remembered waking up briefly, but his father wasn't sleeping next to him as Mike had claimed. This was backed up by Dr. Angelo Perrotta, who said Mike was sleeping next to Emilio when he went downstairs to use the restroom, but that Mike wasn't there when he came out."

D'Amico appeared puzzled, clearly searching for a link in the series of events JB had presented. "When you returned home yesterday, your husband was alone with Emilio?"

"No, Mike was having a drink with Gianni Cuomo's wife."

"Excuse me?" Their mouths popped open as D'Amico's eyes met Sullivan's. "Talk about burying the lead. What did she want?"

JB grimaced. "Something about thanking Mike for being nice to her husband. She even gave him a medal."

Sullivan chuckled. "They give out medals now for extramarital affairs?"

"Why?" JB snapped. "Are you asking for a friend?"

D'Amico redirected JB back to Cuomo's widow. "Could she have drugged your son?"

"I don't know."

D'Amico rubbed her tired eyes. "Ever heard of a *vendetta?*"

"Like an eye for an eye? I can't imagine Mike would've allowed her to wander around our house unsupervised."

D'Amico stood up. "Will you let us search your house now?"

"Absolutely."

"We should speak with Cuomo's widow," Sullivan suggested.

D'Amico nodded enthusiastically. "Good idea."

"Too late," JB interjected. "Cuomo's widow flew back to Palermo last night. Besides, Emilio never mentioned meeting her."

"If Cuomo's widow came by your house seeking revenge, there's a possibility she poisoned your husband's drink, and your son consumed it as opposed to your theory, which implicates Mike."

JB was silent, his body heavy and his mind whirling with guilt and confusion. "I don't know what I think anymore."

"Let's start with your house," D'Amico said.

"Shit!" JB squeezed his eyes. "Mike emptied all the liquor bottles last night and threw them out."

D'Amico slapped her knee. "He did what?"

"He said he quit drinking." JB stood up now, too. "Don't you think that's suspicious? It's like he was trying to get rid of the evidence."

"Where is your husband now?" Sullivan asked.

JB shrugged. "I have no idea."

Chapter Twenty-Seven

wo uniformed officers searched the Pulaski residence, taking photographs and collecting evidence. JB explained again that Mike had poured all the liquor down the sink and had thrown the bottles into the trash, which, unfortunately, had been collected by a private sanitation company earlier that morning. Sullivan had officers visit the site in the hopes of identifying the trash bags that were collected from JB's home.

D'Amico confirmed that Daria Nicoletta Cuomo boarded a flight to Palermo the night before. When the police questioned Emilio, he corroborated what JB had assumed, that he hadn't met Gianni's wife. He hadn't known Mrs. Cuomo had visited until his father informed him. D'Amico found it suspicious that Emilio had slept through her visit, likely indicating he'd already been drugged by then.

"That means the only person who could have drugged Emilio was Mike," JB insisted.

D'Amico squeezed her eyes, shaking her head. "We'll question your husband, but something doesn't add up." She started for the door and stopped. "Oh, one more thing—how about that DNA sample?"

"Is it absolutely necessary?"

A uniformed officer handed Sullivan a manila envelope. After a peek inside, he handed it over to his partner. D'Amico took the envelope and withdrew a photocopy. "You want to explain why these photos were found in your study?"

JB flushed with violent embarrassment in the face of being confronted

"

with images of Gus Beltram performing oral sex on Gianni Cuomo. The same ones that had been leaked online.

"I don't know anything about those photos," JB insisted.

D'Amico fixed her skeptical eyes on him. "Here's what we do know: you were the last person to see the victim alive, the autopsy identified fibers in the victim's head wound that are consistent with the wood used to make the baseball bat your son brought with him to the costume party—a bat that has magically gone missing, and after Gus Beltram backed up your husband's accusation that you killed Gianni Cuomo, photos of him pop up online. Photos like the ones we found in your study."

"Why would I let the police search my house if I was hiding incriminating photos in my study? Ask yourself, where would I have gotten my hands on them in the first place? Isn't it conceivable that Mike found the photos on Gianni's phone and murdered him once he realized he'd been hustled like Dale and Alfie?"

D'Amico grinned. "The finger-pointing continues."

"Okay," JB went on. "What about your theory involving Gianni's widow? She didn't come by the house to give Mike a medal. That's something we can all agree on. She came here to avenge the murder of her husband, which means she believes Mike was Gianni's killer."

When D'Amico's phone rang, she excused herself to answer it.

JB was annoyed that it appeared he was accusing Mike of murder in a petty game of tit for tat, but who else besides Mike had the motive and the opportunity to kill Gianni and drug their son?

"She's only doing her job—"

JB regarded Sullivan with contempt. "Spare me the good cop, bad cop routine."

A text pulled JB from this showdown:

It's Andy. I need to speak with you.

D'Amico returned. "That was the ME. We gotta go." JB saw the conflict in her expression. Weighing her options, her unblinking eyes stared him down. "Oh, but before we go, I'm gonna ask you again for that DNA sample. It's absolutely necessary, so I suggest you comply voluntarily."

Throughout his adult life, JB had considered himself lucky. At least he'd been told so often, and objectively he knew that to be true. But now his luck, it seemed, had run out. "Like I said, I'm happy to cooperate."

A swab of his inner cheek, and minutes later, the detectives were gone.

JB collapsed into his chair, the leather creaking under his weight. "They're building a case against me," he whispered to the empty room. "First-degree murder."

His DNA under Gianni's nails—what if they find it? Those incriminating photos that had somehow materialized in his study. And the missing baseball bat—the murder weapon—last seen in his son's hands.

JB's phone buzzed—the fifth time in the past hour. Another text from Luca:

I need to speak to you, PLEASE!.

Each message had arrived with escalating urgency, puncturing JB's determination to cut all ties with the man. Now, with Emilio safe, that determination hardened again. Whatever game Luca was playing—whether he was genuinely trying to help or simply manipulating JB further—it needed to end.

Quickly, JB wrote:

I never want to speak to you again!

* * *

The shingle-style cottage home Angelo and Jason rented was located on Bluff Point Lane. Angelo greeted JB with a hug. "I heard about Emilio. Why didn't you call me?"

"I try to keep my private life private. I guess I'm not doing such a good job."

"Private life?" Angelo repeated harshly. Then he caught himself and gave JB another hug. "Come in."

JB sank on the sofa, rested his head back, and sighed. "Angelo, my life is a mess."

Jason stepped out of the bedroom, wearing only boxer shorts, his blond hair tousled.

JB surmised quickly that the two had been having sex when he texted Angelo from the car. "Am I intruding?"

"No," Angelo insisted. "Honey, would you mind?"

Jason nodded and entered the bathroom. Seconds later, JB heard the shower. He turned toward the oversized window and gazed at the placid water of the salt marshes, spiraling away from the shore like a ribbon, flanked with beach and cord grass. "I could stare at this view all day."

"It's Sag Harbor's answer to Monet's *Water Lilies*."

"How are you two doing?"

"Much better." Angelo flushed with embarrassment, but JB noted, as well, a sense of relief. "Now, tell me about Emilio?"

"He's good." JB took a cleansing breath. "Emilio denies it was a suicide attempt. Initially, he blamed it on Mike, but when the psychiatrist questioned him further, he seemed less certain."

Worry etched on Angelo's face. "Do you believe Mike was involved?"

JB steepled his fingers in front of his mouth. "I don't want to, but Emilio also believes he may have been drugged the night Gianni Cuomo died."

"For what reason?"

"To support Mike's alibi," JB ventured. "What if Mike drugged him both times to cover his tracks?"

"Why would Mike kill Gianni Cuomo?"

And then, out of nowhere, a fist clenched in JB's throat, choking him. He turned away, shielding his face with his hand.

"JB, you don't have to hide your emotions from me." Angelo scooted over and hugged JB's rigid torso, and in that moment of quiet, JB sobbed.

"Goddamn it." How JB hated showing emotion, but in light of everything, he was unable to contain himself. "Maybe Mike found out Gianni was a hustler, and he felt betrayed."

"Betrayed?" Angelo repeated. "Do you think Mike was actually in love with Gianni?"

And that question felt so much worse hearing it spoken out loud, though it had been gestating in JB's mind since he'd first met Gianni. But JB refused to believe Mike, the man he married, the father of their son, could fall in love with an opportunist.

"I don't know what to think anymore," JB said. "When I came home last night and found Mike speaking to Gianni's wife…"

"What?"

JB realized Angelo didn't know the entire story. Once he quickly got him up to speed, including the part where Gianni's widow presented Mike with the medal of valor and the compromising photos of Gus Beltram were found in JB's study, Angelo collapsed against the sofa cushion, speechless. "Gianni's wife came to your house—" Angelo's voice, hoarse and shaky, stumbled to speak before giving up.

"What is it?"

"Gianni's wife came to your house to give Mike a Saint Christopher medal. It makes no sense." Angelo sat up as if waiting for some grand theory to dawn. "What if she was the one who planted the photos of Gus Beltram in your study and poisoned your son?"

"That's what Detective D'Amico thought. Something about a vendetta. An eye for an eye."

"*Occhio per occhio.*"

"I've been so focused on Emilio, I didn't think Cuomo's wife could have planted the photos in my office."

A phone rang in the bedroom. Jason stepped out of the bathroom, a towel wrapped around his waist. "Excuse me."

JB smiled at Angelo. "I'm so happy you two are okay. I like him again."

"Me too."

Jason appeared in the bedroom doorway. He had thrown on board shorts with a palm tree pattern, toweling his blond hair dry. "That was Sullivan."

"Sit." Angelo patted the space beside him on the couch. "What did he say?"

"Gianni's death was declared a homicide."

How much longer until the ME matches the DNA under Gianni's nails with mine?

"In addition to the concussion," Jason continued, "the toxicology report found traces of Rohypnol in Cuomo's blood."

JB squeezed his eyes. "What's that?"

"The date rape drug?" Angelo began to explain. "Rohypnol is a benzodiazepine like Valium, but stronger."

"Wasn't Winnie handing out sedatives the night of the party?" Jason asked.

JB's brows tensed. He was lost in the ebb and flow of his thoughts. "Benzodiazepines," he repeated. "That's what the doctor said they found in Emilio's blood."

JB couldn't help but think that it wasn't a coincidence.

Chapter Twenty-Eight

There was no escaping it. The pull of dread as JB drove to the hospital after leaving Angelo and Jason to meet with the Chief of Psychiatry. Moments of absolute certainty in life were few and far between.

Why did he allow the detectives to take a sample of his DNA? Was it to avoid further suspicion? Was it to be polite? No, it was because JB Pulaski was innocent. Except he knew his DNA would match the tissue recovered from under Gianni Cuomo's nails. Innocent of murder but guilty only of assault. A story no one would believe.

Dr. Clifford Laird was long and lanky, a blond with a sparse grayish beard; his slim face seemed perpetually pleasant. "I've come to the conclusion that Emilio did not attempt to take his own life."

JB's heart filled with the helium of relief. "Can I take him home?"

Laird's gaze sharpened. "What's the status of your living situation?" JB explained that Mike had moved out. In light of their separation, Laird agreed to discharge Emilio but suggested he not return to school in the fall. "Although he's doing better, this has been quite a traumatic experience for him. I'll release Emilio only if he remains in your care and agrees to therapy three times a week."

JB gnawed his lower lip. "Why does Emilio need such intensive therapy?"

Laird shot him an appraising look. "Mr. Pulaski, your son overdosed and accused his father of drugging him. In addition, you were diagnosed with cancer last year. That had a significant impact on your son."

JB groaned, fretting over the difficult road that lay ahead for Emilio. "What have I done?"

"Often, when someone undergoes a traumatic experience such as cancer," Laird explained, "they neglect to understand how their trauma affects those closest to them."

"Are you saying I've been neglecting my son?"

Laird leaned forward, smiling placatingly. "I'm merely suggesting that although you've come to terms with surviving cancer, perhaps your son is not as far along in his journey as you."

How blind had JB been not to consider Emilio's feelings? The Pulaskis maintained a stiff upper lip during a personal crisis, but he'd neglected to consider his son's reaction to his potentially fatal diagnosis. Mike, too, had accused JB of pushing him away, though JB understood that only as an excuse for his extramarital affairs. Emilio was another story entirely.

"My understanding," Laird continued, "is that your marriage has become quite...toxic, to use Emilio's word."

It was gutting to hear his son's opinion about his marriage from a stranger. But Laird appeared nonjudgmental. It was clear he acted only as Emilio's advocate. "I take complete responsibility for that, and you have my word, Emilio's well-being is my only priority from now on."

Relief washed over Laird's face. "Good."

Funny how saying it aloud made it real. If only he'd said it to Emilio months ago, they might not be in this situation. JB had often questioned what course his life would have taken had he separated from Mike after his affair. The answer was always the same. He wouldn't have been happier as a single father, wouldn't have been able to live a carefree life as a wealthy eligible bachelor, and certainly wouldn't have had what he wanted most: the comfort of a family. JB was quite straight with himself on this matter. He would have become a sad and lonely recluse. That was no longer true.

"Now, what about you?"

How much time do you have? JB cleared his throat. "I'm sure you heard. I've found myself in the middle of an...awful situation. You see, I attended a party where my husband's lover was murdered."

"I heard about Mr. Cuomo's death." Laird appeared impassive, as if he'd heard the rumors but decided to remain impartial. "That's why I'm asking what you're doing to take care of yourself. You see, in many ways, this murder is as traumatizing to Emilio as your cancer diagnosis. I'm suggesting you consider your well-being as an extension of your son's. Think of the safety instructions flight attendants give—put your mask on first before aiding others. Does that make sense?"

Laird's example hit JB with an unexpected lurch of unease. "I hadn't thought of it that way, but it makes complete sense." JB made out the spokes of light blue in Laird's irises. He experienced a thudding in his chest. Was this reaction genuine, or was JB defaulting to something more visceral to avoid acknowledging his emotional responsibilities as a parent?

"Thank you, Dr. Laird. You've given me a lot to think about."

"Call me Cliff."

* * *

Emilio was sitting quietly in the car with his eyes shut. JB imagined he felt like a man wrongfully accused of a crime who had been sprung free from prison. What long-term effect would this unwarranted ordeal have on his son? JB didn't know. "You want to grab cheeseburgers and fries?"

"You?" Emilio's head twisted. "Eat carbs?"

"Sky's the limit." JB buckled his seatbelt.

Emilio pressed his face against the glass, obliquely looking out. "You don't have to do this."

"Do what?"

"Overcompensate," Emilio muttered quietly.

JB reached over and squeezed his shoulder. "I'm not overcompensating."

Outside, it began to rain—a typical Hamptons summer storm that moved in quickly, drenching everything in warm showers. Steam on the scorching asphalt created swathes of mist that rose to obscure the view of the road. They drove in silence, with the only sounds being the patter of rain on the hood and the hypnotic whoosh of the windshield wipers. JB glanced over and noticed the dimple in Emilio's chin seemed more prominent, and his unruly curls tamed. He had the patchy stubble of a five o'clock shadow. Had he grown so much in only two days?

"Dad? What's going to happen?"

JB frowned over at him. "I don't know exactly, but I promise nothing will happen to you. Not ever again. Do you believe me?"

"I never stopped."

Emilio reached over, and JB felt the warmth of his hand on his. For the first time, he felt hope. How was it possible JB had believed he wouldn't be happy as a single father when, in the span of this short drive, he'd never felt more confident about his happiness? "Can I ask you a question?"

"You can ask me anything."

"I can handle most things, but your marriage is insane. It's affecting you in ways you don't even know. Can't you see that?"

"I see that now."

"Then why do you put up with Pop?" Emilio's question shook JB's confidence. "Sometimes, I see you as someone weak when I know you're not weak. You're strong, Dad. Why do you let him make you look so weak?"

JB, peering over at his son, couldn't distinguish the flush of emotion he experienced. He could hardly comprehend how to manage the worry on Emilio's face. "The police are going to want to speak with you again about the accusation you made."

Emilio stared at the window. Rivulets of water slid along the glass. "I know."

"They're going to ask why you believe Pop drugged you."

"Not drugged. Poisoned. Pop poisoned me."

JB sat up straight, unnerved by the ferocity of his reaction. "Do you recall Pop giving you something?"

"No, but I was drinking a soda. He could have spiked it while I was in the bathroom."

JB sensed a prickliness in Emilio's tone, a defensive reaction that told JB this was a road worth exploring. "And you're sure you had no contact with Mrs. Cuomo?"

"Dad, I didn't even know she was there until you told me. I was already out cold."

JB couldn't imagine how traumatizing it must be for a child, how unbelievable—how your sense of safety would implode, and the hurt would be too great to feel, too huge to understand.

"One more question," JB pursued. "You're sure that when you woke up in the Beltrams' basement the night of the party, you didn't see Pop sleeping next to you?"

Emilio swerved to stare straight into his father's face. "Dad, I was in the basement watching television when I fell asleep. I woke up briefly and saw Dr. Perrotta coming out of the bathroom. Pop wasn't with me."

JB stole seconds to look at his son, but the rain was intense. He had to keep his eye on the road. "What time was it when you saw Dr. Perrotta?"

"I don't know. I was so groggy. All I remember was that he was wearing a gold bathing suit."

What time had everyone decided to go swimming?

It was after Winnie had chosen the winners of best costume. JB recalled asking Angelo where Mike was. His response corroborated what Emilio had told him, that Mike was napping with Emilio when he went to use the bathroom, but that Mike was not there after he came out.

JB squinted through the windshield. The rain was easing up. The mist from the asphalt had drifted off the road toward the bay, so that JB could see clearly. "That's all for now. What's it going to be: pizza or cheeseburgers?"

"Sushi!"

JB offered an impressed nod. "Sushi it is, then."

JB tried to smile, concerned that the grimace he'd been wearing might only disturb Emilio more. He could only imagine the full implications of Emilio's accusation, complicating an already messy situation. What nagged at JB was why Mike had cleaned up after Emilio accused him of drugging him. Was Mike trying to make a statement about having given up alcohol? It made no sense, especially since Mike had already decided to move out. In the end, Mike would have to handle the consequences of his son's accusation on his own.

"Stop beating yourself up." Emilio tapped his father's temple. "You make that face."

"Got it. No more thinking." JB drove on, wondering: when had his little boy become such a perceptive man?

* * *

JB waited in the car while Emilio ran into the restaurant to pick up their order. They shouldn't dine in public; the scrutiny would be unbearable. The stares and whispers—JB refused to put Emilio through that.

Their lives were becoming smaller and more insular, confined to the walls of their home. Through the windshield, he watched a family laughing as they entered the restaurant, so casual and unaware. How he longed for this to pass, for some form of normalcy—whatever that was—to return, but even as that thought formed in his mind, he knew that until the police caught Gianni's killer, it wouldn't happen for a long time.

Across the street, the liquor store called to him. He jogged across the road, picked a bottle of Scotch off the shelf, and handed the cashier his credit card.

"JB?" He turned around to find Andy. "What a surprise."

JB cast a judgmental glance at the case of wine by Andy's feet.

"I texted you, but you never responded." An uneasy silence descended. "How's your son?"

"Good." JB signed the receipt, his hand tensing slightly around the pen. "He's actually in the car, waiting."

"I need to speak to you about Rakesh." Andy's voice had a pleading tone, appealing to JB's sense of empathy, but the timing couldn't have been worse. "We're having problems."

JB moved away from the cashier. "Rakesh is my best friend. I don't feel comfortable talking about him with you, especially in a liquor store."

"It's about that night." Andy squeezed JB's arm, nearly causing him to drop the bottle. "After we got home from the costume party, I woke up, and Rakesh wasn't in bed with me. I mean, he wasn't home. I looked everywhere. The car was gone."

JB snorted with disbelief. "What do you mean, he wasn't home?" He was already angry with himself for engaging in this conversation. "As I recall, you were pretty intoxicated at the party. Is it possible you were dreaming?"

"No. I waited up, but I fell asleep on the couch."

"Did you ask Rakesh?"

Andy leaned in and whispered, "He said he went out for a drive."

JB tore his arm from Andy's grip. "Well, there's your answer."

"I'm going to the police." Andy's voice wavered like a car swerving on black ice.

"Might I suggest you invest in some introspection before broadcasting your struggles to friends?"

"Funny how you share your opinion when no one asked, and yet, here I am begging for help, and you turn your back on me."

"I have to go. My son is waiting."

In the car, JB took several cleansing breaths, wondering if he'd been too harsh. He glanced at his reflection in the rearview mirror—and saw his father staring back. Those familiar eyes burned through him. JB didn't want to succumb to this anger, but at the same time, he felt a turbulent sensation in his stomach. Emilio had been discharged from the hospital after an overdose. For Andy to approach JB in public, to discuss his best friend—JB had hit his breaking point.

Breathe. In through your nostrils. Out through your mouth.

Emilio exited the restaurant. JB reached over to open the passenger side door. His cell phone dinged. It was another text from Luca:

I need to talk to you. PLEASE!!!

"The place was packed." Emilio strapped on his seatbelt. "What's the matter? I can tell something is wrong."

JB chuckled exhaustedly. "You really are an amazing kid...I mean, young man."

As he backed out of the parking spot, JB caught sight of Andy outside the liquor store in the rearview mirror. He was speaking to a man roughly his size, wearing dark sunglasses. Andy thrust the case of Chardonnay against the man's chest, and then he followed Andy to his car.

"Is everything all right?"

"Never better." JB shifted the car into drive and sped away.

* * *

They sat in the living room, watching television and eating sushi with chopsticks. JB sipped Scotch, feeling a warm, calming sensation run through his entire body as though he had been anesthetized. The rain continued throughout the evening. Emilio retired to his bedroom early, opting to watch a movie on his iPad. JB poured himself another drink and sat in his dark study, remaining still, listening only to the rain pelting against the window.

His cell phone rang. "Hello, Rakesh."

"How are you?"

"I hate that question."

"Understood, sir!" Rakesh shouted with military affectation. "I'll take out an ad in *Hamptons Magazine*: don't ask JB how he is. A sort of Leave Britney Alone campaign."

JB sat back, laughing at the sheer stupidity of it all. Only Rakesh could distract him from the troubling circumstances that had engulfed his family, even if only for a little while.

"Why don't I come over?" Rakesh suggested. "We'll have a sleepover like old times. You can spoon me."

"Not tonight, old friend. It's just Emilio and me for a while."

"Well, let's get together tomorrow. I'm not taking no for an answer."

"Okay," JB replied, "but come here. I'm not leaving Emilio alone." A bolt of lightning shot through the sky like an electrified bifurcating vein. "This rain is coming down, isn't it?"

Through the window, a figure loomed in the driveway. The face obscured in shadow. He moved closer to the glass, but the rain fell so hard that he could hardly see who it was—only that it was a man. An icy shiver of fear ran down JB's spine. The man stood in the driveway, staring at him.

Another bolt of lightning zigzagged through the night sky, causing JB to drop the phone. He started for the door, his heart racing. The kitchen light was on, and the bottle of Scotch left open on the counter was now empty. The front door was ajar, and rain poured into the foyer. Lightning struck again. The mysterious man stared up at the sky. JB reached over to turn on the exterior lights. As he squinted against the rain that blew against him, JB finally saw the man's face. He charged toward him. The gravel driveway was rutted with puddles.

"Emilio," JB shouted. "What are you doing out here?"

"Where am I?" Emilio didn't sound like himself—he sounded slow, wary. He didn't look like himself, either; his eyes were vacant, and his expression was dull. He didn't even smell like Emilio—there was a hint of burnt caramel.

JB escorted him inside, sat him down on the couch, and fetched towels. When he returned, Emilio was sleeping in an awkward position, snoring. JB removed his wet clothes and toweled him dry as best he could. The open bottle of Scotch in the kitchen crossed JB's mind—Emilio certainly had the smell of liquor on his breath.

There was no use in confronting him now. He would talk with him in the morning. However well JB thought he knew Emilio, it was obvious now he knew very little. Dr. Laird's words echoed in his head: *Consider your well-being as an extension of your son's.*

It was apparent JB had to do exactly that for Emilio's sake.

Chapter Twenty-Nine

JB flipped through a tabloid, the glossy pages sticking to his sweaty fingertips. Every few seconds, his eyes darted to the office door, willing it to open. The small waiting room with its sage walls, mid-century apricot chairs, and geometric paintings felt like a cell. No sound penetrated the thick silence. It was well before normal office hours—the sky outside still held the gray pallor of dawn. After finding Emilio outside, face upturned to the pouring rain, JB had called Laird's service. Thankfully, Laird had called him immediately.

JB's world was falling apart. At any minute, he expected Detectives Sullivan and D'Amico to burst through the doors, badges flashing, handcuffs jangling—ready to arrest him for murder. His thoughts raced in desperate loops: If only the DNA results would be delayed. If only he could have a few more days to secure Emilio somewhere safe. If only he'd chosen different paths to escape the consequences of his worst decision. If only...

Emilio's well-being was the only fixed point in JB's crumbling world. While waiting for his son's therapy session to end, JB called the dean at Columbia, his voice carefully modulated to hide his desperation. He explained that under the circumstances, he would not return for the fall semester. The dean sounded relieved. The scandal would be "too much of a distraction." It would be best, they agreed, to wait until… "everything got sorted out."

The metallic click of Laird's door opening snapped JB to attention. He stood up immediately. Emilio met his gaze and offered a weak smile. Even now, the image of his son standing in the dark, rain-soaked night haunted

JB. The next morning, as JB suspected, Emilio's recollection was fuzzy. Only that he'd admitted to drinking the Scotch. "To fall asleep," Emilio had said, voice small, like a child confessing to stealing a cookie.

"Can I speak with you?" Laird asked.

JB glanced at Emilio, who had slumped into a chair, arms folded tightly across his chest. "I'll only be a little while."

JB sat perched on the edge of the chair, his right knee bobbing. Recently, he'd fallen into the habit of tremoring his limbs as if they were malfunctioning electric equipment instead of appendages.

Laird cleared his throat and straightened his spine. "As I suspected, your son is suffering from a severe case of post-traumatic stress disorder. Drinking your Scotch was his way of self-medicating." Laird's clinical tone made the diagnosis both detached and grave. "Emilio admits to having nightmares. They began shortly after your cancer diagnosis. The alcohol helps him sleep."

"Emilio has been drinking all this time?" JB's voice cracked on the last word.

Laird offered a curt nod. "I know this comes as a shock. His alcohol misuse is a warning sign that he's struggling to process these traumatic experiences."

The room felt vacuum-sealed and superheated. Stifling air pressed against JB's skin, drawing beads of sweat along his hairline. "It's funny," he muttered, the words scraping his throat, "you try so hard to protect your children, but it's not easy." He peered up at Laird. "Do you have children?"

"No, but you shouldn't blame yourself, not completely."

"Why not?"

Laird leaned forward. "Describe what it felt like seeing your son outside in the rain."

JB blinked at the unexpected redirection. "I felt frightened, I suppose..." he began, the words, feeling inadequate. "Frightened is the best way to describe how I felt."

"Frightened of what?"

"Frightened my son had hurt himself."

"What else? What are you feeling right now?"

"I'm feeling uncomfortable." JB shifted in his seat. "I'm uncomfortable talking about myself. It makes me…"

"Go on," Laird urged, voice gentle but insistent. "Say the first thing that comes to mind."

"Frustrated," JB spoke as if the word were a bone in his throat that he'd finally dislodged. "I feel stifled and frustrated with this"—he gestured vaguely—"this difficult situation."

"Do you feel like a frustrated father dealing with his difficult child?"

"You don't get to talk to me like that. You're not my father!" JB's spine stiffened, hands gripping the chair arms.

Laird held up his hands, his expression carefully calibrated to convey understanding. "My only concern is for Emilio, but I strongly believe you need to work on yourself. It's the only way you and your son will move past these traumatic experiences. If you don't put in the work now, you're only setting a poor example for Emilio."

"Tell me what I have to do."

"Have you thought about seeing a therapist?"

JB squeezed shut his eyes, the darkness behind his lids providing him with no escape. "Can we focus on Emilio for now?"

"For now," Laird conceded with a slight nod, "you must support and encourage Emilio to confront the truth. Only then will he have any hope of recovery."

"What truth?" The question felt dangerous like stepping onto thin ice.

"Your son is extremely protective of you. He blames Mike for everything that happened this past year. When Emilio woke up in the hospital after drinking your Scotch, his intense anger toward Mike may have motivated him to implicate your husband."

Intense anger?

The unresolved murder of Gianni Cuomo pointed at Emilio again. JB had brushed aside his suspicions once he learned the baseball bat had been stolen, but he never quite forgot Emilio's reaction—the raw ferocity with which he swung the bat—that night after Mike stormed away from them at the party.

But now, knowing that when Emilio woke up in the emergency room after an overdose—an overdose likely intended for JB since it was his Scotch that had been tampered with—his son had immediately concluded that Mike was behind it all.

"My son is not angry," JB insisted. "He's frustrated and confused. That's all, Dr. Laird."

JB would have preferred not to sound defensive, but they were speaking about his son, after all. Now that he was essentially a single parent, both mother and father to Emilio, JB felt compelled to defend him at any cost. Even if it meant defending him from the truth.

"I'll see Emilio on Monday," Laird said with finality. "I'm available by cell if anything comes up over the weekend."

The unspoken message was clear: *And something will come up.*

* * *

In his study, JB crafted a list while Emilio sunbathed by the pool. Lists had always been JB's salvation—a way to impose order on chaos, a checklist to keep him regimented, sane.

1. Inquire about finding a tutor to homeschool Emilio.
2. Email the completed syllabus to the dean at Columbia.
3. Follow up with Angelo about lab work.

His cell phone shattered the silence, making him jump. JB stared at the unknown number, his pulse galloping. "Mr. Pulaski, it's Detective D'Amico."

Here it comes. The results of the DNA report that will implicate me.

"Sorry to bother you, but we can't locate your husband."

Her words took a moment to register. JB glanced out the window and saw his son sleeping on a lounge chair, face peaceful for the first time since his overdose.

"Mr. Pulaski, are you there?"

"I have no idea where Mike is, and quite frankly, I couldn't care less."

"I would think you would care very much under the circumstances."

JB's father's voice clawed its way up from memory's depths, as sharp and cutting as ever: *Only cowards and weak-minded men put their families in harm's way. You must be strong, but I don't think you have it in you.*

The silver clock ticked relentlessly. JB let the silence stretch, willing himself to prove his father wrong. "Mike has a sister. I'll call her. Maybe she knows where he is."

"That would be most helpful."

The phone barely rang once. "JB, my love, what a pleasure hearing your voice. I won't ask how you are. You must be a wreck. What can I do for you?"

Leslie's directness didn't surprise JB. Mike's eldest sister had always been a control freak—efficient, bossy, and brutally honest. Throughout his chemo and radiation, Leslie had checked on him often, never hiding her disgust at Mike's infidelities. It was the main reason she stopped visiting. Leslie couldn't bear to be around her brother and his strays. During her last visit, JB had noticed the siblings often whispered, their conversations animated and charged with mutual antipathy.

"Mike moved out," JB explained. "Emilio…" He faltered, a lump rising in his throat, threatening to choke him. "Emilio was in the hospital after an accidental overdose. The police want to question Mike, but he's disappeared."

"Jesus Christ," Leslie breathed. "Not again."

This statement hit JB like the great swing of an ax on an old tree trunk. "What do you mean, *again?*"

"First of all, how is Emilio?"

JB explained what had happened and reassured her that Emilio was stable. But he immediately wanted Leslie to explain what she meant by, *again.*

"You remember Alex, poor, poor Alex?"

JB had never met Mike's older brother. He only knew that Alex had killed himself when they were teenagers. An overdose.

"Alex and Mike were so close when they were younger," Leslie explained.

"My mother referred to them as her 'Irish twins' because they were born eighteen months apart. I don't know why or when it happened exactly, but Mike began to resent Alex. We chalked it up to plain old sibling rivalry. Once they entered high school, they experimented with drugs and alcohol. Typical teenage stuff." She paused. "It's funny. I always thought Mike was the out-of-control one. That's why it surprised everyone when Alex overdosed."

Terror crashed over JB. His fingers began to tingle. "Leslie, what are you insinuating?"

"My love," she replied, her voice softening, "Mike can be a selfish prick, but I love him. What he did to you during your hour of need pissed me off, but it didn't surprise me." She sighed. "After Alex died, Mike developed an irrational fear of dying. Soon after the funeral, Mike disappeared. It pulled everyone's focus away from Alex, but then I noticed that Mike reacted the same way after our father died."

JB's mind drifted, struggling to connect this decades-old family tragedy to his son's current crisis.

"It's Mike's way of coping with his fear of mortality," she continued. "He did the same after you were diagnosed with cancer. Distracting himself with those silly men instead of being a supportive husband. And now, it seems, he's run away again after Emilio's overdose. It's what Mike does when confronted with the possibility of death."

JB's eyes drifted to the window. Emilio was swimming laps. Each stroke, precise and determined. "Well, if you hear from Mike," JB said, still processing everything Leslie had revealed, "please, tell him to call me."

"If you want my advice, don't worry about Mike. He's fine. Let the police do their job, and you do yours. Take care of my nephew."

JB hesitated, then asked the question that had been crystallizing like ice in his veins. "Leslie, one last thing. What did Alex overdose from?"

"Xanax, I think. Or was it Valium?" Leslie's voice wavered slightly before hardening with certainty. "Either way, he overdosed on benzodiazepines."

The phone turned to lead in JB's hand. Benzodiazepines—the same class of drug found in Emilio's system, the same drug reportedly in Gianni's bloodstream. Not a coincidence, but a pattern.

The pieces aligned with sickening clarity. JB had been staring at a family legacy of tragedy without recognizing its dark echoes in the present.

"JB? Are you still there?"

"Yes," he managed, though his mind was already reexamining every memory through this new, terrible lens. "Thank you, Leslie. I think I understand now."

And he did understand—perhaps for the first time since this nightmare began. The question wasn't whether Mike was capable of such acts—it was whether JB had spent years willfully blind to the monster sleeping beside him.

Chapter Thirty

There were flickers of moments when it felt like this endless journey through human misery couldn't get any worse, and the only bright spots were seeing his son acting normal. As JB watched Emilio swim, he felt encouraged things could be good again. They could be normal.

Right after JB hung up with Leslie, Rakesh pulled into the driveway. He retrieved two large canvas bags full of groceries from the back seat. *What's he doing here?* And then he recalled their conversation the night before, and the plans they'd made to spend the afternoon together.

The intense challenges he and Emilio had faced this week blurred time, crowding out the ordinary memories. Emilio spotted Rakesh struggling with the groceries and hopped out of the pool to help. This random act of kindness was not akin to someone who would plot to undermine his father. He recalled what Laird had insinuated about Emilio or rather, what he'd gleaned from their conversation. True, Emilio was traumatized and had been self-medicating with alcohol. Emilio had admitted that much on his own, but beyond inflicting pain upon himself, Emilio was not a violent person.

"JB, where are you?" Rakesh's booming voice heralded his entrance as he stepped through the front door. "Get your ass out here. The sun is shining, I bought ribs to barbecue, and there's a cocktail with your name on it."

Even watching Rakesh unpack the groceries and haphazardly attempt to put them away without concern for where they should go, JB experienced a relief that only his best friend could provide. Emilio buzzed around him like a child marveling at a circus clown, assisting him. Given the demoralizing events of this past week, JB and his son needed this distraction.

"You're making a mess." JB shooed Rakesh out of the kitchen. "Go outside. I'll handle the groceries."

It was noon and nearly ninety degrees Fahrenheit. JB joined Emilio and Rakesh by the pool, handing out glasses of freshly brewed iced tea and gluten-free chips. Rakesh took a sip and spat it out like a sitcom actor. "Where's the hooch?"

"These are hooch-less." JB glowered.

"*Mmm,*" Rakesh feigned with scintillating appreciation. "Delish."

Emilio sat on the opposite end of the pool, sunning and listening to music while JB and Rakesh lounged in the shade.

"How are you?" Rakesh asked. JB scoffed with obvious annoyance. "I'm kidding. I know how much you hate that question."

"Let's go inside and talk." JB offered Rakesh a smiling but steely reminder that Emilio could still hear them even with his earbuds in. "Emilio, we're going to prep for lunch." When Emilio didn't respond, JB rolled his eyes at Rakesh. "Like he didn't hear me. I swear that boy is part canine."

In the kitchen, Rakesh fixed them martinis while JB prepped egg salad sandwiches. "Drink up." Rakesh handed him the glass, "and don't even think about saying no."

JB hesitated briefly before taking a sip, savoring the taste. "Promise me you'll take all the alcohol home with you when you leave."

"About that." Rakesh cleared his throat. "Would you mind terribly if I crashed here for a few days?"

JB noted the physical tension that wiped across Rakesh's face. "What happened?"

"I need a break from Andy. He has demons he needs to resolve, and until he does that, I refuse to be around him."

"I wasn't going to mention this, but I ran into Andy yesterday, stocking up on Chardonnay. He wanted to talk about you, but I had just picked up Emilio at the hospital. Something about you going out after leaving the Beltrams' costume party." JB turned away, thinking. "Come to think of it, he may have been a little drunk when I saw him."

"Andy refuses to acknowledge that he has a problem. 'Everyone drinks out here,' he said, but I explained that most people can hold their liquor. Most people don't throw up in the Beltrams' gardenias during a costume party."

"Well, you're welcome to stay for as long as you like." Never would JB have imagined that he would be sharing a house with his former college roommate. It hardly seemed worth questioning; it was only to be grateful for. "Is what Andy said true? That you went out after returning home from the party?"

This question sat between them like some dull and unpleasant meal.

"I'm going to tell you the whole story." Rakesh sighed with resignation. "After we got home, Andy continued to drink. What you don't know—what you don't see because I've been shielding Andy is that he can be a pretty nasty drunk. Normally, I don't engage, but that night...it got physical."

JB had a burst of memory: days after the party, while Rakesh lectured Angelo about relationships, JB noted bruising on his forearms. "The black and blues on your arms. Rakesh, I'm so sorry you had to go through this alone."

"Love is a battlefield." Rakesh raised his glass. "Thankfully, I have you."

They finished their martinis and eventually joined Emilio by the pool. He was swimming laps again. JB watched his son's arms cut swiftly through the water.

"Emilio looks great," Rakesh said.

"He's becoming a beautiful man, and I truly believe Cliff is going to help us heal."

Rakesh lurched forward, clutching his throat. "Wait. Hold up. Who, pray tell, is Cliff?"

JB immediately regretted mentioning Laird by his first name. "He's Emilio's psychiatrist. That's all."

Rakesh's lips closed like a purse clasp. "I'll leave it at that...for now."

"Will you?" JB was fairly sure Rakesh would circle back to the topic of Cliff Laird once they were alone.

What a coincidence these two best friends found themselves in, both separated from their partners. Even without looking at Rakesh directly, JB wondered if he felt the same.

Emilio appeared, standing before them, dripping wet. His dark curls, his tan skin glistening in the sunlight. "Would it be all right if I go to Montauk with Evan's family?"

"Not today, son."

Emilio dropped his head and walked away. "You can't keep him a prisoner," Rakesh said. "Besides, isn't Evan's father a police officer?"

"You're a bad influence."

"Let him enjoy the final days of summer."

A little while later, a car pulled into the driveway. JB stood up and waved to Evan's parents as Emilio hopped in the car. Rakesh had already run into the house to fetch more alcohol. JB debated whether drinking was completely inappropriate. He knew he shouldn't drink in front of his son. Obviously, Emilio knew they had been drinking. He wasn't stupid, though his internal dialogue was less of a debate and more like encouragement to allow himself to relax on this beautiful day with his best friend. They deserved it after all they'd been through.

An hour and several more cocktails later, Rakesh and JB sat in the shallow end of the pool. The water up to their chins, blotto. "My how the mighty Beltrams have fallen," Rakesh opined.

JB scoffed. "They brought it on themselves."

"What's so unbelievable is that Gianni had the nerve to show up at their party as Mike's guest. Now that's cold-blooded." Rakesh went on to say that the television network had decided to put Winnie's series on pause until the scandal got sorted out. "Guess fans will have to chef's kiss her show goodbye. The Beltrams are done."

At the same time, it annoyed JB to think how this would play out. "You're wrong," he said, standing up. "Mr. Utters will go to rehab. Winnie will disappear from the public eye for a few months, maybe a year, and then the two will reemerge as the sweet couple we all knew and loved, now completely rehabilitated. It's happened so many times before. Martha Stewart. Paula Deen…shall I go on?"

"Not unless one is found guilty of murder." Rakesh handed his martini to JB. "Drink up."

"Murder?" JB hadn't once entertained the thought that the Beltrams were capable of murder. Certainly, Winnie had the opportunity when she ran to fetch Mike another pill. What if she had given them Rohypnol? Now JB remembered something he didn't give much thought to at the time: when Winnie returned with the pills—shaking the bottle like a maraca—she had changed clothes, again!

JB lay slack along the pool steps, staring up at the sun, wondering how long they'd been drinking. "We should eat something." The sound of his voice made him think he was far more inebriated than he suspected, and Rakesh, apparently, was not. What had brought JB to this point? The past few weeks, he'd felt as if he were living life in a disembodied way. Now, he felt heavy. The side of his face pressed along the hot wooden pool deck. "Rakesh," he called out, loudly. "Rakesh, help me. I'm drunk." A pair of dark feet appeared. JB grabbed at his best friend's ankles.

Rakesh squatted, offering him another martini. "Drink this. You'll feel better."

"Why did I do this? I'm a horrible parent."

Rakesh helped JB sit up so he wouldn't spill a drop. "As bad as you feel right now, there are endless versions of worse out there."

This was the most profound wisdom JB had ever heard, and then everything went black.

Chapter Thirty-One

JB shuddered awake.

The room was dark. It occurred to him that he was in his bed. No, not his bedroom. Mike's bed.

What happened?

Somehow, he was able to piece together a series of events—the ones he could remember. Rakesh had come over. They'd drunk alcohol. A lot of alcohol. For a long moment, maddeningly long, he lay still. He heard the low rumble of jagged breathing. Someone was in the room with him.

In the bed, no less!

JB had no thought other than he needed to get out of this bed. He needed to find Rakesh.

Where is Rakesh?

It occurred to him then. He knew that jagged breathing. He was intimately aware of it, having lived with that jagged breather for years. It belonged to Rakesh. When JB turned around, his suspicions were confirmed.

The sight of Rakesh—his face smooshed against the pillow—hit JB with the force of a physical blow. The familiar snoring pattern, the slight whistle on each exhale that had once been the soundtrack to their college years, now seemed a damning indictment of his parental failures.

"Wake up!" JB's voice emerged strangled and desperate. He had invited Rakesh to stay, had poured the drinks, had continued drinking long after he should have stopped, all while his son was recovering from trauma. "Rakesh, wake up!"

"What?" he replied, groggily shifting against the pillows.

"What did we do?" JB leapt out of bed only to discover he was naked.

Rakesh looked up blearily from his side of the bed, squinting. "Why are you shouting? And why are you naked?"

And here JB was, rushing into the bathroom for a towel, having done the very thing he shouldn't have done as a father to a son who had been self-medicating with alcohol to deal with his parents' poor choices.

JB instantly felt wide awake. He reached for the clock. It read six p.m. "Where's my phone?" He groped around the bedroom floor, searching for it. In the process, he located his swim trunks. Clumsily, he pulled them on while hopping on one leg. Then he began scavenging the floor, the chair, and the dresser for his phone.

"It's right here," Rakesh said, holding it up. "It was on your pillow."

There was a text from Emilio:

Going to dinner with Evan's family. Be home @ 10.

Rakesh's grin widened. "You're hysterical."

JB ignored him, texting Emilio back:

Have fun. See you later.

JB collapsed on the bed and started the process of steadying his breathing. He inhaled deeply through his nose, exhaling fully out his mouth. After four or five cycles, he felt in control. "Did we...?"

Rakesh peered up at him with sincere dark eyes. "Doubt it."

"But I was naked."

Rakesh shifted his body so that his cheek was pressed against JB's chest. "And yet, I'm still wearing my swim trunks."

"Thank God." Finally, JB relented and drew Rakesh closer, kissing the top of his head. "More than anything, I didn't want to drink in front of Emilio, and not only did I get shit-faced, I woke up naked with my best friend."

"Technically, you didn't drink in front of Emilio," Rakesh reasoned while twirling his finger in JB's chest hair. "And I recall waking up many mornings naked next to you in college."

"We were in our twenties."

"I miss being twenty." Rakesh closed his eyes, sighing. "Remember when we were roommates and fooled around? No strings attached." Rakesh's hand reached under the covers.

JB grabbed it. "Stop."

"Oh, come on. Let's give it the old college try."

"I said stop! What's wrong with you?"

"What's wrong with me?" Rakesh spoke so fiercely that it sounded almost like a growl. "Excuse me if suddenly I repel you."

"I didn't mean that."

But it was too late. Rakesh stormed into the bathroom and slammed the door. His outburst seemed so out of character, it was jarring. JB was about to knock on the door to apologize when his cell phone rang.

"Jason and I want to stop by in an hour," Angelo said cheerfully. "Is that okay?"

"Okay. See you soon." JB hung up and stood outside the bathroom door. He knocked once. "Can we talk?"

The door flung open. "What?"

"Jason and Angelo are coming over in an hour."

"Lovely."

"Rakesh," JB began. "About before…it has nothing to do with you. Understand?"

"You're not the only one who's suffering, JB. I'm going through my own marital problems. I get you don't want to complicate our friendship with sex, but you could be more considerate of my feelings."

"You're right." JB held Rakesh's hips. "I'm sorry. Can we turn this around and start over?"

Rakesh found a smirk to glue onto his face. "Fix me a drink, and I'll forget all about it."

The bathroom door slammed shut again. JB heard the shower running. He retreated to his bedroom, feeling like such an ass. Rakesh had not expressed such a terse shift in his demeanor in such a long time. It was, he had to admit, an aggressive reaction, and it had JB wondering how much his best friend had been suffering and for how long.

JB changed into white slacks and a fitted blue short-sleeved shirt. He fixed Rakesh a martini and set it on the nightstand in Mike's bedroom. Then he grabbed the ribs Rakesh had brought and started the barbecue.

Less than an hour later, Angelo and Jason arrived. They emerged from their car, appearing chipper as usual. Angelo wore a white tank top over black shorts. Jason had on a black tank top and white shorts. "Do you two always coordinate outfits? Oh, and by the way, Rakesh is here."

Angelo eyed Jason excitedly. "Rakesh and Andy are here? Perfect."

"Not exactly. Rakesh is staying with me for a few days."

"Wait. What?" Angelo clasped JB's wrist. "Rakesh left Andy?"

"Yes, I did." Rakesh appeared, carrying dishes and utensils, to set the table. "That's a new world record, JB."

"I'm sorry, Rakesh, but you were going to tell them anyway."

"That's right. I was going to tell them. The operative word being 'I.'"

"I'm sorry to hear that, Rakesh." Angelo turned to Jason. "We should go."

Rakesh set down the plates so that they rattled against the table. "You two aren't going anywhere. I bought ribs." JB offered Jason and Angelo a tense smile. Rakesh continued to hostilely set the table, ignoring them until he was done. "How long before dinner, JB?"

"About another thirty minutes."

"Lovely," Rakesh replied tartly. "I bought sides. Jason, can you help me?"

He nodded and followed Rakesh into the house, glancing nervously back at Angelo as he walked away.

Angelo whispered, "How much has he had to drink?"

JB mouthed, *A lot.*

Rakesh returned with containers of coleslaw and potato salad. Jason handed Angelo a beer.

"Let's sit," JB suggested.

"Sorry for stopping by unexpectedly," Angelo began, "but Jason and I wanted you to be the first to know."

JB stared at them expectantly. "What is it?"

"Dear God," Rakesh groaned. "You're engaged."

Angelo bounced in his seat. "Surprise!"

The good news was a welcome relief, at least, to move past the awkward predicament JB had manufactured, getting intoxicated and winding up in bed with his best friend.

"Well, if you're hell-bent on torturing yourselves," Rakesh spoke in that inimitably terse way of his that made any further discussion on the topic seem ridiculous, "then this calls for champagne."

"Sorry." The smile on JB's face dissolved. "Mike threw out all the liquor."

"Not a problem." Rakesh stood up. "I'll make us a round of martinis. Jason, don't even think about having that beer. An engagement calls for hard liquor."

They sipped cocktails and ate ribs around the picnic table. There was a silent agreement that no one would bring up Gianni's murder, Gus Beltram's incendiary photos, Emilio's accusations against Mike, or Rakesh and JB separating from their spouses.

They felt poised on a tragic precipice. There were many things they wanted to know, but it was hardly the right time. Life was too precious and too short. All of it, at any time, might be pulled out from under them so swiftly that they would find themselves lying on their backs, helpless, even before they realized what had happened. Sitting with his friends, celebrating Angelo and Jason's engagement, JB, for the briefest moment, forgot his troubles.

But only for the briefest moment.

"By the way," Rakesh started in. "JB had sex with Luca after he left James and John's party. Oh, and Luca is Gianni Cuomo's brother-in-law. Isn't that right, JB?" His grin was as wide as a gator's.

Touché.

It began to drizzle. They hurriedly cleared the table and ran into the house as the downpour hit. They were assembled in the living room when Rakesh started in again, "So, what shall we talk about next?"

Angelo shifted uncomfortably. "I'm still trying to process how JB ended up having sex with Gianni Cuomo's brother-in-law."

"Anyone care for another round?" JB offered.

Rakesh held his empty glass upside down. "Yes, please."

Jason and Angelo declined, and so, JB returned to the kitchen to fix Rakesh another drink. Angelo followed him. "I hate to be the bearer of bad news,"

Angelo began, "but can you come by the office on Monday? The lab messed up, and I need to redraw your blood."

"What else can go wrong today?" JB took two cleansing breaths.

"What's going on with Rakesh?"

JB sighed heavily, his shoulders sagging with resignation. "Andy's situation has been tough on him. We should cut him some slack." He met Angelo's gaze with pleading eyes. "I'll swing by your office after I drop Emilio off at therapy. We can talk everything through then."

JB prayed the conversation had shifted to something pleasant once they returned to the living room. No such luck. Rakesh was interrogating Jason about the Beltrams. "Why haven't they arrested them? They had motive, and witnesses said Winnie was handing out drugs."

"You seriously think Winnie and Gus Beltram are capable of murder?" Angelo asked.

JB let out a snort of laughter. "A question no one in the Hamptons ever thought they'd hear."

"Don't underestimate a woman scorned." Rakesh stood for yet another soapbox lecture. "Hear me out. A poor girl from the Bronx makes it big as a home-schooled cook and marries a closeted queen. Riding high as a TV host and bestselling author, her husband's affair with a hustler threatens to destroy everything she's worked for. Imagine the years in kitchens—peeling, chopping, toiling over boiling water, enduring burns and blisters—and for what?

For some rent boy to worm his way in and blackmail her? No, not Winnie *fucking* Beltram. She's too smart for that. So, what does she do? She invites this piano-playing hustler to a costume party, slips him enough sedatives so that he can barely stand in the shallow end of the pool, and when no one's looking, she bops him on the head with a bat. Problem solved."

"I'll admit," Jason began, offering a slow clap, "you make a great argument. Except the police never recovered the murder weapon, and the rest of your case is purely circumstantial."

Angelo scooted over to kiss Jason's cheek. "Isn't my fiancé sexy when he talks all lawyer-like?"

It was obvious Rakesh had given Gianni's murder some thought. Had he gone public with his theory, JB wondered, or opted instead for the more private sanctum of his best friend's living room? JB assumed the former. Still, he wondered where Rakesh had gone that evening of the costume party. He'd given JB the impression that after rushing Andy home before he could cause a scene, they'd engaged in a physical confrontation. Had Rakesh gone for a drive to clear his head while a drunk Andy passed out in their bed? For now, JB had no reason to question him. None at all.

Chapter Thirty-Two

Monday morning, JB drove Emilio to his appointment with Dr. Laird. Afterward, he stopped at Angelo's office to have his blood work repeated.

"You're going to feel a little pinch," the phlebotomist warned.

"You couldn't hurt me even if you tried."

Once the blood draw was complete and they were alone, JB sat on the exam table, towering over Angelo. "I've been meaning to ask you a question, but I didn't want to add fuel to the inferno Rakesh started regarding Luca. It's about Emilio's toxicology report. It came back positive for benzodiazepines. Is there a way to determine if it was Rohypnol specifically?"

"They don't routinely test for Rohypnol," Angelo explained. "You should ask his psychiatrist if they still have his urine sample."

"Why can't they use fresh urine?"

"After two days, there won't be any trace of the drug in his system." This fact hadn't even entered JB's mind—he'd been too fixated on connecting Emilio's overdose to Gianni's toxicology report. "Do you really think Mike tried to poison Emilio?"

Eyes shut. Three deep breaths. Dread coursed through his body like reverse meditation designed to heighten his anxiety rather than relieve it. "Objectively, I don't believe Mike would do such a thing. Then again, Mike never told me that he'd met Dale and Alfie, let alone sold them a house, and I can't help but wonder if Mike may have had real feelings for Gianni"—his entire body went rigid—"you saw how they carried on at the party."

"They were high."

JB ran his hand along his forehead. "How is it that one day you realize that a sentient husband, with the same priorities and plans as you, is not the man you thought he was?"

"You two have certainly had more than your share of challenges this past year," Angelo replied. "I'm not sure most marriages would have survived."

"Mine hasn't."

"Do you think it's over?"

"I do. I really do."

"I hoped you two would work things out," Angelo added. "As for Rakesh and Andy, I'm not surprised they broke up."

"You're not?"

Angelo turned away, chin down. JB had seen him do this time and again. It was the way he looked when he had to ponder something further before answering. "This may sound bitchy, but doesn't Andy come off a bit... trashy?"

JB wriggled his head for dramatic emphasis. "Well, well, Dr. Perrotta. It appears you are now officially a Hamptons snob."

Angelo's face flushed. "I knew you were going to make fun of me."

JB pressed a hand across his heart. "Look who you're talking to. King of snobs here."

"Now I know you're making fun of me." Angelo buried his face in his hands. "The Staten Island pot calling the Tampa kettle black."

JB pulled Angelo's hands away from his face. "Darling, you are no longer that little boy living on the island of Staten. You are a handsome doctor, soon to be married to a hot lawyer. I'd say you've come a long way."

"Thank you," Angelo said as his normal skin tone returned. "Do you understand what I mean about Andy, though?"

"Trashy? Yes, in a way."

"Isn't it funny?" Angelo paused with a tentative expression. "That you and Rakesh both married..."

"Go on," JB urged. "How did two Hamptons snobs marry poor white trash?"

Angelo blushed again. "I didn't say that."

Now it was JB who turned his head to ponder his reply. His mind drifted back to that night he'd met Mike. They'd spoken for hours, drinking and laughing. "When I think about it, Mike provided me with everything my life was lacking. Over the years, I suppose, my lifestyle rubbed off on him. He became intoxicated by the allure of meeting the right people and attending the right parties, when the only thing I grew to enjoy was staying home with our son. I guess, you could say I poisoned Mike."

"You didn't poison Mike. You grew apart. Cancer does that."

"Anyway," JB muttered. "Water under the bridge."

"And now you have your old college roommate back."

"That's another mess."

"You two seemed at odds on Saturday."

JB heaved a long sigh. "I'm chalking that up to too much alcohol and displaced anger."

Angelo scooted forward, eager to hear the details. "What happened?"

"We got drunk and ended up in bed together." JB held up a hand before Angelo had a chance to jump in. "Nothing happened, but Rakesh was being… more than a little aggressive. Once I made it clear sex was out of the question, he turned embittered as though I had insulted him. Thank God you showed up with good news."

Angelo had an odd smile, lips pressed together in a display of incredulity. "I mean…whatever went on between the two of you as college roommates, it's obvious Rakesh still has feelings for you."

JB swatted his hand. "He does not."

"Come on, JB."

But the memories came hurling at him, unstoppable and absurd: an inseparable friendship, sloppy drunken sex, and an unwavering loyalty. "Yes, we fooled around, occasionally, but that was decades ago."

The disbelieving grin on Angelo's face broadened so that JB sensed he viewed his relationship with Rakesh differently. "As your friend and as an observer, I can only say that Rakesh warmed up to me after he knew I was head over heels in love with Jason. Immediately, I thought, 'This man is not interested in sharing JB.' He's the number one friend, and that's okay, but you must know he still feels a certain way toward you?"

What began as wary roommates had over time morphed into friendship and then to devotion. JB and Rakesh shared a bond borne from their parallel twisted upbringings. Over the years, JB had noticed Rakesh's lingering gazes, his unnecessary touches, but he'd chosen to ignore them.

He'd chalked it up as being another one of Rakesh's collectibles—his precious friend, neatly catalogued and displayed. But hearing Angelo speak so objectively about it, and recalling the cold fury in Rakesh's tone after JB had refused his sexual advances, it was apparent that perhaps he'd dangerously underestimated the depth of Rakesh's feelings.

Yes, they'd had sex, especially after nights of heavy drinking. They were both young, horny gay men with limited options on campus. But to JB, there was nothing especially meaningful—let alone romantic—about those encounters. It was just sex.

Enter Mike.

Right away, Rakesh had voiced his disapproval, and when it was clear that Mike wasn't simply another fling, Rakesh had grown distant, quiet, and became more outgoing with other friends, leaving JB to cultivate his newfound relationship.

"And here I was, thinking the whole time Rakesh had a crush on you," JB offered.

"Me?" Angelo chuckled. "Why would you think that?"

"In a way, you remind me of Andy…physically, that is."

"Maybe a little." Angelo stood up to walk JB out. "And now here you are, the two college roommates reunited under the same roof again, single. Coincidence?"

JB's phone buzzed. "Saved by the bell." Another message from Luca. He'd been texting all weekend, but JB saw no point in hearing him out. What could he learn from him that he already didn't know?

"Everything okay?"

JB shook his head and laughed wearily. "How do you get rid of a persistent Italian?"

"Tell him you're allergic to sausage."

CHAPTER THIRTY-TWO

"Too late for that." JB dropped his head back, exhaling.

"Aren't you curious to hear what he has to say?"

"Not an ounce."

Angelo ran a hand through his dark hair. "That's where we're different. I would love nothing more than to confront Luca, tell him he's the type of Italian who makes us look like stereotypical pieces of shit."

"Why would I tell Luca off? He's not the scumbag. His brother-in-law was."

"Is that so?"

Had he come to Luca's defense too quickly, and even if he had, he wondered if lurking under his own smug indifference, simmering beneath, was a desire to see Luca once more.

No! He's a liar.

And the entire story he'd fabricated and perpetuated—the rich client who once was interested in financing a chain of restaurants for Winnie Beltram, the same client who'd hired him to find a house in the Hamptons—lies.

To what end?

All to conceal that he was Gianni Cuomo's brother-in-law. But what if Daria Cuomo had spoken the truth, that she'd asked her brother to spy on her husband while he was abroad to avoid another scandal?

No! Luca is a liar. "Once a liar, always a liar" was what JB's father always said.

Yet, there was no denying a scintillating spark existed between them, still smoldering amongst the ashes of those blazing lies.

"Have you spoken to Mike?"

Angelo's question shook JB from his thoughts. "He's disappeared, apparently."

Angelo grimaced. "Are you worried?"

JB knew what he was thinking: missing in action after Emilio was found unconscious. Mike's subsequent failure to check in on his son could only be described as suspicious and deplorable.

"About Mike? No. Emilio is my number one priority now." JB rubbed the bandage where the phlebotomist had drawn his blood. "When will you have the results?"

"In a day or so."

"Let's have lunch this weekend," JB suggested.

"I'd like that."

* * *

The entire drive home, JB was absorbed in the question of why Mike had abandoned their son until he was pulled from his reverie by the sight of a red Fiat in his driveway. Immediately, JB felt besieged, his defenses walled up around him. For a while, he sat there staring at the man in his garden.

JB had to confront him. This had to end now. It would only complicate matters if Luca persisted—and from his actions, he was quite persistent.

"Hello, JB." Luca had a jovial expression, but underneath, JB sensed his woundedness.

Good.

"You're mad," Luca continued. "I see it in your face."

"Mad? Why would I be mad?

"Because I didn't tell you Gianni was my brother-in-law."

"Oh, that. I'm not mad. I'd have to care to be mad."

Now it was impossible not to hear the rebuke. JB had never been that person, hurling out insults or banging on tables. He didn't have to be. The cold edge of his wit cut deeper than any blade. From the second they'd met, he'd seen Luca as a titillating thrill, an erotic escape, nothing more. So why was he upset?

"Shouldn't you be with your sister in Italy?"

"I couldn't leave without speaking to you."

"Well, you can check off that box." JB started for the house. "*Ciao.*"

Luca charged toward JB, grabbed his arm, and spun him around. "Talk to me."

"Okay, let's talk." JB wrenched his arm free from Luca's grip. The professor in him—the man who had built a career dissecting human social behavior—knew exactly how to inflict damage with minimal effort. "You mean nothing to me—a blip before flatlining." JB watched his words land, saw the imperceptible flinch around Luca's eyes, and felt a cold satisfaction. "In fact, most people have already moved on. And for those who were dick-*matized* by the Big GC, they were met with scorn, hypocritical as that may be."

JB stepped closer, disgust hanging on every word.

"As we say in America, the wagons have circled. A new narrative has written itself: when attacked by an outsider, the Hampton gays will unite to fend off a threat. You, my friend, are no longer welcome here."

Luca grabbed JB's face and kissed him.

Dazed momentarily by this consuming lust, JB came to his senses and pushed him away. "You need to go!"

"You need to listen to me."

What plausible explanation could Luca give for his presence in the Hamptons—beyond the neat little story he'd fabricated? The one where his sister had begged him to keep an eye on her corrupt husband, to make sure history didn't repeat itself. But Luca had latched onto JB's family like remora clinging to a dolphin: courting Mike under the pretense of house hunting, flirting with JB to sow tension between them, and showing up at nearly every social gathering as if part of a calculated plan.

JB left Luca standing outside without so much as a goodbye or a hint that he planned to have a proper sit-down and hear him out. He closed the door and waited until he heard Luca drive off.

Later, he drove to pick up Emilio. He parked outside the clinic and sat with his head on the steering wheel. The frustration he felt was almost physical, a wave of nausea and fatigue that shuddered through him. And through this all, trying to form some sense of what he needed to know most right now, was the grim truth that his husband might be a murderer.

Where is Mike, and why has he abandoned our son?

Emilio pushed through the clinic doors, smiling. For now, he was all that mattered. And for one glorious moment, JB thought of nothing else.

Chapter Thirty-Three

When Detectives D'Amico and Sullivan paid JB an unexpected visit the next day, panic and dread choked his throat. He wished, suddenly and hopelessly and desperately, to return to the Beltrams' costume party, at the exact moment before he'd decided to use his legs like a vise around Gianni Cuomo's neck.

Right after his father passed away, JB would wake up in the morning and not recall he'd died, and then when he did, it wasn't so much grief he felt as a simple childish desire to travel back in time. He felt like that, standing in the doorway of his front porch that morning, waiting to be arrested.

"Good morning," JB said with a thorough appraisal. "Come inside."

"We've located your husband," D'Amico began. "He's staying with Alfred Hammer and Dale Carnegie."

Alfie and Dale. Surprise. Surprise.

"Your husband volunteered to be questioned without a lawyer," she continued.

It was after ten a.m., and JB noted the perspiration streaking her armpits. Her hair was pulled away from her face except for a thick strand that flopped over one weary eye.

"He denies having anything to do with Gianni Cuomo's death," she elaborated.

"Still blaming me, is he?"

"Actually, no," Sullivan interjected. "Mike is now remorseful that he'd accused you of murder without proof."

Sullivan, too, looked tired. His eyes were red-rimmed, his sleeves rolled up, tie askew, as if he'd been slogging at work for half a day.

They were under gargantuan pressure to solve this murder. The headlines had been relentless: "Murder Masquerade," "Death at Chef's House," and JB's favorite, "TV Host's Killer Party."

"Your husband also denies…" Here D'Amico paused. JB sensed she was choosing her words carefully. "Poisoning your son."

"Then why hasn't he called once to see how Emilio is doing?"

"That I don't know," she replied. "We were able to locate your trash from the sanitation company. Very organized, they are."

"Should be, for the price they charge me."

"The lab found traces of Rohypnol in one of the bottles of alcohol," she said.

"A bottle of Johnnie Walker Black, to be exact," Sullivan added.

A long pause followed, punctuated by confusion and vindication and the very clear confirmation that the poison wasn't intended for Emilio or Mike. "So, the Rohypnol was for me?"

That meant Mike or Daria Cuomo had spiked his Scotch and planted the incriminating photos of Gus Beltram in his study. Had everything gone as planned, JB might have died. A search would have led police to the photos. They would have leaped to the conclusion that JB had killed Gianni out of jealousy and leaked the photos of Gus Beltram out of spite. What a fitting ending. JB could see the headlines now: "Cuckold Kills Self."

"Is it possible your son drank the Scotch?" D'Amico asked.

Although JB knew the answer, he wanted the detectives to hear it from his son. "Emilio," he called out. "Can you come to the living room, please?"

Emilio's face displayed a wary sharpness as if the presence of the two detectives heralded another new snag he didn't deserve to be subjected to.

JB motioned for him to sit down. "I'm going to ask you a question. But first, I want to tell you that you haven't done anything wrong, so answer truthfully. Okay?" Emilio nodded. JB sat next to him. "The day we found you unconscious, did you drink any of the Scotch from the bottle in the kitchen?"

JB waited for his son to get up, storm out of the living room, and slam his bedroom door shut. Instead, he sat absolutely and oddly calm. "Yes, I did. Pop was reading a bunch of papers about a new listing when I snuck into the kitchen and had a shot. Well, two or three."

D'Amico's eyes went wide. "And how soon after that do you think you passed out?"

He grinned uneasily. "Like…right away."

"Thank you," she replied, appearing somewhat satisfied.

Emilio went back to his room. JB stood up, thinking the detectives had all the information they needed.

"Does your underage son normally take a nip or three of Scotch during the day?" she asked with unexpected reprove.

That Emilio could merit suspicion after all he'd been through ignited JB's ire. "My son is currently under psychiatric care due to an attempt on his life. Yes, he admitted to self-medicating with alcohol, which, to me, is a brave thing to do. So, spare me your disapproval. My son is a good boy." D'Amico's expression was unreadable to JB. Her provocative questions seemed like a tactic to incite reactions that might reveal hidden truths. "What about Gianni's family?"

"Mr. Luca Guardia and his sister have been very cooperative," D'Amico offered. "After Mrs. Cuomo returned to Italy, we spoke to Mr. Guardia several times. He organized a conference call with Mrs. Cuomo. She vehemently denies having anything to do with what happened to your son, and according to your husband, Mike said she never left the living room. In fact, she is willing to return to the States to clear her name."

Cooperative. Organized. Words JB hadn't expected to hear.

For one tantalizing moment, he allowed himself to imagine that Luca had played no part in any of these nefarious acts. If anything, Luca had gone out of his way to clear his sister's name.

That left only one person. Mike.

"Mr. Guardia admitted he knew his brother-in-law was blackmailing Gus Beltram," D'Amico continued. "Once Mr. Guardia found out, he met with Mr. Beltram and assured him that the photos would be destroyed and that his money would be returned."

"But the photos weren't destroyed."

"No," D'Amico replied. "We found them in your office."

JB imagined next would come the results of the DNA test, followed by a list of facts linking him to the murder of Gianni Cuomo. When his phone rang, JB excused himself to answer it. "Angelo, I can't talk right now."

"This can't wait."

Amid the mounting tension, JB heard the urgency in his doctor's voice. He indicated to the detectives that he had to take the call and slipped into his study. "What's the matter?"

"I just got your test results." Angelo's tone caused JB's pulse to spike. "I don't want to alarm you, but your PSA has increased."

"What is it?" JB lowered himself into the chair as if preparing for a physical blow.

"After treatment, it was less than one."

"And now?"

Angelo paused, clearing his throat. "It tripled."

Here it was—the shadow that had never truly left, the monster that had merely retreated to gather strength. The thing he'd always suspected lurked beneath the surface of his recovery was back. His cancer had returned, just as the murder investigation closed in, just as his son needed him most. The cosmic cruelty of the timing wasn't lost on him. Cancer, like justice, had no sense of fair play—no appreciation for what a man could reasonably bear.

JB recalled the first time Angelo had informed him his PSA was elevated. He remembered grinning through the pain as the dark blanket of terror descended over him, bundling him up for the angel of death to retrieve. Although the feeling remained with him for months after he was cancer-free, every moment of every day after that, he imagined the tumor hibernating inside, festering with disease.

"So, the cancer is back?"

Angelo cleared his throat again. "I don't know for sure. I'd like to repeat the blood test. Can you come in tomorrow morning?"

"Of course." JB hung up without saying goodbye.

He stared forlornly out the window, at his garden, the cucuzza overwhelming the trellis like the arms of an octopus. He stood up, knees buckling. He sat again, trying to recall how he'd approached his family with his diagnosis the first time, playing it down as though he were having a minor procedure.

Nothing a little chemo and radiation can't fix.

It would have been one thing if he'd managed to handle the diagnosis well then, but he hadn't, and in fact, he admittedly was the poster child for what not to do. Again, JB recalled that day when Angelo first diagnosed him. He'd assumed a defensive posture, bracing himself for the treatment and the long period of recovery ahead while hoping, against all logic, that his family would subsist in an alternative cancer-free reality. That experience had taken a lot out of him, and now, for the first time, he felt enraged by his stupidity.

Not this time.

Before he exited the study, JB caught a glimpse of his reflection in the silver clock, the impact of the summer's tragic events deeply and undeniably engraved on his face. Skin ashen. Expression leaden. A look with something dreadful stirring behind it, a look that passed over his expression like portentous mist over water. The cancer was back. JB was sure of it.

Emilio was standing on the other side of the door when JB opened it. "Is everything okay?"

"Yeah, why?" he replied casually, though Emilio's expression registered the worry he heard in his voice. "Let me finish up with these detectives."

Emilio squinted with suspicion, and he returned to his bedroom.

The detectives were standing by the door. JB hoped that meant they were planning to leave. "Apologies for the interruption. Is there anything else I can do for you?"

D'Amico stared at him with a pained expression. "Is it possible someone else entered your house that day?"

"Of course, it's possible"—JB chuckled—"it's the Hamptons. No one locks their doors."

"I'm sure lots of people lock their doors now," D'Amico said. "Oh, and one more thing."

Here it comes.

"The tissue samples taken from under Mr. Cuomo's nails were inconclusive. The chlorine ate away at whatever he'd been clawing at." She dropped her gaze to JB's thighs before her eyes shot up to lock on his. "Thank you for your time. We'll be in touch."

JB returned to his study and closed the door. He felt relief wash over him now that his DNA hadn't been found under Gianni's nails. But something grabbed JB by the throat and forced him to ask: what had he learned from all this? For starters, he refused to succumb to cancer or to the circumstances Mike had inflicted on his family. No, he would not be a victim. No one and nothing was going to fuck with him or his son, and if they did, he was going to fuck them right back.

Mike had been the one to introduce Gianni Cuomo into their lives, and now, it was time for JB to confront him about his murder and the attempt on their son's life. If Mike wouldn't reach out to him, he would reach out to Mike.

By the neck.

* * *

JB drove with no clear plan but a heavy heart to find Mike. The address on the card Alfie and Dale had given him led to a sprawling mid-century modern house that had been recently renovated with glass additions. Two white Pomeranians barked from behind the front door as he pulled into the circular driveway.

Wisteria draped the entrance in heavy white blooms, and through the glass walls, he could see the pool area. A couple of young men—college-aged, maybe—were lounging naked. One waved when he spotted JB, then both headed toward the pool house.

Beyond them, JB caught a glimpse of Alfie and Dale quickly wrapping themselves in robes when they saw him.

"JB!" Dale's voice carried surprise as he opened the door, the Pomeranians circling his feet. "What a pleasant surprise. Come in, come in."

"I hope I'm not interrupting anything."

"Just afternoon drinks by the pool," Dale said, leading him through the minimalist interior. The dogs followed, their nails clicking on the polished concrete floors. "Can I get you something?"

Alfie appeared, still adjusting his robe. "This is unexpected. Everything all right?"

JB got straight to the point. "I'm looking for Mike. I heard he might be staying with you."

The silence that followed felt loaded. Dale and Alfie exchanged a look.

"Is something wrong?" JB asked, reading their hesitation. "I need to speak with him. Our son was in the hospital, and—"

"Oh my God," Alfie interrupted, his hand going to his chest. "We had no idea. Is he okay?"

JB realized Mike hadn't told them about Emilio's overdose. The concern in their faces seemed genuine, and suddenly, both men were reaching out to comfort him.

"This was a mistake. I should go." JB was already turning toward the door. "Tell Mike to call me."

"The thing is," Dale said carefully, "we're not sure when that will be."

"What do you mean?"

Another uncomfortable pause. Dale looked to Alfie, who shook his head slightly.

"He's… out for the evening," Dale finally said.

Something cold settled in JB's stomach. "Out?"

"On a date," Dale blurted out, then immediately looked stricken. "I mean—"

"We don't know that," Alfie clarified. "Only that he was meeting someone at The American Hotel."

The words hit JB like a physical blow. His husband was on a date while their son was barely out of the hospital, while their marriage was falling apart, while JB was desperately trying to hold everything together.

"I knew we shouldn't have said anything," Alfie whispered.

"It's fine," JB managed, though his voice sounded distant to his own ears. "I'm fine."

CHAPTER THIRTY-THREE

"Please sit down. Let Dale make you a drink."

"No, I should go."

The cumulative weight of this embarrassment took JB's breath away, rendering him frozen. He remained immobile for so long that Dale had to shake him. "JB?" Dale's voice seemed to come from far away. "Are you all right?"

JB forced himself to move, to open the door, to walk to his car. Behind him, he could hear Alfie and Dale talking in low, concerned voices. By tomorrow, he realized, this story would make the rounds. The sad husband who came looking for his cheating partner while their son recovered from an overdose.

As he drove home, one thought kept circling in his mind: I need to get out of this town. I need to start over somewhere else, away from all the people who know our business, away from the gossip and the pity and the failure of everything I thought my life was supposed to be.

Chapter Thirty-Four

Stubbornly throughout his life, JB had rebelled against his punitive father, coming out at Christmas, marrying a man, and adopting a mixed-race child. He'd dared to imagine a happy family in a well-padded life. He understood that misfortune struck at random, having witnessed the tragic deaths of his parents within the space of six weeks. He also understood that he was susceptible to calamity as well, but he had not conceived that bad luck could strike every member of his family at the same time.

JB sat motionless in his car parked outside The American Hotel, cursing himself for allowing another interloper to infest his family. His gaze locked onto one of the hotel windows, imagining Mike sprawled on his back.

What the hell am I doing here? The thought was immediately followed by, *You're pathetic. Confronting Mike will solve nothing. Go home. Be with your son.*

JB drove up Main Street, overwhelmed by a crushing mix of exhaustion, humiliation, and frustration. As he passed the black-and-white striped awning of Page Sag Harbor, he saw them. Mike was talking animatedly, flicking glances at Luca like a cigarette in the general direction of an ashtray. Luca hunched over the table, listened while absently spinning a saltshaker. A piercing realization blinded JB, as if a window shade abruptly yanked upward, flooding a dark room with harsh light. Mike Fogarty intended to steal Luca from him out of spite.

Luca met JB's eyes, his jovial expression cracking with shock. JB sped away before Luca could approach.

* * *

Rakesh was on the telephone when JB entered the house. He hung up almost as soon as JB closed the door behind him. "Where were you?"

JB sat next to Buckley on the couch, smiling at the dog as if they'd shared a funny joke. "I'd rather not talk about it."

"Emilio's in his room. I made pasta Bolognese, but with pasta made from hearts of palm because I know you don't eat carbs."

"I eat carbs." JB sounded annoyed and exhausted. "I simply prefer not to."

"Whatever. I now have to run home and check on Andy. I just got off the phone with Hank Lawson. Andy hasn't been to work, and he's not responding to my calls or texts." Rakesh retreated into the kitchen in frustration. JB wouldn't have been surprised to hear the crash of pots and pans in the sink or the sloshing of wet pseudo pasta in the trash.

"Are we celebrating something?" JB asked when Rakesh entered the living room. He had ditched the apron and was holding his keys.

"What?"

JB aimed his chin toward the dining room table. It had been set with the Tiffany dinnerware and Baccarat crystal.

"Oh, that." Rakesh sighed. "You know dinner for me isn't simply a meal. It's a time to reconnect with loved ones. I suppose Mike stopped doing that years ago, but I felt it was my duty to resurrect a sense of family for your family."

JB stared at the dining room, recalling the many holidays they'd spent seated around that table. "Why don't I come with you?"

"You mean that?" The tension in Rakesh's face dissolved. "Apologies for the drama, but I keep a stash of pharmaceuticals in my old footlocker. I won't rest until I know Andy hasn't broken into it."

"Don't worry." JB gave a little laugh. "It's the least I can do for you, old friend."

There was no sense in telling Rakesh about Mike and Luca. For now, JB had to remain fully present for his best friend. Who knew what they would encounter upon arriving at Rakesh's house?

* * *

JB watched his former college roommate hunched over the steering wheel, gripping it tightly so his knuckles blanched. What tormented him was uncertainty. Not knowing what lay in store at the house was tantamount to waiting for his doctor to confirm his cancer had returned.

All the lights were on as they pulled into the gravel driveway. Andy's car was parked outside. The door was unlocked. Rakesh charged in, calling out for Andy, but there was no response. They split off, looking for him. JB found Andy in the kitchen, sitting on the floor, empty wine bottles scattered around him. Andy was propped against the cabinet underneath the sink, wearing only his boxer briefs, clutching Rakesh's running shoe as if he might hold a child.

JB called out. "He's in the kitchen."

Andy's upper eyelid had a small gash. The cut had congealed and swelled, so the outer edge was swollen and blue. Rakesh kneeled beside him. "Are you okay?"

JB grabbed ice cubes from the freezer and wrapped them in a dish towel. "Take this."

The second Rakesh applied the ice to Andy's eye, he opened them both. Wincing, he pushed his husband away, staring at him confusedly. "It's me, Rakesh."

The confusion on Andy's face washed away, leaving him visibly surprised. "Rakesh, you're home." When Andy met JB's eyes, his expression soured. "Oh, it's you." Turning to Rakesh, Andy groused, "Figures you'd bring him."

"We need to go to the emergency room," Rakesh said softly.

"Get away from me!" Andy pushed Rakesh, knocking him off-kilter so that he fell backward, striking his head on the terrazzo floor. Ice cubes skittered on the tile. Andy pulled himself up, gripping the edge of the sink, but JB threw his arms around him, rendering him immobile. "Get off me!"

"What's gotten into you?" Rakesh stood up and headed for the bathroom. The pallor of his face concerned JB. He returned, holding a washcloth to the back of his head. "I'm bleeding."

"Let go of me!" JB debated whether he should, and ultimately, he did. Andy rushed toward Rakesh and hugged him. "I'm sorry, baby. I'm so sorry."

Rakesh held his sobbing husband. "You've got to stop drinking. It's killing you."

Andy rested his head on Rakesh's shoulder. "Okay, I promise. Anything. Just come home."

"We have to get you to the emergency room." Rakesh looked at JB. "Take my car and go home."

"Why don't I drive you?"

"I can manage. Go be with your son."

Once Rakesh and Andy drove off, JB mechanically began cleaning up. He moved throughout the house, collecting empty bottles. The living room couch was a repository of old magazines and a variety of hamburger condiments. Empty bags of potato chips and crumbs littered the carpet. JB hauled two overstuffed trash bags to the garage, where Rakesh kept the garbage containers since the deer always found a way to get in them outside.

Rakesh maintained the garage like JB's father—meticulously clean, with everything in its place. The shelves were stacked with labeled bins: Christmas lights. Halloween decorations. Legal documents. A trunk on the bottom shelf caught JB's eye. It was the one Rakesh had in college. He was reminded of what Rakesh had said earlier, that he kept a stash of pharmaceuticals and worried that Andy had gotten his hands on them.

JB pulled it from the shelf. The lock hadn't been secured. As expected, the trunk was neatly organized with smaller plastic bins labeled: Postcards. Letters. Photographs. Even an assortment of pills in small plastic baggies. Though JB had no way of knowing if Andy had taken any, it didn't seem as if anyone had tampered with them.

JB sat on the floor and flipped through the college photos. They told a story of their friendship. From the first day they'd met while registering for classes. Group shots with various people, JB couldn't even name anymore. It was as if he'd lived an entire life that was now nothing more than a distant ring of a bell once tolled decades ago.

A strip of four black-and-white photos caught JB's attention. Playful poses captured in a photobooth: *Charlie's Angels*, Blue Steel, and Deuces! JB couldn't recall when they were taken. The final image showed them kissing on the lips—a moment entirely absent from his memory. Clearly, these photos held some sentimental value to Rakesh. The discovery stirred Angelo's recent comment in JB's mind: *Rakesh still has feelings for you.* Another set included group shots with Andy and Mike. In each one, Mike's face was violently scribbled out in black ink.

JB felt like an intruder rummaging through his best friend's precious things. He replaced the photos in the bin. In his haste to return the footlocker to its place, he dropped it, spilling the contents everywhere. JB collected everything off the floor. As he was about to place them back where they belonged, though JB knew he would never achieve Rakesh's level of organization, something at the base of the trunk caught his eye. An object wrapped in a hunter green blanket. It seemed out of place amongst everything else, which had been neatly packed in smaller bins. This blanketed object was placed on the bottom with smaller bins set on top to camouflage it. JB peeled the edge of the blanket aside. A sense of confusion washed over him.

"Jesus Christ!"

JB stared down at the Louisville Slugger split in two jagged pieces. Dark strands of hair embedded in a splotch of dried blood at the splintered edges. The cold embrace of panic overwhelmed him—not just in his mind but in his physical form. The garage floor seemed to pitch beneath him like the deck of a storm-tossed ship. He collapsed, his muscles surrendering all at once, his body spread against the cold concrete floor.

The sight of the murder weapon filled him with disgust. Marrow-deep disgust, the kind that changed you, because lying on the floor, there could be no other reason why Rakesh had the murder weapon in his college footlocker. The motive was obvious: kill Gianni Cuomo, end his best friend's humiliation, and have Mike take the fall.

JB bolted out of the house after placing the footlocker back where he'd found it, holding the two pieces of the bat wrapped in the hunter green blanket under his arm. There was no other choice. *This is Rakesh after all. My best friend.* He drove home in Rakesh's car. It had been a long day filled with disappointment and indignities. JB wasn't thinking straight. He needed time to think, but first, he had to get rid of the bat.

The light in Emilio's room was off when JB pulled into the driveway. The entire house was dark. He headed for the garage and retrieved the lighter fluid off the shelf. The fire pit was located by the garden. Buckley barked once. JB let him out, and the dog followed him quietly. The pit had two logs in it. Another one of his father's rules: *If you used the firepit, you had to make sure there were fresh logs in it afterward.* JB walked to the car, where he retrieved the two pieces of the bat wrapped in the hunter green blanket. He doused the wood with lighter fluid. Then he struck a match. The blaze shot up with a mini-Hiroshima mushroom cloud. Buckley backed away, barking. JB stared at the yellow flames, thinking of the bat his father had gifted him. The same one he'd given to Emilio was used to murder Mike's lover. And JB felt not an ounce of guilt. It occurred to him that in destroying this bat, he was not only protecting his best friend, but he was also relinquishing the hold his father had retained over him in death, and in doing so, freeing himself from the toxic legacy that had haunted his entire adult life.

Buckley snagged the hunter green blanket out of JB's hand and ran toward the house. JB turned to chase him, he saw Emilio standing on the porch. "Dad, what are you doing?"

JB hadn't the least idea what he was going to say next and was aware with a sudden overwhelming apprehension that his expression—eyes wide, jaw agape—told Emilio everything. JB attempted to smile, but even that felt wrong.

Buckley sat at Emilio's feet, the blanket still in his mouth. JB observed his son as he retrieved the blanket from the dog, inspecting the wood splinters and the dried blood. Emilio gazed at his father this time with comprehension.

"It's not what you think," JB insisted.

The fire blazed in the pit, illuminating JB with red and orange hues. Emilio was bathed in the blueish tones of the moonlight, standing on the porch. Buckley nipped at the blanket, tugging at it, but Emilio held a firm grip.

"That's my bat you're burning. Isn't it?"

"Let's go in the house, son. I can explain."

Emilio took a step or two backward as JB approached him. Buckley, seizing the opportunity, snatched the blanket from Emilio's hand and bolted. JB instinctively lurched for the dog as Emilio ran heedlessly in the other direction.

"Emilio!" he shouted, but his son had disappeared.

JB chased after him, then paused. The deer fence encircled the property, meaning Emilio would have to funnel toward the road to escape. Changing course, JB sprinted down the driveway to intercept him. Before he could reach the end, Emilio streaked past with an easy loping gait.

"Damn it!" JB wheeled around and ran to Rakesh's car. He navigated the dark, winding road—a river of asphalt cutting through the night. Lowering the window, he called out his son's name, his voice carried away on the night breeze. No answer came back across the void. Then, a figure among the trees ahead caught his eye, swaying like a buoy in shallow waters.

Emilio?

JB accelerated just as a figure emerged from the shadows, darting across the road. Their eyes locked in the blinding white gleam of the headlights. JB jammed on the brakes but not soon enough. The sound of crunching metal mixed with an agonizing scream of pain. The windshield splintered into a giant spider's web before it showered down on JB. Airbags deployed. It took several long seconds before JB attempted to get out of the car.

What have I done? Jesus Christ, what have I done!

He ran to the front of the car. Twitching and groaning, a deer peered helplessly up at him. Its belly was split open, and its organs spilled out. JB moved closer, but a voice called out from behind him. "Don't touch it." Emilio's tone was definitive and resolute.

"I'll call 9-1-1." As JB dialed, fingers trembling, his son disappeared again into the woods. "Hello, my name is Joseph Pulaski. I hit a deer."

While JB's voice rose with each panicked syllable to the emergency operator, Emilio materialized from the darkness. The boy's silhouette resolved into view as he approached, clutching a gnarled oak branch thick as his forearm. Without hesitation, he positioned himself over the wounded deer.

Emilio's eyes hardened with a cold intensity. In one fluid motion, the young man raised the makeshift cudgel high above his head. The branch hung suspended for a heartbeat against the night sky before Emilio brought it down with terrible precision on the deer's head.

Again.

And again.

A crimson jet spurted in rhythmic arterial arcs. Each pulse emerged weaker than the one before, the diminishing pressure making the countdown of the animal's final moments until, finally, the deer's frantic twitching ceased altogether.

JB stood paralyzed, the phone slipping forgotten in his hand. The emergency operator's voice faded to insignificance. What hollowed JB's chest wasn't the violence itself but Emilio's expression—impassive, methodical, showing neither revulsion nor remorse as he stepped away from the dead animal.

The operator's tinny voice called out from the phone, but JB couldn't summon the words to respond. He was transfixed. His eyes remained locked on his son's, searching for any flicker of the little boy he knew.

"Yes," JB replied finally. "You'll send someone? Thank you."

JB put his arms around his son. They stood in the street for a long while. Emilio clutched his father—jagged breaths, heaving sobs—before rescue arrived.

* * *

JB sat motionless in his study. The house was silent except for Buckley's soft snoring at his feet. Through the window, he could see embers still pulsing in the firepit. The splintered Louisville Slugger and the blood-soaked blanket now reduced to ash. The murder weapon destroyed for good.

After they'd arrived home, Emilio had showered methodically. JB stood in the hallway listening to the water run for nearly forty minutes. He imagined scarlet rivulets spiraling down the drain, his son scrubbing until his skin was raw, until every trace of blood had been cleansed.

JB had gathered his son's clothes and double-bagged them before burying them at the bottom of the outdoor trash bin. Each movement deliberate, as if performing a ritual. Now, with nothing left to clean, nothing left to burn, he nursed a generous pour of cognac in the darkness of his study.

His phone's sudden vibration against the wooden desk sent a jolt through his body. Rakesh's name illuminated the screen. "We just got home," Rakesh said, his voice weary but relieved. "All stitched up. Thank you for cleaning. You didn't have to go to all that trouble."

JB's grip tightened around the phone. "It was no trouble."

"I mean, you really cleaned up. Andy and I couldn't believe it."

JB's laughter emerged brittle and hollow. "I know how fastidious you are."

"I'm going to sleep here tonight. Andy and I need to have a sober conversation in the morning."

"That's a good idea. Let's talk tomorrow." JB hung up without mentioning the deer. That would have to wait until morning.

A shadow drifted past the doorway.

"Dad."

JB's heart hammered against his ribs. He pressed a steady hand to his heaving chest. "You're up."

"I can't sleep." Emilio stood perfectly still, a pale apparition in the darkness. Only his hands betrayed him, trembling by his side like autumn leaves.

"I think I know why." JB straightened, fingers clasped tightly together on his desk.

Emilio remained silent, hands still trembling.

"I found the bat," JB continued, each syllable measured, deliberate, "and I knew it was used to murder Gianni Cuomo." He drew a cautious breath. "But I didn't kill him. I only destroyed it to protect someone. Do you understand?"

Emilio didn't respond. He barely dared to breathe.

"However, what I did is illegal. I tampered with evidence, and for that, I may pay a price. But just as I burned the bat to protect someone I love, I will protect you since you witnessed my crime."

A mutual understanding solidified in the darkness—an unspoken pact sealed in the charged silence of JB's study. His son retreated with an almost imperceptible nod, disappearing down the hallway like a ghost. JB knew Emilio would never speak of this night.

From Emilio's reaction, JB understood that this tension would stretch between them like a taut rope for years to come. His son might never forgive him. Certainly, he would think less of his father for breaking the law, for compromising the principles he'd always preached. As for himself, JB would say nothing, not even to Rakesh. He would pretend he'd never seen the bat, bury it beneath layers of justification until it sank like a stone in Hampton Bays.

In sleepless nights to come, he'd wrestle with his choice, untangling the knots of his decision and working through the complex rigging of his morality. He'd deal with those nights when they came—consoled with the thought that some secrets were better left sunken at the bottom of memory's ocean.

Chapter Thirty-Five

JB got up the next morning and knocked on his son's bedroom door. "Time to get up." He heard Emilio ruffling the sheets. Then, the solid sound of his feet on the floorboards. Once JB heard the shower running, he entered the kitchen to fix breakfast.

Emilio sat, elbow on the table, head propped up by his fist. He pushed his eggs around using the tines of his fork, leaving an oozy yellow trail. His expression appeared vacant as though he were gazing down a long, dark hallway. JB didn't want to say the wrong thing, so he remained quiet, sipping coffee until it was time to leave.

Emilio seemed like a different person, staring out the window with his forehead pressed against the passenger side window. JB resisted the urge to fill the space with chatter, though the silence was roaring unbearably around him. Once JB pulled into the clinic parking lot, he turned to Emilio. "I'll pick you up after my appointment with Dr. Perrotta." His son opened the car door and walked inside the clinic without saying goodbye.

JB's head began to throb as he drove. He wondered if Emilio would talk to Laird about what had happened last night. Maybe not the part about burning the murder weapon. Certainly, Emilio would share the tragic event involving the accident with the deer. All JB could think about was his son's sudden burst of violence. The memory of it sent a stab of icicle chill up his spine.

How was he going to face Angelo? JB was determined to say nothing about finding the bat. He'd leave Rakesh to tell him about Andy. For now, he had to focus on repeating his PSA and the implications of the results.

* * *

"How soon will you know?" JB asked Angelo as the phlebotomist drew his blood.

"A day or two." Angelo sat still, observing JB. "I can see how upset you are. Your hands are shaking."

JB laughed inwardly. *If only you knew the whole story.*

"I need to ask you a personal question. It's about Luca."

"Angelo, I love you, but I don't care to discuss him."

"Hear me out." Angelo waited until the phlebotomist left them alone. "You had sex with Luca before you had your blood drawn last time, correct?"

"Yes." JB turned away, crossing his legs.

Angelo cleared his throat. "Did you engage in receptive anal sex?"

JB stood up to leave. "I have to pick up Emilio."

"Answer the damn question!" Angelo spoke with such exactitude it startled JB.

Slowly, he sat back down again. "As a matter of fact, I did. Happy?"

Angelo's face rippled with relief. "I didn't think to ask you at the time. Had I known, I wouldn't have drawn your blood."

"You're talking in circles, Angelo."

"Your elevated PSA might have nothing to do with a recurrence of cancer."

JB's gut contracted. "Anal sex can elevate your PSA?"

"Yes."

As JB's comprehension solidified, the churning in his gut began to ease.

If JB could scratch cancer off his list of nightmarish problems he was facing, it would almost make the entire humiliating experience with Luca worthwhile—a cruel cosmic joke with an unexpectedly merciful punchline.

JB hugged Angelo with such force they nearly toppled backward. "That's the best news I've heard in weeks."

* * *

A subtle whiff of adrenaline percolated through JB's body now that he may have been given a reprieve from cancer. The morning's relief about his health now collided with his concern about Emilio's psychological state. The boy had already been through so much—witnessing his father's cancer treatments, enduring the fracturing of his family, and now last night's disturbing incident with the deer. JB wondered if Emilio's uncharacteristic behavior might somehow be connected to overhearing that phone call about his PSA result. Perhaps beneath his son's methodical composure lay a terror JB hadn't fully recognized—the fear of losing his father.

He sat in Laird's waiting room, flipping through an outdated tabloid once again, when the office door opened. "JB, please come inside," Laird said with a minimal but palpable sense of urgency. "I'd like to talk with you in my office."

"Is everything okay?" JB asked as Emilio brushed past him.

"Please, come in."

The roller coaster ride that had been the last twenty-four hours of JB's world suddenly came to a screeching halt when he saw Mike. JB observed his appearance as he struggled to see clearly through his anger and confusion. Clear blue eyes and trimmed blond hair. Mike wasn't just sober. He was as dry as gluten-free bread. "What's going on here?"

"Emilio texted me late last night," Mike explained. "He asked to see me. Dr. Laird and I spoke this morning, and he suggested I join Emilio's appointment."

"I thought my office would be a neutral place for them to reunite," Laird filled in.

"How nice of you to make time for our son."

Laird held up a hand to halt Mike from firing back. "JB, I believe Emilio experienced a breakthrough. Reaching out to his estranged father means he wanted to resolve the issues between them."

JB absorbed that, trying to accept that his son was showing signs of maturity beyond his years. But for Mike not to tell JB felt like another form of betrayal. "So much for co-parenting."

Mike turned to face JB directly. "I want a divorce."

"Divorce?" JB froze as if even the slightest movement might shatter his entire body.

Instead of grief, a strange cocktail of emotions swirled within him: relief that Mike had finally said it out loud; resentment at the presumptuous timing; and an odd, hollow sense of anticlimax—as if a long-anticipated blow had finally landed, but with less force than expected.

"We both know our marriage ended a long time ago," Mike explained, his watery blue eyes welling. "When Emilio accused me of poisoning him… that's when I knew I had to separate from our family, for his sake."

"For Emilio's sake?" JB's eyes went wide with exaggerated disbelief.

"Emilio admitted that he made up the story that Mike had poisoned him." Laird hesitated, but he slowly went on to say, "When he woke up in the ER, he panicked, knowing that he'd drunk the Scotch, and so he accused Mike of drugging him to cover it up."

"I'm aware my son drank Scotch that day." What JB wasn't prepared to tell them was that the police had found traces of Rohypnol in the bottle, indicating someone had meant to poison him.

"I understand there was an accident last night," Laird probed further.

JB informed them he'd hit a deer, but he was cautious not to overemphasize Emilio's reaction in putting the dying animal out of its misery.

"Emilio feels extremely remorseful over the incident," Laird continued. "I believe his impulse frightened him."

Emilio. My son, Emilio.

The baby who slept through the night, the docile toddler with a perpetual smile, the little boy all the teachers adored—what had he and Mike done to him? Parenting meant putting their child's needs first always, but clearly, they hadn't done that.

"Have you ever heard of the fight-or-flight response? It's a physiological reaction to an event that is perceived as stressful or frightening. The body releases adrenaline and sets off a chain reaction that increases heart rate, blood pressure, and breathing. After you struck that deer with your car, Emilio said you got out to assess the situation, and he responded with a violent reaction."

"But Emilio isn't violent," Mike insisted.

Laird sat back, staring expectantly at JB.

"Emilio was trying to protect me," JB added quietly.

"Protect you from a dying deer?"

Laird turned to Mike. "After JB struck that deer, Emilio observed his father approach the injured animal. That's when his sympathetic nervous system took over. There was no way to predict how that animal was going to react. Emilio's body went into fight mode. I suspect his body has been primed ever since JB was diagnosed with cancer. The thought of losing a parent can be quite traumatizing for a child. Not to mention, the effect his illness had on your marriage."

"What happens now? Besides the quickie divorce, Mike's asking for so he can resume his philandering guilt-free. I mean with Emilio. What happens now with Emilio?"

Laird cleared his throat. "We resume therapy as planned. Emilio has made it clear he wants to continue to see me. I believe he's making progress. Today was a step in the right direction."

JB thought about how hard it must have been for Emilio to live with these emotions he was ill-equipped to comprehend. And to have witnessed his father burn evidence must have pushed him over the edge. What JB found so incongruous with Laird's explanation was that Emilio didn't display any of the classic symptoms consistent with a fight-or-flight response. The boy JB witnessed last night hadn't been frantic or panicked. Instead, Emilio had been eerily calm—methodical even. Nothing about his behavior suggested an instinctive reaction to danger.

JB didn't want to bring it up with Mike in the room. "Can I talk to you alone, Dr. Laird?"

"I'll wait outside with Emilio." Mike squeezed JB's shoulder before exiting.

JB stared into Laird's eyes, wondering what he must think of his family, and then chastised himself for worrying about what other people thought. "Is my son going to be all right?"

Laird drew his fingers to the small patch of stubble under his lower lip. "Death, even the accidental death of an animal, forces us to reflect. At that moment, Emilio's brain triggered a response to end that deer's misery much in the way he wishes he could end your suffering."

"There's something else. The other day, Emilio may have overheard me on the phone with my doctor. My PSA came back elevated, but I learned today, just now, that it might not be a recurrence of my cancer, but something called prostatitis."

"That's interesting." Laird continued to rub the stubble as though the action itself stimulated his analytic process. "So, you think Emilio overheard your doctor informing you that your PSA was elevated and that he may have understood this to mean you have cancer again?"

"Exactly."

"First, I'm glad to hear you're all right. Overhearing your conversation with your doctor likely triggered Emilio's anxiety. I hope you plan on having this conversation with him as soon as possible. The news will do him good."

"Yes, I will."

Emilio appeared skittish when JB entered the waiting room. Mike stood up first. "Hey, can I speak with you for a second?"

JB handed Emilio the keys and asked him to wait in the car.

"Would it be all right if I came by the house tomorrow? Andy dropped off specs on a new listing the other day. I forgot them when I moved out."

"Sure." Despite everything, it didn't escape JB's attention that Mike had made changes for his son's sake, though he continued to humiliate him in public with his strays, Luca now being his latest.

"There's one more thing."

JB sighed. "If it's about the divorce, I need time to think."

"I know it's none of my business, but I'm trying to turn over a new leaf."

"Can this wait?"

"You should speak with Luca," Mike cut in abruptly. "Now hear me out before you go on one of your long-winded monologues about liars. Yes, Luca kept a secret from us, but for good reason."

"And what's that?"

Mike gripped JB's wrist. "The reason you saw us together wasn't because we were on a date. He wanted to meet me to discuss the money I gave Gianni."

"It's been a rough twenty-four hours. I don't have time for this."

Mike moved in front of JB to stop him from walking away. "Luca wants to pay me back. He returned Dale and Alfie's money. Well, at least some of it."

"Why are you doing this? Our life is complicated enough."

Mike bit his grin. "New leaf."

"A few days of sobriety, and now you're enlightened?"

"Emilio accused me of poisoning him. I've spent a great deal of time reflecting on that. I know I still have a long journey toward enlightenment. I'm trying to see life through other people's perspective."

Then, as if this day couldn't get any worse, JB exited the clinic as Luca emerged from his Fiat. The universe was determined to orchestrate these collisions with meticulous cruelty.

Luca stood frozen by his car door, the summer breeze ruffling his dark hair. It was hard not to see the remorse in his eyes—a particular shade of regret that seemed genuine, even beautiful in its intensity. For a brief, treacherous moment, JB felt the magnetic pull between them, that inexplicable current that had drawn him to Luca's hotel room.

But beneath that momentary weakness came something stronger: indignation. JB didn't feel sorry for Luca. He felt waylaid—ambushed by these coordinated appearances, first Mike inside the clinic and now Luca outside it. The orchestration felt suspicious, as if the two men had planned this pincer movement to catch him at his most vulnerable.

JB's eyes shot over to his car, where Emilio sat watching this unfold, his gaze unflinching and observant. The boy who had methodically ended a deer's suffering was now studying his father's response to emotional confrontation with the same clinical detachment.

Emilio's words echoed in JB's mind: *Sometimes, I see you as someone weak when I know you're not weak. You're strong, Dad.*

Luca took a step forward, mouth opening to speak words JB decided he didn't need to hear. Without acknowledging Luca's presence with so much as a nod, JB strode to his car with deliberate steps, his spine straight, his gaze fixed forward. He slid into the driver's seat, closed the door, and started the engine.

Emilio had shown strength today by confronting his other father. Now, JB would show strength by refusing to engage with the complications Luca represented. Some doors were better left closed, some explanations better left unheard. Some strengths came not from confrontation but from the simple, decisive act of driving away.

Chapter Thirty-Six

Something in JB took over, some kind of ferocious parental instinct. He wanted to believe he had struck a blow for the underdog—that he'd stood up for the betrayed and brokenhearted—that he'd done it for Emilio. The truth, he knew, was that Emilio had stood up for himself. JB had only followed his example. Somewhere along the way, they had swapped places.

He saw that now, driving home.

"Dad, are you mad at me?"

JB pulled off the road at a nearby farmer's market. "Mad at you?" He stared squarely at his son. "Why would I be mad? If anything, you should be mad at me."

Emilio raised his eyebrows. "But now you and Pop are getting divorced."

"That's true, but you're not to blame."

"But it is my fault. I made you believe you were weak because of the way Pop treated you."

"I was weak, but I'm not weak anymore. And I'm not going to die." JB reached over and gripped his son's shoulders. "You hear me? I'm not going to die. I went to see Dr. Perrotta this morning. He doesn't think I have cancer. Understand? I'm not going anywhere."

Emilio stared back, but he couldn't speak.

JB hugged him, feeling his son's body shudder until Emilio was no longer sobbing. They sat in the car a while longer. Exhaustion ascended JB's body, from toes to knees to hips to chest. He wondered if he would be able to move from this position again. "What do you say we buy some corn on the cob? I'll grill steaks and make confetti corn. Would you like that?"

Emilio nodded in that childlike way JB remembered whenever he'd asked his young son if he wanted ice cream. They got out of the car and stretched. Emilio retrieved one of the canvas bags they kept in the trunk for grocery shopping. They bought corn on the cob, basil, and red bell peppers.

"Are you going to date that Italian guy?"

JB smiled, taking in his son's curious expression. "Do you think I should?"

Emilio shrugged, sheepish. "Don't know."

"Well, if it's all right by you." JB walked back to the car, "I'll pass on dating him or anyone else for now. Let's just focus on us."

A short while later, they emerged from the car, breathing in the warm air and hoping for some respite, but the dramatic and unexpected events were far from over. Andy's car was parked in the driveway.

They entered the house and were immediately assailed by two aggressive and competing senses: the fragrant aromatics of Indian spices and the instrumental genre of *choro* that Rakesh had discovered while vacationing in Rio de Janeiro.

JB grinned uneasily at Emilio, who bounded toward the kitchen. "Finally," Rakesh shouted above the music. JB walked over and turned the volume down. Rakesh emerged wearing Mike's *Chef's Kiss* apron. "Too loud? My bad."

"Are you making curry?"

"Your favorite," Rakesh gushed as if he were talking to a toddler.

"Can you give your Uncle Rakesh and me a few minutes alone?"

Emilio dropped the bag of groceries on the kitchen counter and headed toward his bedroom.

"Would you like a glass of wine?"

JB followed him into the kitchen and stood in the doorway. "What are you doing here?" Rakesh was leaning over the simmering pot, fanning the aroma to his nose. "Where's Andy?"

Rakesh did not meet his gaze. "Home."

"I assumed after last night—"

"You assumed after Andy attacked me in a drunken fit that left a two-inch gash on the back of my head that we would reconcile?" Rakesh glanced over, a beaming smile of condescension on his face. "Why don't you wash up before dinner?"

JB observed his old friend in the stillness of that moment. "So, how did you leave it with Andy?"

Rakesh stared up at the ceiling, inhaling sharply. "I told him he should go to rehab, and that I would pay for it, but afterward, he needs to move out."

"Andy agreed?"

"No, he refuses to go to rehab, and he refuses to move out." Rakesh peered at JB with a wounded expression, which shifted quickly into one of control. Pleasant, calm, and utterly in control of the situation, except JB sensed a deep-rooted frustration in his best friend.

"What are you going to do, Rakesh?"

"It's all been taken care of."

"What does that mean?"

"It means Andy is no longer a problem for us."

Us?

JB didn't realize how chilling a word could sound. Rakesh dressed in that ridiculous apron, grinning into a boiling cauldron of lamb parts, JB heard the voice inside his head scream, *run!*

The memory of the splintered Louisville Slugger hidden in Rakesh's footlocker surged through JB's mind. He'd burned the evidence to protect his friend. Now, watching Rakesh slip so easily into Mike's role, JB felt a creeping horror.

"Where will you go?"

"Go?" Rakesh turned to JB as if called out of a daydream. "I'll stay here until I get things sorted out."

"I see," JB replied, though watching his old friend mechanically uncorking a bottle of red wine like a gay Stepford wife, he thought, something was definitely wrong. "Emilio had a breakthrough today at therapy, and I don't want to—"

"Don't want to what?" Rakesh cut in. "You don't want me to upend the happy home you've created for your son?" JB sensed he may have struck the wrong tone because Rakesh's demeanor had shifted, reminding him of the way he had reacted after they'd woken up after passing out in bed together drunk. "Let's face it, JB, you need me," Rakesh continued. "Now more than ever. Mike has made a mess. Look at your life. Look at your son's life."

"I am thinking about my son." The calm in JB's voice had been replaced by an all too familiar shakiness. "My only concern now is for Emilio. Mike has asked for a divorce."

"What?" Rakesh's eyes fluttered shut; then he took a deep, satisfied breath as if he were inhaling something fragrant and delicious. "That's wonderful news. All the more reason for us to celebrate."

Us, there's that word again.

Rakesh handed him a glass of wine. JB accepted it, but all the while he was thinking, *Who is this man standing before me?* Rakesh clinked his glass and drank. "I can press the reset button and bring some order to this family while you and Emilio begin the long and difficult process of uncoupling from Mike. You're about to get knee-deep in an ugly divorce. Don't let Mike fool you. That bitch is not walking away with just the clothes on his back. I should know. Andy and Mike are cut from the same cheap cloth. No doubt they'll want to take us to the cleaners, but that's no longer a problem for me. Not like it will be for you." Outside, the sun sailed behind a cloud. JB watched its shadow pass over Rakesh's face.

"What's that supposed to mean?"

"Leave everything to me, okay?" Rakesh turned away and resumed cooking. JB stood there, having held his breath the entire time Rakesh ranted. Another glance around at the dining room table, set for a holiday dinner from the night before and the homemade lamb curry stewing on the stove. It was as if Rakesh had hit his breaking point and had assumed a new role. A role he'd always coveted, the newly vacant role of JB's husband. "Why don't you get washed up for dinner?"

"Good idea." JB heard the break in his voice.

"We need each other. Don't you think?"

"I've always needed you." JB almost heard a smile in those words, drowning out his fear.

It was a widely accepted belief across many areas of sociological research and theory that people in despair grew calm once they'd decided to take the final step, their spirit at peace with the prospect of the sweet release of death—that some desired objective would only be realized once an obstacle had been eliminated.

JB stopped outside of Emilio's door. He crept in with a finger held to his lips. "We're leaving." Emilio hopped off the bed without asking why. JB entered his bathroom and turned on the shower. He pulled out his cell phone and texted Andy. Rakesh turned up the choro music. JB waited for Andy to respond, staring at his phone in the dim light of his bathroom. JB experienced a strange, inexplicable fear. Thoughts churned like a turbine in his head, splintering and slicing them into fragments that, when pieced together, told him something he refused to believe.

After several more seconds, JB decided he couldn't wait for Andy to reply. JB and Emilio had to get away. They needed to distance themselves from everyone until Emilio was safe and JB could think rationally.

Emilio followed JB as they took the stairs that led to the garage from his bedroom and exited the side door. "Is everything okay?" Emilio asked as JB backed his car out of the driveway.

JB stole a furtive glance. "I don't know."

He fell silent, pensive while driving toward North Sea Road, thinking they could be in Manhattan in two hours, where they would be safe. He had to think. He had to sort this through. Rakesh was not acting like himself, but with all that he'd been through, it seemed somewhat expected.

When JB's phone rang, Emilio picked it up off the console. "It's Uncle Rakesh. Do you want me to answer it?"

"No!" JB's reaction had more of a smack than he'd intended. "Call Uncle Andy."

JB sighed heavily once Emilio informed him that it went straight to voice mail. The GPS calculated that Manhattan was less than two hours away. There, they would be safe in their Tribeca apartment, but what about Andy?

Was Andy safe?

"Hang on." JB made a wide U-turn.

"Where are you going?"

"To do the right thing, I hope."

Chapter Thirty-Seven

A long pause followed a knock on the door. JB exhaled once he heard the stomping of feet approaching. Andy appeared pleasantly stunned, as if greeted by someone holding a huge Publisher's Clearing House check. "JB, what are you doing here?" Andy's bright blue, bulging upper eyelid had thrown his face into a gruesome asymmetry like a Picasso portrait. "Is Rakesh with you?"

"No," JB replied. "We happened to be in the neighborhood and thought we'd check on you."

"Aw, that's so sweet," Andy said, yawning. "Hey there, Emilio. Haven't seen you in a while. Come in." Andy glanced up at the sky. "Looks like rain."

"If now is not a good time," JB began, but Andy had already pulled Emilio into the house.

"I fell asleep watching TV," Andy explained. "What can I get you, boys?"

"Go back to sleep," JB insisted. "I only wanted to check on you. I tried calling and texting but when you didn't answer, I got worried."

"Aww," Andy sang. "That's so sweet. I'm up now. Emilio, care for a soda?"

"May I use your bathroom first?"

"It's down the hall." Andy pointed to his left. "I'll make some tea. It's chilly tonight. Isn't it?"

JB sat on a barstool, staring at Andy from across the marble island. "How have you been?"

"Good, all things considered." Andy filled the tea kettle with hot water and set it on the stove. "I mean, my head hurts." His eyes veered toward his injury. "That will heal. Can't say the same thing about my marriage now, can I?"

JB hesitated, not wanting to engage in a conversation about his best friend's marriage without his best friend being present, but Andy looked so pitiful that he made a concession.

"Based on my conversation with Rakesh, it seems the ball is in your court. I think you two can still work things out."

"Do you really think so?" Andy strained to smile. "Then why is Rakesh at your house?"

"Andy, what's going on between you two has nothing to do with me." JB heard his phone ring. He reached into his pocket, but it wasn't there. *Where's my phone?* But then he remembered that Emilio had it last when he asked him to call Andy in the car.

"It's just…I love him so much…" Andy's voice crumbled away.

JB got up and walked around the island. He held Andy's shoulders. "Then go to rehab."

"It won't be enough," Andy sobbed against JB's chest. "I'll never be enough."

"Why would you say that?" JB gave him a tentative one-arm hug. The kettle was coming to boil, the water rumbling in its depths, a faint whistle building from its spout. Andy pulled it away and turned off the stove. "How do you take your tea?"

JB shook his head. "We're not staying long. Emilio and I are heading back to the city."

Andy resumed fixing tea as though he hadn't heard JB. "Why are you heading back to Manhattan?"

Because your husband is acting like a psychopath.

"Emilio had a breakthrough today at therapy. I think it's best if we're on our own for a little while."

Andy set about arranging mugs, a small brass bowl of sugar, and a white porcelain milk jug on a tray. "You left Rakesh alone at your house?" Steam rose to meet Andy's face as he poured hot water into each mug. "I'm confused."

JB steeled himself. "Like I said, Emilio had a breakthrough today."

"Yeah, but why would Rakesh stay at your house…alone?" Andy's tone had shifted, become accusatory.

"I-I'm not sure."

Andy narrowed his eyes. "What aren't you telling me, JB?"

Andy's cell phone rang—Rakesh calling. "Do you want me to answer it?"

JB forced a chuckle. "Go ahead."

Andy stared at him, his eyes crackling with suspicion. As he moved to answer, JB slapped it out of his hand.

"I'm so sorry. I'm under enormous stress."

For an instant, JB saw fear—an intense withering fear—cross Andy's features. Then it was gone. He knelt down to pick up his phone. The screen had cracked. Andy looked up at JB. "Go sit down," he said in a soothing voice. "We'll have some tea."

JB walked to the living room, hearing Andy speak quietly to Emilio in the hallway. "Why don't you watch TV in the den?" Moments later, Andy entered with a tray. "It's jasmine. If I had anything stronger, I would have offered you a drink."

JB took a long sip. "Did you put sugar in this?"

"What do you take me for? Everyone knows JB doesn't eat gluten or sugar." Andy's voice mimicked Rakesh's cadence perfectly, vowels rolling off his tongue.

"You've got Rakesh down." JB sipped again, licking his lips. The sweet aftertaste was undeniable. JB set the mug down and moved to get up. "I should go."

"You can't go now," Andy insisted. "Please, tell me what happened."

"I need time alone to think."

Andy huffed in frustration. "Something must have happened. Please, I need to know."

JB exhaled, squeezing his eyes shut. "I'm not thinking clearly."

"You know how much Rakesh hated the way Mike humiliated you." Andy sat back, crossing his legs. "He went on and on and on about it." Andy launched into his imitation of Rakesh again. "—'I can't believe JB puts up with him. Why doesn't he do something about it?'—On and on and on, he worried about you. *You!* It's always about you."

JB's head felt fuzzy as he lifted it. "Rakesh loves you."

Andy sighed. "No, Rakesh loves you. He's always loved you. Do you want more tea?"

JB's shoulders felt impossibly heavy. His throat felt like a collapsed accordion trying to expand. "No, no more tea."

"The funny thing," Andy said like a gossipy neighbor, "is that you don't acknowledge Rakesh's obsession with you. Do you know why?"

"Why?" JB managed to say, although he felt like he was sinking into the sofa.

"Why?" Andy repeated mockingly. "Because you're a selfish, entitled snob. You always have been. My God, JB, haven't you tamped enough nosebleeds looking down at the rest of us from that high moral pedestal you stand on?" Andy took JB's mug to the sink and rinsed it. He set it in the dishwasher and started it. "You really look tired. I doubt you're in any shape to drive now."

JB nodded, the simple gesture draining what little energy he had left. To fight against whatever was happening to him seemed pointless now. His mind struggled to solve the riddle—Andy's sudden hostility, the sweet aftertaste of the tea, the alarming numbness creeping up his limbs. The answer was slotting into place with horrible clarity.

Rohypnol.

Yet, there was something JB couldn't understand. He found he was becoming increasingly incapable of concentrating at all. The words he was searching for were far away. They floated high above him like an unbound bouquet of balloons.

Why can't I reach their strings?

"You probably want to know why," Andy said, which was true, but JB could hardly speak by now. "Being married to a pharmacist has advantages."

Andy returned from the kitchen with a small plastic baggie containing pills.

"The night of the party, I snuck into Winnie's bathroom and replaced her pills with the Rohypnol I stole from Rakesh's stash."

JB struggled to focus on Andy's face, which wavered like a reflection in rippling water.

"Rakesh taught me so much about drugs like Rohypnol, which is really hard to spell. Then there are other drugs like ipecac, which are spelled almost exactly as they're pronounced. Do you know what ipecac is for?"

JB wanted to ask what the point was, but he was barely conscious.

"Ipecac induces vomiting. That's what I used to make myself throw up all over that fat bitch's gardenia bushes. I knew once I made a scene at Winnie's costume party, Rakesh would drag my drunk ass out of there. Alibi accomplished. Even drugged your son to get his bat."

JB was so confused. His vision was blurring.

"The second time was meant for you," Andy continued. "Spiked your Scotch when Mike was on the phone. Planted those photos."

"To fra—frame me?"

"You ruined everything." Andy's voice turned venomous. "That dinner party where you told Jamie and Tom to be careful? Do you have any idea what you cost us?"

"Wha...?"

"Wha...?" Andy repeated mockingly. "You have no idea how your words can alter outcomes we spent months planning."

"Wha...?"

"Confused? Well, you're in luck." Andy stood up. "Emilio, can you come in here?"

The sound of feet shuffled along the floor like someone being forced against their will.

"Dad!"

JB could hardly crane his head. By the marble island, Emilio stood with a man holding a Bowie hunting knife to his neck. The stranger's face bore a distinctive scar running through his left eye—a jagged white line that pulled the lid into a permanent squint.

"JB, meet my brother," Andy said with exaggerated formality. "RJ."

Chapter Thirty-Eight

JB's consciousness returned in fragments. Vibration beneath him. The rumble of tires on asphalt. His tongue probed something foreign—duct tape across his mouth.

The car hit a pothole, jolting him fully awake.

Andy's eyes flicked to the rearview mirror. "Oh, you're up."

JB tried to speak but only managed a muffled grunt. Zip ties cut into his wrists and ankles. Reality crashed over him: Andy. The tea. The knife.

Emilio! Where is Emilio?

A muffled thudding from the trunk answered his question, sending terror through his drugged system.

"Don't worry about your son."

The man in the passenger seat glared at Andy. "Stop talking."

"Shut up, RJ. You're the one who can't keep his mouth shut, Mr. Jailhouse Confessor."

Through the receding fog of Rohypnol, JB understood. *RJ is Richard-Jay Santiago. The Jailhouse Confessor. The Sag Harbor murderer.*

"You fucked up everything, JB," Andy snarled. "That dinner party where you told Jamie and Tom to be careful? Six months of work, gone."

"They took your stupid advice!" RJ screamed. "Cut us out completely!"

The car turned onto a sinuous two-lane road: a golf course on the right and the bay to the left. It had begun to rain, hard drops pelting the roof like a fusillade. JB found himself looking around in fear; there was nothing to see but manicured lawns and beyond them, carefully maintained forests. White vapor wafted among the trees like phantoms. The car swelled up and down, swerving along waves of pavement. JB couldn't feel his hands. The thudding in the trunk only increased in rapidity, a gruesome reminder that his son was locked in a steel coffin.

"I know you found the bat. Why'd you take it? Protecting your boyfriend?" Andy glanced in the rearview at JB for several fraught seconds. "Well, it ends tonight."

JB ripped his eyes from Andy to observe his brother, who stared unbothered out the window, stroking the scar along his left eye.

The car tunneled forward along the narrow strip of road. JB squinted past his kidnappers into a rising tide of steaming fog, lustrous smoke in the headlights.

Andy grunted. "Looks like we're gonna have to drive farther east to get ahead of this storm."

An oncoming car whitewashed the interior and doused the windshield with a thick splash of water as it drove past. Andy braked to slow down, sending the car into a skid.

A pair of headlights appeared in the distance like two white flames, growing closer with every second. JB tilted his head back. Closing his eyes, he stared at the red of his eyelids. JB saw his chance. He threw himself backward, swinging his bound legs over the seat and around Andy's head. The zip tie cut into the driver's throat like a garrote.

The car veered into the other lane. Andy thrashed, suffocating. RJ grabbed the wheel as they skidded off the road and plowed through a series of arborvitaes. Branches slapped the windshield, cracking it.

Trapped in the back of Andy's car, an overwhelming, all-consuming rage that had been building for months finally reached its crescendo. Every humiliation, every betrayal, every moment of weakness—JB channeled it all into his legs, tightening the plastic strip around Andy's throat, which would have sliced his head off—if only JB had spotted the knife sooner.

Pain exploded in his ankle. The duct tape tore free against a gut-wrenching scream. RJ had lodged the tip of his Bowie knife into JB's ankle. The car struck a utility pole and lurched toward the water. RJ severed the zip tie with a flick of the blade. The knife glinted in RJ's hand. He raised it to strike

JB again. And there it was, the dark voltage in RJ's eyes, leering at him. He reared the knife overhead, but JB kicked him desperately, his heel connecting with RJ's scarred eye. Bone cracked. Blood splattered the windshield as the car plunged into the bay.

Airbags deployed.

RJ stumbled out, clutching his ruined eye, disappearing into the night with agonized moans. Water poured in. JB had to reach Emilio. He kicked out the rear window and squeezed through, glass slicing his back. A shard still stuck to the frame—he used it to cut his wrist restraints.

"Hang on, son!" He popped the trunk.

The car lurched in the current, pinning him underwater. Panic flooded his lungs. Then a hand grabbed his arm—Emilio, pulling him to the surface.

They plodded through the shallow, choppy water like partners in a three-legged race, collapsing on the shore. JB's phone rang—Rakesh calling.

"Uncle Rakesh—" Emilio sobbed into the phone. "They were going to kill us!"

JB slumped against a rock, his ankle throbbing mercilessly as he watched his son crumble into exhaustive relief as he spoke on the phone. Other than his son's voice, everything was eerily quiet—even the rain had taken a break—except for the electric wire that had snapped free from the utility pole after Andy had struck it with the car, its raw end emitting white sparks in the black sky. The fog, thick as smoke, coiled across the road. Through his exhaustion and pain, JB's senses suddenly sharpened.

Something was watching him. Waiting there—at the edge of visibility, where the fog met the darkness. Two lambent black eyes emerged suspended in the nothingness. JB blinked, trying to clear his vision. The eyes remained, and slowly a form materialized around them. For a moment, the world held its breath.

Then the creature turned and melted into the darkness.

The fog shifted again. Where beauty once stood, something else emerged. Andy, his face twisted with murderous rage, stalking toward them.

"Dad?"

"Don't move."

A sharp crack split the air. The damaged utility pole groaned, toppled, and crashed down—directly onto Andy. White sparks died in the rain.

Silence.

Chapter Thirty-Nine

JB stared at the sunlight shimmering on the pool's surface through his study window. It had been a blurring of days. Images flew past like scenery viewed from a train window: sirens blaring toward them along that dark sinuous road, the dense forest bathed in red and blue lights, a series of endless questions by first responders and the police that carried on until they were transported to the hospital.

Hours after the encounter, when JB and Emilio were safe inside the antiseptic walls of the emergency room, he rode a foaming crest of relief. The world around him glittered with sudden serendipitous hope.

The police found Richard-Jay Santiago in the woods about a quarter of a mile from the accident. "He sustained complete globe luxation." This from D'Amico, who then rushed to explain that JB had kicked his eyeball right out of his socket. "RJ confessed to murdering Gianni Cuomo and that couple last summer."

JB didn't have to ask about Andy. He'd witnessed the loud crunch and swift shift from menacing life to brain crushing death.

Over and over, JB's mind replayed one scene. Each time, he asked himself the same questions: was it truly a stag that emerged from the darkness, or something more—a premonition manifesting itself in physical form? Though not one to believe in predetermined fate, preferring instead the philosophy that humans forge their own destinies, JB couldn't deny that something mystical had reached through the misty darkness and touched him.

Who could say with certainty what he'd actually seen? And perhaps the specifics no longer mattered. Even now, sitting in his study, the silver clock ticking, JB experienced the disquieting thrum of unease—a low voltage of electricity traveling throughout his body. A sensation, he knew, would remain with him for a long time. A keen sense echoing below the surface that he and Emilio had narrowly escaped death.

JB imagined a period in the distant future when he'd return to teaching. He planned to use Andy as an example to illustrate an interactionist's perspective to his students, of someone who was not only influenced by how he engaged with everyone around him but also, how the world chose to interact with him. Andy had operated with a sort of radar about the people in his orbit.

Thinking back, Andy had never volunteered much about his past, and JB had never thought to ask. Considering this, JB realized that he'd treated Andy no better than Rakesh had treated Mike. Perhaps even worse, since Rakesh had made no effort to hide his disregard for Mike, unlike JB, who had been blind to his dismissiveness toward Andy. The way JB saw it, Andy believed life had dealt him a bad hand. Instead of playing those cards, he'd tried to cheat life, a foolish mistake that proved to be fatal in the end.

JB grimaced, limping into the kitchen. He fixed a pot of coffee and, gazing out the window, wondered about Rakesh. It wasn't like him to go into hiding. He was the kind of person who jostled through the throngs to take his rightful place front and center, absorbing every detail. Never shielding his eyes, no matter how ugly, gruesome or disgusting the situation, Rakesh remained a steadfast and voracious observer. But Rakesh was no longer viewing this scene from the sideline. This tragedy had thrust him unwittingly in the middle.

Rakesh never visited them in the hospital. He never responded to any of JB's texts or calls. The silence stretched for days as both men retreated to lick their respective wounds—JB nursing physical injuries while Rakesh grappled with psychological devastation.

Under the circumstances, JB couldn't fathom the torrent of emotions his best friend must be experiencing. To discover your husband was not only dead but the architect of a plot to frame your best friend for murder—to realize you'd shared your bed and your life with a sociopath—was a betrayal so profound it defied conventional consolation.

Still, he couldn't bear the thought of Rakesh alone in that house—the house where Andy had hidden his true self for years, where every room must now feel contaminated by deception.

JB texted him again:

I'm thinking about you. When you're ready, I'm here.

The seconds crept by as he waited, a lump rising in his throat, until three dots pulsed on the screen. His heart galloped.

Rakesh wrote:

Hey

That single word—so casual, so inadequate—spoke volumes about Rakesh's state. He wasn't just alive; he was reaching back across the chasm that had opened between them.

JB replied:

How are you?

Rakesh sent back two vomit emojis.

JB typed:

I want to see you.

As JB waited—he hoped Rakesh would call—he thought about what he would say first. Or whether he should say anything at all or just listen.

Rakesh wrote:

I'm not leaving the house.

JB typed that he would be over within an hour.

After a quick shower and a change of clothes, JB poked his head into Emilio's room. "I'm dropping by Uncle Rakesh's house for a bit. Care to take Buckley to the beach later?"

Emilio nodded, unable to tear his eyes away from his phone.

"What's going on? You seem happy, all things considered."

Emilio burrowed his face into his pillow. "Remember that girl I was telling you about?"

"The one from school?"

Emilio nodded. "We've been texting. She heard about what happened and said she feels bad about the way her parents acted."

JB sat next to his son on the bed. "That's great." He patted Emilio's knee. "I think that's a good sign. A very good sign."

"Yeah, we'll see." Emilio clasped his hands behind his head. "Tell Uncle Rakesh I said, Hi."

"I'll text you on my way home."

JB experienced a flicker of hope as he made his way to the front door. A glimpse that eventually they could move past this nightmare. He tried to convince himself that the worst was behind them, matters couldn't get any stranger, and then they did.

The smile on JB's face dissolved once he opened the front door. Luca stood on the porch, poised to ring the bell. JB stepped back—speechless—but Luca was standing staunchly in the doorway with those pleading dark eyes.

"I know you don't want to see me," Luca began, "but when I heard what happened, I had to see you for myself. To make sure you and your son were all right."

JB stepped outside, closing the door behind him. "Well, as you can see, I'm all right."

"You're not alright. You're limping."

JB shook his head. "That's temporary. Now if you'll excuse me."

"When can I see you again?"

JB looked at him, at his gray stubble, his shaggy brows, and regarded him as one of those pathetic, moony-eyed characters in those romcoms Mike adored. Except what part did JB play in this clichéd plot that had become the tragedy of his summer in Sag Harbor?

"What did you hope to gain by coming here?" JB said with such bluntness it surprised even him.

"Your trust."

"My trust!" JB smirked, a quick flair of his eyes like a faulty pilot light, which roared into flames. "You lost my trust the minute you lied to my face."

"Have a drink with me." It was obvious Luca wasn't taking no for an answer.

"I'm not going anywhere in public, least of all with you." JB pushed past him and headed for the car.

"Wait!" JB jolted with evident shock, glancing over his shoulder at Luca as he said, "I love you."

"What?" JB blinked in perplexity. "No, you don't."

Luca charged toward him and kissed JB with such intensity. But the kiss was not returned. "Give in," Luca moaned against his mouth. "Please, JB."

The feel of Luca's lips on his, the light prickle of his stubbled cheeks, sent a familiar shudder through JB's body, awakening a desire he'd extinguished once Luca had revealed himself a liar.

Luca pulled away, still cupping JB's face. "I'm returning to Italy. Unless..."

"Unless what?"

"I can't leave you like this. We shared something beautiful. Yes, I did not tell you the whole truth, but I never lied."

JB was in the midst of a struggle, a crossroads in which either direction ensured obstacles ahead. The sensible part of him screamed to walk away, put this man behind him, but the pull of passion had tethered itself to Luca so that his selfish side begged him to give in if only to experience pleasure with him one last time.

"Let's take a drive to Montauk," Luca suggested, "have a drink on the beach, and talk."

Talking was all JB had done these past few days. What more was there to say to Luca? After coming so close to death twice in one year, JB had gained a perspective no book could teach him. For now, his only concern was for his son, and not even the allure of a passionate distraction could dissuade him.

"I'm done talking," JB said. "Please, leave me alone."

Without another word, he drove away.

Chapter Forty

Life had become complicated that summer to an extreme JB had never imagined possible. Even with the murder solved and Richard-Jay Santiago in prison, JB couldn't catch a break. What he longed for was to fast forward six months so that this entire tragedy would be behind him and his son. But his life had hit a new snag in the form of a seductive Italian. He realized that his physical surrender to Luca had created a deeper connection between them. Something he hadn't experienced in a long time.

JB decided to make a stop at the Beltrams' house. Up until now, Gus and Winnie had been secondary characters in this tragedy written by Andy, and one thing vexed JB. Something he couldn't explain. How had Andy gotten his hands on those salacious photos of Gus Beltram and Gianni Cuomo?

As he pulled into their driveway, the sensible side urged him not to pursue this. *Leave it alone. Move on.* But JB had already rung the doorbell as the sensible side faded away, and the selfish side took over.

"JB, what a surprise." Winnie clutched her chest with dramatic flair. "When I saw you from the window, I almost couldn't believe my eyes."

"May I come in?"

"Please." Winnie seemed as spry as usual, though her hair was grayer since he'd last seen her.

About Winnie's career, JB knew only the basics—that it had collapsed like an underbaked soufflé.

"How are you?"

A bark-like laugh escaped her lips. "You're kidding, right?"

"I broke my own rule. I can't believe that question came out of my mouth."

"Would you care for anything? Aperol Spritz?"

JB waved his hand. "No, thank you. I'm actually here to speak with Gus if that's all right."

Winnie held a fist to her lips, her eyes brimming with tears. "I think that could be arranged." JB followed her to the study. She knocked on the door, opening it. "I come bearing a visitor." Gus sat behind the desk, appearing dazed. He had lost weight, his cheeks sunken. Deep craquelure lines marked the corners of his eyes.

"Well, look who the cat dragged in." Even Gus's voice sounded shucked of its usual wry timbre. Replaced now with a hollow pang of pain.

"I'll leave you two boys to talk." Winnie closed the door behind her.

The light was low in the study. The room seemed slightly smaller to JB. Gus's laptop sat squarely in the center of the glass top desk beside the silver-framed photo of the Beltrams embracing.

Gus gestured for JB to have a seat. "What can I do for you?"

"This is none of my business, and you can ask me to leave, but I'm here to talk about Luca, Gianni's brother-in-law. What do you know about him?"

"Not much, honestly." Gus looked away, inhaling slowly through his nose. "The time you saw us together at The American Hotel lounge, we were negotiating."

"My understanding is that he paid you back the money Gianni had extorted."

"Word sure does get around." Gus stood up and walked behind his chair. "Here's the thing. Luca had contacted us prior to that night. Said he knew all about his brother-in-law, and that he only wanted to make things right. I agreed to meet him at the lounge because Luca insisted. Something about Gianni wanting to apologize. I said that wouldn't be necessary, but Luca said Gianni wanted to apologize in person. Regain my trust."

Trust, it seemed to JB, was something of great importance to both Gianni and Luca.

"Trust my ass." Gus let out a condescending snort. "I only agreed because he promised to pay me back the $50,000."

"Is that why you invited Gianni and Luca to your costume party?"

"You know Winnie and me. Always the gracious hosts," he said with a hint of bitterness. "We played along with the pretense. Unfortunately, we never anticipated our blackmailer was going to be murdered at our party."

"Who knew it was Zorro all along? Funny how there were two of them."

"Two?" Gus questioned. "I only remember the one."

"Did Luca ever pay you back the money?"

"Not exactly." Gus walked to the front of the desk and sat on the edge. "Luca paid me half what Gianni stole, but…I don't know how to tell you this…the money came from Mike."

"Mike? My Mike?"

Gus leaned forward slightly, his expression urging patience. "In all fairness, I don't believe Mike knew, and before you ask, I'm going to tell you how I know."

JB fidgeted in his seat.

Gus hesitated. "I assume you heard by now that Mike had given his commission to Gianni."

"No, I had no idea."

Gus turned somber but there was more there—pity. "Apparently, Mike was in love with Gianni. He gave him the commission to avoid declaring it to you. My understanding was that Mike planned to leave you for Gianni."

JB's mind lurched backward to the night of the costume party—Mike sobbing uncontrollably as the emergency personnel worked on Gianni's lifeless body. That night, JB had dismissed it as a performance, a calculated display to deflect suspicion. But Gus's explanation—though painful—cast Mike's breakdown in a new light.

Was it truly love, though?

Mike confused attention for desire, and desire for love—fostering strays, mistaking their attentive gaze for genuine connection. Perhaps his tears were real that night, but they revealed more about what he'd lost than who he'd loved.

"If you haven't heard it by now, Mike and I are getting a divorce."

Gus nodded. "Like I said, word does get around. I'm sorry."

"It's for the best."

Gus reached over and squeezed JB's knee. "I know the truth stings, but this only confirms you've made the right decision to separate."

"Thank you." JB stood up to leave. "One more thing: any idea how Andy got ahold of those photos of you and Gianni?"

"Not a clue."

"For what it's worth," JB offered, his voice cracking a little. "I'm sorry for any embarrassment I may have caused you."

Gus appeared as if he was trying to embolden himself by making eye contact with his former nemesis. JB could see the wistfulness in his eyes, as though he were staring at a mirror. "Maybe we can start over. Winnie and I would love to have you and your son, Emilio, over for dinner one night."

"I'd like that."

A sudden urge overcame JB. He hugged Gus, heaving a long sigh as he clung to the man. Gus returned the gesture, embracing JB for several long seconds. "There, there," Gus whispered. "You'll get through this. I promise."

JB imagined that this was what a father's love must feel like, and how he had longed to experience such love from his own father.

* * *

Rakesh opened the door looking like a slob: faded Columbia University T-shirt, sweatpants, bare feet, and the scraggly makings of an early beard. "Come in quick." JB followed him into the living room where days earlier, Andy had drugged and kidnapped him and his son. JB hovered uncertainly in the entranceway. "What's the matter?"

JB took a shaky breath, feeling lightheaded. "Give me a minute."

Rakesh smacked his forehead. "What was I thinking, bringing you back to the scene of the crime?"

"No, seriously, I'm okay."

But JB's knees buckled. He sank to the floor, feeling strangely numb. Rakesh knelt beside him. JB felt a heaviness pressing down on his chest. Rakesh pulled him close as JB attempted to even out his breathing until the episode passed.

"There, there now, old friend," Rakesh whispered as he held JB in his arms. They sat embracing one another on the floor for a long while. The house phone rang. Rakesh cursed under his breath.

"Aren't you going to answer that?"

"Why? So, another reporter can ask me if I care to comment on my dead psycho killer husband?"

"Unplug the damn thing." JB got up and made his way to the sofa where he sat down, propping his injured foot on the coffee table.

Rakesh remained puddled on the floor, holding his face in his hands. "What am I going to do? I can't go outside. I can't go to work. I can't show my face in town. My life is over."

"Your life is not over."

"JB, I married a sociopath! I have to be the stupidest human being alive." When JB turned to meet his gaze, Rakesh's expression bore a profound anguish. "I can't believe it. Me, Rakesh Singh, duped by a pair of bumbling con artists. Do you know Andy has been plotting his revenge against you for a year, but after I left him, he changed his mind and decided to frame me instead?"

"Nothing surprises me anymore. Mike was planning on leaving me for Gianni Cuomo."

Rakesh scoffed. "This is no time to play lets one up Rakesh, okay?"

"You're right. I'm sorry."

Rakesh stood up and fetched a bottle of Pinot Grigio from the refrigerator. After handing a glass of wine to JB, he plopped in the chair opposite him, hugging a yellow satin pillow.

"Who told you Andy decided to frame you for Gianni's murder?" JB asked after taking a long sip.

"Clark Kent and Lois Lane. Better known as Detectives Sullivan and D'Amico. They informed me that my brother-in-law, in his confession, said that once I left Andy and moved in with you, they decided to change the master plan. Who changes a murder plot halfway through a mystery?"

"Does it even matter at this point?"

It had been an insidious plot Andy had concocted. To think he'd changed his mind due to jealousy. JB wondered if he would have gotten away with it had JB not burned the bat.

"What am I going to do?" Rakesh clenched his jaw, nostrils flaring. "No one is going to believe I didn't know my brother-in-law was Richard-Jay Santiago. I have to move. I have no choice. I'm done here in Sag Harbor."

Rakesh dissolved into tears. A sobbing punctuated with guttural moans. It was hard for JB to observe his best friend in such a state.

Though they had survived this nightmare, JB sensed there was something permanently wrong inside his own body. It was beyond his comprehension, some critical electrolyte imbalance running through his veins, throwing his organs into entropy. Rakesh was suffering from it too. You only had to look at him to know he felt rage. An anger so gutting because it was directed toward himself, for his hubris and stupidity.

"Come home with me," JB offered. "I don't want you to be alone. We are family after all."

Silence of contemplation followed. Rakesh tried to pull himself together, squaring off his shoulders and clearing his throat.

"Did D'Amico and Sullivan explain how Andy got his hands on those photos of Gus and Gianni?"

"After Alfie and Dale told Andy their story about the Big GC, Andy pushed them on Mike, hoping they'd regale him with the same tale. He figured once Mike realized he'd fallen for a con man, he'd run back to you. When that didn't happen, Andy stole Gianni's phone and leaked the photos of Gus Beltram online."

Now it made sense why Mike had allowed Gianni to use his cell phone.

"What I want to know is, who stole the bat from Andy?" Rakesh fixed JB with gimlet-eyed scrutiny. "Do you have any idea?"

JB experienced a flicker of unease cross his face before he could control it. He stood up and set his hand on Rakesh's shoulder, squeezing it, perhaps a moment too firmly. "Enough with the questions. Let's go home."

Rakesh held his gaze for a beat longer than necessary, as though trying to read something in JB's expression, before finally nodding. "You're the best friend in the whole wide world, Joseph Byron Pulaski." A sob burst from Rakesh's mouth. "How will I ever repay you, old friend?"

"You'll repay me when the time is right."

Chapter Forty-One

The setting sun dappled the water. A light rain chased away the remaining beachgoers. With the wind on their backs and the sand between their toes, it occurred to JB that he and his son had entered a new phase in their lives: a mature relationship where silence felt comfortable, having both undergone the same traumatic experience and in doing so, came away with a perspective no words could define.

"How's your ankle?"

"It's getting better. Thanks for asking."

"How's Uncle Rakesh?"

"Not as good as my ankle. I asked him to move back in with us for a little while so he's not alone."

"Cool."

Buckley ran to them, carrying a piece of driftwood in his mouth. Emilio pried it from his jaw and hurled it toward the water.

"How did your virtual session with Dr. Laird go?"

"He wants me to continue the virtual meetings for another week or two. At least until everything calms down."

JB listened, his ears brimming with the sound of waves crashing on the shore.

"He asked about you," Emilio added.

"He did?"

Emilio nodded eagerly. "I think he likes you."

"I think you're reading into things." JB pulled his arm across his son's shoulder.

"Maybe."

JB's phone dinged. It was a text message from Luca:

When will I see you?

JB put his phone back in his pocket, sighing.

"Who's that?"

"Gianni Cuomo's brother-in-law. He wants to have a drink with me."

Emilio fell quiet. Unlike so many people JB knew who listened with their mouths ajar, eager to seize the opportunity to speak, his son possessed the appealing and rare quality of the silent listener. "I always thought you and Uncle Rakesh would end up together."

JB cocked his head. "What made you think that?"

"You two are inseparable. I just thought, if I ever got married or whatever, I hope that person would be my best friend."

"I can't speak for Uncle Rakesh, but I don't think either of us is thinking about marriage *or whatever* for the foreseeable future."

"Dad, do whatever makes you happy. You deserve to be happy."

Happiness? What an odd concept.

On the drive home, something nagged at him. It occurred to him that there was one last stone to overturn. Two people he needed to speak with who could shed light on this situation—free him from this lingering sense of resentment once and for all.

* * *

"JB," Dale said, opening the door with a look of surprise. "Come in."

Alfie appeared behind him, offering a cautious smile. "We weren't expecting you."

They gestured him inside, and JB could sense their curiosity—and wariness. After his last visit, when he'd learned about Mike's date, he imagined they weren't sure what to expect from him now.

"Can we get you something to drink?" Alfie offered.

"I'm fine, thanks." JB settled into a chair, noting how they watched him carefully. "I need to ask you about Gianni Cuomo."

Dale's expression hardened slightly. "What about him?"

"You mentioned two con artists at James and John's party. I initially thought you meant Gianni and his wife, Daria."

"We never actually met her," Alfie said, moving to pour drinks. "Our private investigator did, though, when he went to Sicily. She apparently gave him quite a story about being destitute, having hungry children. Even gave him some kind of religious medal for protection."

"A St. Christopher's medal?"

"Sounds right," Dale confirmed. "We're not particularly religious, but yes, I think that was it."

JB leaned forward. "So if Daria wasn't the second con artist you mentioned, who was?"

Dale and Alfie exchanged a look.

"Surely you've met him," Dale said carefully. "He was here this summer, supposedly trying to make amends for what Gianni had done. Very charming, very apologetic."

"Luca," JB said.

"That's the one," Alfie confirmed. "Handsome man. We almost bought his act at first."

Something cold settled in JB's chest. He'd been so close to meeting Luca again, so ready to believe someone might actually be interested in him for genuine reasons.

"The whole thing was orchestrated," Dale continued. "Luca used the money Gianni had extorted from Gus Beltram to pay us back, probably hoping to keep us quiet. Then they used the money Mike loaned Gianni to pay back Gus. Classic shell game."

"A Ponzi scheme," JB said.

"More like robbing Peter to pay Paul." Dale's voice carried a bitter edge. "They must have thought we were easy marks—rich gay Americans with more money than sense."

JB set down his untouched glass, his mind racing. "We know now that Andy and his brother changed plans partway through. Instead of framing me, they decided to frame Rakesh."

Dale looked skeptical. "That's unusual. Con artists don't typically alter their plans unless something forces their hand."

"Maybe something did," JB said quietly, more to himself than to them.

"Your guardian angel was watching over you, JB," Alfie interjected.

A sudden thud against the glass wall made them all jump.

"Christ," Dale muttered, his composure cracking for a moment. "I hate that sound."

"What was that?" JB asked, looking around.

"Birds," Alfie explained wearily. "They keep flying into the glass walls like aviary kamikaze pilots."

Dale rubbed his temples. "We find dead birds on our doorstep daily. It's…unsettling."

As JB got up to leave, he noticed the smudged bloodstains on the glass, the small feathered body near the door. The house that had seemed so impressive now felt like a trap—beautiful but deadly.

"We're thinking of moving," Dale said quietly as he walked JB out. "Sag Harbor isn't what we thought it would be."

JB nodded, understanding the feeling completely.

Chapter Forty-Two

"What's all this?"

But even as JB asked, he knew the answer. The answer was in Luca's eyes, burning with the ferocious longing of a soldier returning to his bride after the war. The answer was the scent of firewood and anisette softly blowing in the breeze right outside his door. The answer was a Fellini movie starring Marcello Mastroianni, standing in the doorway, greeting JB with roses, wine, and kisses.

"You have no idea how happy I am. When you called me yesterday and invited me to dinner, I almost didn't believe you."

"Well, I realized something." JB looked at Luca closely. "Let me fix you a drink."

Luca sat on the couch as JB entered the kitchen. "Your ankle. I see you're not limping so much."

"Hardly feel any pain at all." JB returned with two tumblers of amber fluid over ice. "To new beginnings."

"Negronis!" Luca stood up to make a toast. *"Cent'anni!"*

"What does that mean?"

"May you live a hundred years."

"I like that." They clinked glasses and drank. JB watched Luca's face as he swallowed.

"Sweet. But not too much," Luca said.

"I hope you like braised short ribs with cucuzza made two ways."

"My favorite. How did you know?"

JB shrugged. "Lucky guess."

"So, tell me. What changed your mind?"

"Like I said on the phone, after all that's happened, I realized it's time I focused on myself." JB gestured for Luca to sit down. He grabbed a dining room chair and sat across from him. "You don't know this but last year, I was diagnosed with cancer."

The color drained from Luca's face. "That's horrible."

"I'm cancer-free now, but it changed everything. Mike started seeing other people." JB paused. "You may have heard of them. Jamie Friend and Tom Fitzsimmons. They were murdered last summer."

Luca nearly choked on his drink. "No, I heard nothing."

"Just as well because my husband didn't stop having affairs after they were murdered. Earlier this summer, I did something stupid. I tried to scare away my husband's strays." JB caught himself, chuckled. "By strays, I mean the men my husband was sleeping with."

Luca took another swig of his Negroni. "Okay."

"It doesn't matter what I call them. What matters is what I did earlier this summer." JB crossed his legs, taking a deep breath. "Have you ever heard the story about the boy who cried wolf?"

Luca offered an uncomfortable grin as if JB were questioning him as part of his naturalization interview. "Um…"

"It's about a boy who's tending sheep. Every time he shouts, 'Help, there's a wolf!' the farmers would come running only to discover that what the boy said was a lie. Then one day there actually was a wolf, but when the boy shouted, '*Wolf*', no one came."

"Ah." Luca nodded in recognition. "*Il ragazzo che gridava al lupo.*"

"Of course, there's an Italian version of this fable." JB planted both feet on the floor, leaning forward. "Earlier this summer, I started telling my husband's *strays* that I had killed Jamie and Tom."

JB laughed as if everything—the cheating, the cancer, the conning, and the killings—was some of the funniest stuff he'd ever experienced.

"Some people actually believed me. Imagine that. Me, a murderer." The laughter died. "Of course, that didn't last long. RJ Santiago confessed to those murders while in prison."

Luca nodded slowly. "I read about what you and your son went through with that man and his brother."

"Andy and RJ originally planned to frame me for Gianni's murder." JB watched Luca's reaction carefully. "But they changed their mind."

"Frame you for Gianni's murder?" Luca took another sip. "Because you were the jealous husband?"

"Instead, they decided to frame my best friend, Rakesh."

Luca stifled a yawn. "What time is dinner?"

"Let me go check." JB retreated to the kitchen and returned with fresh drinks. When he nudged Luca's hand with the new cocktail, the man's eyes popped open like a ventriloquist dummy.

"Drink up. We're celebrating, remember?"

Luca squeezed his eyes, shaking off fatigue. "What are we celebrating?"

"The beginning of my new life. You see, I had a guardian angel watching over me." JB's voice grew softer. "You were that guardian angel, Luca." Luca coughed, holding a hand to his throat. "You were the one who convinced Andy and RJ to change their plan."

"I didn't do it—" Luca's words came out slurred.

"Gianni couldn't return to Fire Island this year? That's why you chose Sag Harbor. But when Alfie and Dale moved here too…" JB shook his head. "You had to pivot quickly."

Luca frowned, rubbing his forehead. He slapped at his cheeks, struggling to focus.

"That story about finding a house for your secret client—why choose Lawson's? Why specifically ask for Mike?" JB's voice remained conversational, almost gentle. "You must have thought you'd hit the jackpot. A wealthy soon to be ex-husband, fresh from surviving cancer."

Luca reached for his phone but fumbled it. His hands shook as he clawed it from the floor.

JB kicked it away. It slid across the room with a satisfying whoosh.

"You won't be needing that." JB studied Luca's deteriorating condition with clinical interest. "The costume party—you were there as the first Zorro, weren't you? Made sure the hosts saw you, then slipped out when RJ arrived as the second Zorro."

Luca lurched forward, his hand clutching JB's ankle. "You're going to kill me?"

"In the Hamptons, we have a saying." JB's tone remained pleasant, almost sweet. "Interlopers are as ubiquitous as deer ticks. The only way to remove one is to apply steady, even pressure on the head and pull."

The terror in Luca's eyes was absolute.

JB bent closer, speaking in a near-whisper. "Remember that fable about the boy who cried wolf? The irony isn't lost on me—when I tell everyone I killed you, no one will believe me." He smiled thinly. "I can't say I blame them."

Luca's breathing had grown shallow, his skin ashen. He looked up at JB with pleading eyes.

"I know this is a shock. You thought I was a good person." JB's voice carried an almost tender quality. "But I'm not. I have evil inside me. I've just become skilled at burying it so deep no one can see it."

The doorbell rang, slicing through the moment.

JB straightened, adjusted his shirt, and walked calmly to the door. He opened it with a smile.

"On time as usual."

"Wild horses couldn't drag me away."

"Thank you for coming."

"Happy to return the favor, old friend."

Chapter Forty-Three

Naked Tourist Found Unconscious

SAG HARBOR—Police responded to an unusual incident early Thursday morning after the owner of the Corner Bar discovered an unconscious, nude man in a wheelbarrow parked by the historic windmill at the entrance to Long Wharf.

Gianluca Guardia, a 46-year-old Italian tourist with reported connections to the late Gianni Cuomo—whose murder at the Beltrams' costume party last month shocked the Hamptons community—claimed he was the victim of a robbery. According to police reports, Guardia alleged someone had drugged and stripped him before abandoning him in the public display, elaborately arranged among a collection of Sicilian gourds known as cucuzza.

Toxicology reports confirmed the presence of unspecified sedatives in Guardia's system, but police have been unable to determine the perpetrators or motive behind what they described as an "unfortunate prank."

Guardia reportedly departed for Italy immediately following his release from Stony Brook Southampton Hospital, vowing never to return to "this godless place again."

Epilogue

The April sun was high, splashing bright light over the guests. A cellist began playing "I Will Always Love You." When Jason and his mother, Eileen, exited the French doors, the guests stood up to watch them walk down the aisle. They were followed by a procession of Jason's three sisters, each wearing identical rose-colored dresses. Finally, Angelo and his sister, Camille, appeared on the rear porch and walked arm in arm.

The wedding was held at the Beltrams' home in East Hampton, where Winnie and Gus offered to host it, though at first Angelo and Jason refused, not wanting to sully their special day with the memory of the tragedy that had occurred the summer before. Winnie and Gus had insisted, arguing that they would be doing them a favor. The gay wedding of a doctor and lawyer was exactly the publicity they needed.

It was a small affair with twenty guests. A curly willow wedding arch adorned with peonies and white roses framed the couple. Angelo and Jason presented a striking contrast—Angelo in a white tuxedo jacket with black bow tie and trousers, while Jason wore the reverse, a black jacket with white bow tie and trousers. As they joined hands at the altar, the officiant invited the guests to be seated, and the ceremony commenced.

"I can't believe our little girl is all grown up," Rakesh whispered in JB's ear. "Soon Emilio will be next." JB shot Rakesh an admonishing grin, noticing how handsome he looked—hair slicked to one side, a trimmed beard—in a satiny butter-yellow tuxedo. Single life had been good to him.

Rakesh had sold the pharmacy and taken a job as a global medical director for a pharmaceutical company. He worked remotely, so that meant he didn't have to leave Sag Harbor. The only downside was the traveling, but he got used to that quickly once he realized his colleagues were a bunch of lushes who expensed drinks at the hotel lounge where they debriefed nightly "for work."

"Where is Emilio?"

JB held a finger to his lips. "He's spending spring break in the Dominican Republic, building a school for college credit."

Angelo and Jason read the vows they wrote. Afterward, the guests were escorted to a tent on the beach where Winnie had assembled a long table draped in an ivory cloth. Silver lanterns hung from above at different lengths. Everyone took off their shoes and sat down. Camille made the first speech, though she could barely read her notes, her hand as shaky as her voice. Jason's sisters took turns, recalling the childish antics of their beloved baby brother.

Finally, it was JB's turn. He stood up, pausing to even out his breathing before he introduced himself. He'd worried over what to say, giving ample thought to whether he should say anything at all. Preparing for this special event felt like crossing from a familiar realm into a foreign one. In those days, he thought often of what he was hoping to accomplish in writing a toast—celebrating marriage as someone who was no longer married. But his son, ever the cajoler, talked him out of giving up and rightfully shamed him for thinking of such a thing. So, JB tried. As each day passed, bringing him closer to this moment, he gained clarity. When he stood up at the reception, he knew, looking at Angelo and Jason, he was ready.

"Today we're here to celebrate the union of Angelo and Jason because we believe everyone deserves love in their life," JB began. "While marriage isn't for everyone, it often enriches our lives in ways we can't fully appreciate. Let this day be a testament to the hope marriage provides us all. Without love, life loses much of its meaning. Aristotle once said we are social creatures, and in marriage, we find our deepest connections—not just to another person, but to parts of ourselves we might never discover alone."

The sunlight caught in the crystal glasses, scattering tiny rainbows across the white tablecloth—ephemeral beauty like so many moments in a shared life.

"Spouses can be exasperating," he continued, "but they can also cuddle, fill us with love, and connect us with a sense of purpose beyond ourselves."

JB paused, his gaze drifting to the mental image of the wall in his Sag Harbor house paneled with photographs. The wall chronicled memorable milestones from the seventeen years he'd spent with Mike, tracing a journey that began on that transformative Christmas evening when he'd met a young blond man with watery blue eyes. Perhaps it was madness to believe marriage could last. Yet, standing before Angelo and Jason, he believed they were not mad for trying.

"Seize upon the happy moments. Hold them up as proof that life can be filled with happiness, and may you draw upon those memories when life challenges you. May you always be this much in love, and may you never be further apart than you are right now. Cheers."

The guests applauded as JB took his seat. "Well done," Cliff whispered, his hand finding JB's beneath the table.

JB caressed Cliff's face, allowing his fingers to linger along his jawline. "Thank you, Dr. Laird."

Cliff smelled of lemons and the ocean—clean, uncomplicated scents that had come to represent everything JB valued in this new chapter of his life: transparency, simplicity, and the absence of elaborate deceptions. Their relationship had developed gradually, cautiously, with the measured pace of two men who had witnessed firsthand how quickly seeming perfection could implode.

The sun had nearly set. Overhead, string lights glowed golden yellow orbs. The music echoed in JB's ears as he glanced across the crowd. Everyone was happy. Finally, he thought, everyone—including himself.

Acknowledgments

I am deeply grateful to Shawn Reilly Simmons, who gifted me her amazing editorial vision, and to Deb Well and the entire Level Best Books family for shepherding this story into the world. Josephine Spinelli, Lisa Daily, and Larry Higgins must be thanked as well—I'm indebted to them for their encouragement and precious time. This novel was conceived after reading *Deep Water*, and so I thank Patricia Highsmith for writing it. Finally, my biggest thanks and love go to my husband, Chad, who fulfills every meaning of that word and tolerates my writerly obsessions with endless patience. And to Frankie, the best companion a writer could ask for!

About the Author

Frank Spinelli is a New York physician and author of the Angelo Perrotta Mystery series. He has appeared on ABC News, NBC Nightly News, and MTV. A resident of Sag Harbor, he lives with his incredibly patient husband and their four-legged adopted son in a house where the neighbors are just close enough to hear you scream—if they're paying attention.

AUTHOR WEBSITE:
  www.frankspinelli.com

SOCIAL MEDIA HANDLES:
  https://x.com/spinellimd
  https://www.facebook.com/frank.spinelli.581
  https://www.instagram.com/fspinellimd/
  https://www.tiktok.com/@fspinellimd

Also by Frank Spinelli

Nonfiction

Advocate Guide to Gay Men's Health and Wellness
Pee-Shy: A Memoir

Fiction

Perfect Flaw (Angelo Perrotta Mysteries Book One)
No Angels Wept (Angelo Perrotta Mysteries Book Two)